Also by Robert Lautner

The Road to Reckoning
The Draughtsman

QUINT

ROBERT LAUTNER

THE BOROUGH PRESS

The Borough Press
An imprint of HarperCollins*Publishers* Ltd
1 London Bridge Street
London SE1 9GF

www.harpercollins.co.uk

HarperCollins*Publishers*
Macken House,
39/40 Mayor Street Upper,
Dublin 1
D01 C9W8

First published by HarperCollins*Publishers* 2024
1

Hardback ISBN: 978-0-00-864746-9
Trade Paperback ISBN: 978-0-00-864747-6

This novel is entirely a work of fiction.
Wendy Benchley and Benchley IP, LLC appreciate the ongoing enthusiasm
for the book entitled *JAWS* by Peter Benchley and its characters. We respect
the imagination and energy that has been demonstrated in this book, but we ask
that there is an acknowledgement of the limits that must be set on this project.

This book is not endorsed by, sponsored by, nor affiliated with Benchley IP, LLC,
the owner of the worldwide copyrights in *JAWS* by Peter Benchley.
No alleged independent rights will be asserted against Benchley IP, LLC.
PETER BENCHLEY® is the registered trademark of Benchley IP, LLC.
The author of this book supports shark and ocean conservation.

Set in Minion by Palimpsest Book Production Limited, Falkirk, Stirlingshire

Printed and bound in the UK using 100% Renewable Electricity
by CPI Group (UK) Ltd

MIX
Paper | Supporting
responsible forestry
FSC™ C007454

This book is produced from independently certified FSC™ paper
to ensure responsible forest management.

For more information visit: www.harpercollins.co.uk/green

Sometimes a man stands up during supper
and walks outdoors, and keeps on walking,
because of a church that stands somewhere in the East.

And his children say blessings on him as if he were dead.

And another man, who remains inside his own house,
dies there, inside the dishes and in the glasses,
so that his children have to go far out into the world
toward that same church, which he forgot.

'Sometimes a Man Stands Up'
Rainer Maria Rilke

"Shall I tell you something?" asked Pinocchio, who was beginning to lose patience. "Of all the trades in the world, there is only one that really suits me."

"And what can that be?"

"That of eating, drinking, sleeping, playing, and wandering around from morning till night."

"Let me tell you, for your own good, Pinocchio," said the Talking Cricket in his calm voice, "that those who follow that trade always end up in the hospital or in prison."

The Adventures of Pinocchio

Carlo Lorenzini

Prologue

Amity Island, January 1977

Everyone remembers our summer of '75, and even those who weren't residents at the time have heard the stories.

Our chief of police had taken it upon himself to hire, from our dollars, a local fisherman to go out with some oceanographic fellow to hunt a suggested shark that had supposedly injured some bathers along our beautiful shores in the days before our Fourth of July weekend here on our beloved island.

Reluctantly I myself sanctioned his request, if only to placate the concerns of a small minority of our residents and to exercise every available option if indeed there was any risk to the populace's and visitor's beach activities over the holiday weekend.

What followed was a terrible disaster which resulted in not only the loss of a vessel but the death of our very own Captain Quint, the owner of said vessel. Fortunately the season was not too unduly spoiled and Amity still remains the choice destination for our discerning friends everywhere. Amity, as you know, means friendship.

As it was I, in my former capacity as realtor on the island, who had originally leased Mister Quint the land from which he operated his charter business, and the deceased having no known living family, I appointed myself his executor as is within my remit as freeholder of his land.

Although not a popular islander Mister Quint was certainly known and respected throughout our community and his death saddened a fair few of us, particularly Salvatore, a local fisherman who sometimes assisted Quint with his charters.

It was only after I accepted his estate and effects that I established that Mister Quint was a war veteran and, surprisingly, a survivor of one of the greatest naval tragedies in US history.

This manuscript, written sometime around 1968, was part of his effects and thus in my ownership. Apart from some artistic embellishments from the publisher it is as I took possession of it.

Larry Vaughn, Mayor

1

Merritt Island

I says a woman should take you as she finds, and if you found her in a bar with her elbows in whiskey, on a stool too small for her ass, she should be more grateful that you found her at all. Carried that ass home, even bought it a bed, and watched the moon over her shoulder as she humped on top of me and tried to break my hips every night.

That woman could go, and she took it righteously, never made a sound, concentrated as a Chinaman. I was twenty-seven when I wed her. My wife since leaving the navy. My last wife. My third.

You might think it young for a man to have three wives by twenty-seven but that's because I'm better than you. I married the women I screwed.

That would be '51. Good year. Great summer for dolphin. Must've been a good Gulf Stream. And lots of dolphin is good for fishing. Pregnant dolphin make good shark-bait.

Always got a good run of college boys off Merritt—that's Merritt Island, Florida. Those frat boys didn't care what they caught. Hardly anyone lets a dolphin free on a day-boat, not when you've traveled a hundred miles to game-fish.

They'd haul her in a-whooping and a-hollering and they all looked like Kennedys before Kennedys. William Holden. That was it. They all wanted to look like William Holden in those days. Guess Kennedys did too. All sunglasses and white shorts. I don't need sunglasses. I like to see everything.

Anyways, I'd show 'em the cunny on the catch and the domed pregnant white belly. Those idiots didn't even know it weren't a fish. Split between its thighs like their mothers.

They'd chug from the cool-box and I'd wait till they reached for the cold-cuts to slice the belly open right at their feet. All over their new deck shoes.

I take out the fetus, running white and red down my bare arms and over the ice of the box. I don't give a damn; ain't my food or beer. I drink my 'Gansett from my own box. I show 'em its limbs, just like a kid's arms at that stage.

They yell, berate, or laugh as they cough on their beer. They thought me ignorant 'cause I had a buzzcut back then. My hair's not navy habit. Can't grow it much. Haircut twice a year when it starts to grow into those Irish curls and cow-licks. Sideburns I got under my cap that makes it look like I got hair. Don't need the cap for the sun, not anymore. I had nothing but sun for five days with only my head above water. Those five days when I had engine oil over my head which helped stop it from sun-burning. Looked like one of them minstrel shows. Couldn't recognize each of us. I don't burn anyways since then. I got scars from it. My skin's like a rasp file.

Them kids on my boat were confused mostly, confused by the violence. But that's what they were there for. Game-fishing ain't peaceful. Hours of nothing and then twenty minutes of blood and cruelty or "romance" if you're Hemingway inclined. All that

4

gladiatorial happy horse-shit. Quick thinking and quick killing. Like the war. The boys laugh anyways. When you're young you butch-up by laughing. When you're a man you get quiet. You ever been in an Okie bar when it goes hushed? You better pick up a bottle.

They watch my reaction for a lead.

"Sharks," I say. "Best thing for sharks is calves. That's what you want ain't it? You done play-fishing? You done killing man-fish?" I say, dumping the body in the bucket.

Someone always loses it over the side at that blood everywhere. Kids. I always make that asshole take the bucket. If he takes it he goes up a notch. If he don't I give it to the little guy. Always a little guy. Some city-boy trying to keep up with his rich buddies. His clothes bought the day before. Packet creases all over 'em. Spot 'em like bluefish. Just some poor Jewish kid out of place. Sucking up to the people who might get him connected. Show Daddy that his business degree was worth it. He never wanted to be a lawyer. He wanted to be Wall Street. Now he's on my boat with a scuttle and a bucket of chum filled with a dead calf. He brought a Pan-Am comb and no gloves. He'll be shopping for coal-tar soap tomorrow. Take him days to get the stench out.

But that ain't it. I was talking about my Seminole wife, Effa. My last wife. We'd settled down off a jetty at Indian River, Merritt. Built our shack myself. I've built every home I've ever lived in. As a man that is. I fetch a wood-stove and some barrels and tubs. Make everything else. Real *Grapes of Wrath* stuff. That's what comes from being born in '24. Real simple living. Reared on potatoes, the whole thing mind, leaves and all, and clay biscuits, then thrown into a war at nineteen. I never ate so good as when Washington was paying, and I'd been married before as I said. But that's for later.

Me and Effa were raised the same that way. If you couldn't

hunt it, fish it or grow it you didn't know it. I didn't eat beef till I joined the navy. Never liked it less it was minced. I can eat corned beef all day mind.

Don't you think we were poor. It don't work like that. I grew up in the thirties and so did Effa. I see the kids come out on my vessel for the weekenders and they don't know they're born. I know you think that sounds like bullshit, something an old guy says, but it's true of anyone who went through what we had to, and we knew no better. I never saw a fat guy in my life until I saw an admiral; I thought he would blow up. I still can't put meat on my bones. Bony-assed bog-trotters, my old man would say. That's what we were.

My father was a Limerick man. Brought to America when he was twelve, since '02, and I grew up with an Irish sentiment in Boston. I remember him cursing the Republican papers that complained that there were more Irishmen in New York than in Dublin. Feel sorry for Jews and Blacks? How about being handed a flyer outside your school showing an Irish flea sucking Uncle Sam's tit. God knows how they thought up that shit. Tits on their own icon. Madison Avenue Republican shit. Jesus H. Christ.

You needed us, just like the English did. That racist bull quietened down when old man Kennedy started shaking his wallet. But I don't care for any of that. I was American-Irish. And American first. All that paper-Paddy shit curdles me. I didn't know anything but fishing until I signed up for the navy. The navy liked the Irish. And the Poles. Jews and Italians for the army, for the infantry. Nothing more segregated than an American army. Fighting for freedom and building Black barracks and concentration camps for American Japs. No army for Pat. He's a fisherman. Paddy's bones float. You remember that.

Paddy's bones float.

I never paid for a boat either. Built my own home and shape-up my own boat that I'd find abandoned. I learned that in the navy. People abandon boats. You just need to know where to look.

Own a boat and you got work and a home. Don't get much purer than that. Americans don't fix shit. That's an Irish thing. We don't throw nothing away. I seen a record player turned into a spinning wheel and the same back again. No such thing as a broken chair in an Irish house. There's just the good chair and the rest. The first thing I ever bought new was a cap. A marine corps cap. Bought that to stop folks asking about my navy one. And beer. Couldn't make beer. Make any other brew. Beer took too much work. Cheaper to buy. But I'm going on too fast. Been drinking. Let's cut that now.

Effa went of pneumonia in '53. I wasn't there. She was ill but she wouldn't let me stay at home. We needed earning while the weather was good. I had our boat, *Akron*, belt-drive engine, my belt mostly, and took those rich kids out on weekends. I'd spend the week fishing and hunting and bleaching shark jaws for Charlie Hawt to mount and sell in his store. Every weekend from spring to September I would have a boatful of happy assholes. That was my own plan.

See, the good boats, the advertised captains, would be booked up months in advance. Full of old men with money to put in their pipes and fat guts to sit in the stern with their Maker's Mark thinking that marlins jumped into the boat.

I took the stragglers and the Friday boys who decided to jump down to Florida off the cuff. You could make money if you went out on a Friday. The old boys think it bad luck to go out on a Friday. Ruin your whole season. Horse-shit.

All the bellhops and bait stores knew me. Gave 'em a five to know me.

"Quint's your man," they would say. "Boy, you sure can't get a boat now. Quint might be free though. He'll be in from Merritt at noon. Say, why don't you boys get some drinks while you're waiting?"

That was my life. Fishing, chartering, shooting game fish. I had an M1 that was real cheap after the war as the government tried to claw back some cash—hell, every home had something surplus—and I had a Lee-Enfield that you could lay in mud for a week and she'd still pluck your eyebrows.

Shooting sharks was easy work. The kids loved it. Fishing too hard. Blowing holes in snouts when they came up for the chum was what they wanted. Felt sorry for their sorority girls when they got home to 'em. Bet they couldn't walk for a week after. Nothing like blowing meat out of something for a hard-on. I didn't like it so much when the archers came in the sixties. That was cruel, though a fish don't care. His whole life is cruel. He expects it; they even mate fighting. But bolts fired into their bodies looks mean, and everything about fishing is mean so for me to dislike it, well, that made it gruesome. Ghoulish. Ain't that a great word?

After six or seven bolts them fish look like Jesus on the cross with arrows sticking out every which way and running with blood. And the shooter enjoys it too much. If it ain't a crossbow, if it's a regular bow, and the shark comes close, they get too excited and the bottom of it gets trapped on the gunwales as they aim down right along the side and they can't see it. You yell at 'em, "Hey your bow's hitting the boat! Your bow's stuck!" and they ain't listening and they fire anyways, fire high. Happy idiots. Thing is if you shoot or arrow a fish you can't claim no record no matter how big your catch. Some docks won't even let you weigh 'em. Fishing's got rules. It ain't hunting. It's line and reel. Muscle and skill. Your arm against the Monsters. The way it should be.

So I got a librarian I knew, Tom Gelmas, to write Effa's folks. She had her book with all their business. I couldn't meet 'em.

Couldn't meet her folks square. They hated our getting married and she had brothers that would flat out kill me. Nothing as bigoted ignorant as an Indian. I'd learned that much and knew when to steer away.

I paid for the funeral and asked Tom to straight it with her family for me and I was done with Merritt and Florida. I had two wives living and one dead. I knew how to deal with the living ones but the dead ... well ... that was a new thing. I'd had enough of that.

I'd set that I'd work and drink my way to California, to Mare Island. That's how I dealt with it. After the war, after my time with the dead and the living, I wanted nothing to do with it. You may find that without heart but Effa would understand and I only needed her to judge me. I never saw her dead and she would have wanted that. Indians like open coffins. She wouldn't want me to see that.

I took my '39 Dodge pickup, my rifles and reels in the back, buried the boat up at Moore Creek and took my home-wine up the road and ferried over into Titusville; no Bee Line those days. We were true islanders.

Maybe someone would take the boat. Or maybe I wanted to come back to her. The why I buried her so deep. I hoped that some good poor family would have use of our shack. I had painted it white the spring before, when Effa started coughing. She's gone and I still got whitewash on both my pants.

And I said to him, "Careful, Cricket;" and he said to me,
"You are a Marionette and you have a wooden head." And I threw
the hammer at him and killed him. It was his own fault, for I did
not want to kill him.

2

Vallejo

Let no one tell you that a bottle hurts. I had no friends who might give kind words. I'd done with that. I came out of the navy a dead man walking, a priority dead man, and never went home. I had no brothers or sisters and if my parents lived I didn't think of it. I was only a burden at their table anyhow and my old man always reminded me so. As for my mother I have only one good solid memory that has held me well whenever I get something in my eye.

I got sawdust in it when I was about nine 'cause my father was always sawing something that he'd abandon that afternoon. I was crying and she took me outside and held my head up to the light to see.

"Close your eyes," she said. She was wearing that blue dress that went from her collar to her calves that she always wore. "Look up. Keep your eyes closed." She held my jaw. "Look right. Look down. Look left. Look up. Open your eyes." She was bright above me. "Has it gone?"

I wiped my eyes. "Yes."

She smiled, let go my chin and wiped her hands on her hem.

"You see?" she touched my hair. "There's nothing that can hurt that you can't fix."

I was twenty-nine when Effa died. I could afford a few years to punish myself a little. That's the same as some of us felt after the war. Effa must have been part of that. Her dying a page of mine. I felt I wasn't to be happy after what I had done. Wasn't permitted. My service. My judgment. I can't write about that yet. I have to get there. Through it all.

I drank myself across to the west. When money was out I worked until I had enough for six bottles of anything and one tank of gas and then I'd move on. Not a lot better feeling than a full tank when you're broke. Even if you can't eat you can cross mountains.

I can fix anything. Once you work a boat you know engines. Trucks and cars are nothing. You don't have salt water to worry.

Hayseeds can fix their own field machines but not automobiles. Most people don't know shit about engines. I don't think I ever came into a garage that didn't need help with something. I was set to be an engineer on a battleship and I rebuilt my own boats' engines with junk from scrapyards. Common threads all. Pumps, that's all they are. And once those overalls in them motorshops took in the drink on me and my Irish they knew they had me cheap.

Aye, there be some fixing in drink. Don't let anyone say against it. I'd be dead if it weren't for the drink.

I was aiming for Mare Island, Vallejo California. Thought I'd sign back into the navy. Back to Mare and the sea. Leave America behind me. But I had no idea how big the country was. You don't till you try on our own. Last time Washington was in charge of the transportation. Trains and buses and a big group

12

of kids. Like traveling with a circus. America, on your own, sitting in a burning seat and looking out a dirty windshield, is the whale's back of the earth. I was drunk most of the time on the road but I remember those mirror lakes and the endless fields of cattle. Don't see cattle in Florida. And those iron giants pumping oil for hundreds of miles. Just land. Never ending. An ocean of dust. Whole days without seeing another soul. Nothing sweeter than that. Slept in the back of the truck under the stars. That was sweet too but I always liked to keep an edge in my eyeline. The side of something. Something to block out the horizon. The steel side of the truck, a window frame in my shack, the gunwale of my boat. Spent five days in the sea looking at nothing but horizon. *In* the sea, you understand? In the water. In the deep. Nothing but a kapok life jacket and a daisy-chain of hands. Never want to see the horizon again unless there's something between me and it. Something more than dorsal and tails.

I'd stop with a wake of brake dust at a tin sign and stumble drunk out of my truck. I always had two dollars in my jeans. Make sure you keep two dollars for every morning. Buys you gas or coffee and toast, or four beers for a fight.

Aye, a fight. Have to wait for night for that.

I thought nothing of fighting. Grew up fighting. Fought over a beet once and broke Andy Ayling's collarbone. I was eleven he was thirteen. I picked him up and slammed him sideways into a gate. I was so scared with his hollering that I ran to his house instead of mine and dragged his father to help. I told his father it was Dan Levi that done it and Andy was so scared of me that damn if he didn't say it was so.

Andy's father went to Dan's house and he and Dan's father beat Dan with their boots over their fists like boxing gloves. Dan Levi was terrified of me after that. No one ever came to my old

13

man to complain about me. My old man was a drinking Irish. He would fight you for saying his name.

But I felt bad for 'em for what I'd done. Still, they always gave me their old shoes after that, me not having any ever, what with no older brothers and all. I made up to them boys by protecting them for one summer from any scrap they got into, win or lose. Lose mostly because it was always older kids who cornered us in alleys or our fishing places which were theirs first and they were just trying to hold onto being boys. Drinking and smoking but playing swing on tire ropes. Hard to be a man when there ain't no work to go to.

I didn't fight for money. The fighting was a calculation. I was robbing. I'd pick a fight with some Okie and take it out to the lot. No one pays no mind to two young bucks. I'd make sure he didn't have any pals by keeping an eye on him for a spell with my two dollars of beer then make him spill some and drag him out and beat the shit out of him. He'd be drunker than me; I might kill him else or him me. I'd draw him to my truck so I could use it against his head then take his wallet and get out of there before a crowd drew. If I did two or three bars in a night I could have myself forty dollars by dawn. I don't remember ever losing, but then you find that you don't mind if you do it often enough. There ain't no real losing in a drunken fight anyways, just whoever gets tired first, like wearing down a fish. Use that beating for another bar thirty miles up the road, for another fish.

I detoured once.

Amanda, my first wife, had written a coupla times before '43. I'd postcarded her with a return address and she obliged. All polite and distanced, like women do.

She'd gone back to her folks in Blanchard, Oklahoma, after we'd gone our ways. I figured if I was making my way across the country I'd stop by and say hello, maybe get a lunch at least. I never got any reply from Carole anyways, my second wife. Her folks might have moved, of course, or her father might have tore up my postcard.

Besides, me and Amanda had more ties. We'd lost a baby once. That counts even if you ain't together no more. A "stillborn". What do they mean by that? That it didn't move? Didn't shiver and cry blue with the cold air when it came out? Or do they mean it was *still*born, didn't *not* come out. Was still—despite its trauma, its non-existence—born. Born somehow. I know that you "still" have to get a birth certificate, give it a name and then line up to get a death certificate the same day. All their boxes have to be ticked. And then they ask you if you want to bury it yourself or they say it will go in a mass grave and the hospital preacher will say some words over it and you can attend if you want. And all you can think about is that they have the word "mass" attached to this. No one tells you when you make a baby that there might be a mass grave at the end of it. I think of those newsreels about Auschwitz and all those camps that we got to see after the war, all those mass graves. I think, I hope, that it's not wrong to think them pits of graves to be the lucky ones. What would you rather do? Survive and come home to find your wife and children dead, your home gone, family gone, country a pile of shit. Or gone yourself. Gone when there was still hope. "Still".

To be dead can be lucky. To be dead before you knew life can be lucky. I'd be waving my son off to war now if he and I weren't so lucky that day. Lucky we had all them life jackets in the water. That's the only way to look at things.

I was never going to be popular with Amanda Hesk's old man. He was a builder and in real estate and had got real rich before the depression, and richer after when he didn't have to pay so much for workers, and he sent Amanda to the "Academie Moderne" in Boston. This was a finishing school where Oklahoma girls could learn poise and diction. They didn't teach 'em how to "poise and diction" their hormones. We boys hung around that school like flies on honey. She didn't like it there anyways. Too Jewish and starchy for a girl with red knees. She weren't her old man's daughter anyhow so she didn't break too much bond when I wooed her with a wink. She was always a running sort. I had to chase her up the street or stairs half the time. Some women are like that. Always running.

Took me two times to find the house; half the street signs were missing. I parked up the street so my Dodge wouldn't draw any curtains twitching. They had a nice two-story white wood home and I began to blush at the rank of my clothes. But I just wanted to say hello and get a sandwich from my ex-wife. Any man should expect that. It was only as I pulled the bell that I thought that she might have remarried and be long gone.

She answered the door before I'd thought of an excuse for her mother and I must admit I took a breath. She'd be thirty-one now and had put on just about that many pounds. I thought I looked the same except for wearing the war and my sun-scars. It was an old woman that opened the door.

"Oh, My Lord," she said, like I was a coffin set on her porch.

I took off my cap. "I was just passing through." As if that would be enough for the decade. "How you?"

"Quint. You sonofabitch. You dog." She opened the door wider and leaned on it. "What the hell, you sonofabitch . . ."

"I got your letters," I said. "Thought I'd say hello. I'm on my way to California. Thought I'd stop by."

I could see the years melting away in her eyes. They at least were the same. Still ready to giggle and run.

16

"I'll get you some milk. Come on through."

And that was it. I came in real shy but the years soon fell away. I never said that she looked well. I don't speak to many women.

A linoleum and wipe-clean kitchen. Good and clean.

"How you been?" I said. "You married again?" I'm blunt like that.

She pulled out a store cut-loaf. "No," she smiled and pushed her hair back from her ear. "I look after Mom. Papa went off. I ain't got time for men."

She went about making me a baloney sandwich like I'd just come home from work. I'd done looking about the kitchen and pulled out a stool.

"How's your mother?" I'd never met the woman.

"Oh, she's got the rheumatism and her pains. Keeps me busy."

"So your old man went?"

She shrugged and I didn't press.

"What happened to you?" she asked.

I thought she meant the war or the whole ten years, but she touched her face to indicate my bruises that I'd forgot. I mirrored her touching and grinned bashfully.

"Oh thems. I been fighting that's all."

"Fighting still?" she smirked and became the girl again and my heart warmed a little. "You ain't changed."

"World ain't changed." The sandwich and milk was pushed toward me. "Good to see you, Am." I always called her Am. Not Mandy. Only Amanda when I was mad.

She said nothing on that. She put her arms across her bosom and sighed.

"So what you at?"

I chewed on my bread and looked out the window. "I'm gonna sign up again. I was in the navy. For the war."

"You were? What did you do?"

I gave time to swallow.

"I was on a ship. It went down. We were the last battleship to go down. And the bastard that sunk us we were his first hit in the whole war. Believe that? Our last. His first."

"That's kinda funny," she smiled again.

"Ain't it?" I ate more but started to feel uncomfortable. I hadn't been in a kitchen for a long time. Hadn't been alone with a woman since Effa. I could feel her around me.

"Did you get hurt?" She already started packing away the baloney and wiping her knife.

"No," I said, drank my milk. "I did OK."

A call came from upstairs and a stomp of a cane.

Amanda blushed. "That's Mama. You came at her lunch."

"She know who I am?" I said.

"No," and she went to the oven. "I never told anyone. No one needed to know."

I stood up. "I'll get going. Didn't mean no bother. Thanks for the sandwich, Am."

"You marry again?" She wiped her face as she said this.

"No," I lied. "Didn't find no call for it."

She took out a bowl from the oven and moved around real quick for cutlery and tray. Not looking at me now.

I put the rest of the sandwich in my pocket. I'm always squirreling food.

She wiped her hands on a cloth and her face was flushed from the oven.

"You remember when we went to see that movie? That cartoon?"

"Aye."

"Remember how you used to fall asleep at the movies?" She laughs. It fills me up.

"I saw it in Guam too. Last movie I've ever seen."

"Where's Guam?"

I blinked and looked out the window at the paved backyard. "You know? I don't really even know. Ain't that a bitch? Pacific Ocean that's all. Biggest sea there is."

She sighed and shook her head.

"That was real nice of you back then. The movie and all. Better than the sonofabitch you usually were." She nods and we're done. "Real nice."

My hand is on the back door. "I'll go out this way. No trouble. Good to see you, Am."

She shushes me with a flapping wrist. "Just quit fighting, you sonofabitch." There's more stomping from upstairs. "You look a fright! Go and look after yourself."

I tip my cap. All I ever do.

"No war now, Am."

She turns away from me and I shut the door behind and I catch my breath on the stoop. Not one of my best days.

By the day I reached the ocean I'd drunk and fought Effa out and I was the navy boy again. Nobody died, I never got too high, and I'm sure some of them shit-kickers deserved it. Wouldn't be drinking alone else.

I had shipped out of Mare Island for the war so came back there again. Four months it had taken. I went slow because I needed gas money. Had to work weeks here and there to get it. November now, not that you'd know it that much in California.

But my bad luck was that I never got used to telephones. Never had anyone to talk to or ask for anything from anyone who might have had one. Never had one growing up. One wife before the war, one during, no phones. Radio-phones on a ship. Ship to shore. Big lot of whirs and clicks and voices like they were coming out of a locked room. Had to have a two-way on my boat later

19

for licensing, but I'd give you ten dollars if you ever saw me use it and I don't pay ten dollars for nothing so that's a sum. There should be nothing in this world that you start that you can't do on your own. I'd die before I called for help or if the only thing left moving was my mouth and I had to.

So I should have phoned ahead to the Mare but didn't think of it. I wouldn't know how to find the number anyways. Not then. I was in my forties before I got my name in a phone book and that wasn't for personal, just for business. I walked into that wooden building and put in my name pretty much like in '43. Mind I was drafted then. If I had called ahead reckon they might have had a greeting party for me. I'd have been sailing the next day because they would have had my papers by the time I got there. As it was I was just another green boots. That would delay me. And it ain't good for a drinking Irishman to delay in a harbor town. Not for the town anyways.

The young boots, the ensign that called me in, was about my age, which I didn't expect. Last time it had been an old fella. Guess they might all be dead.

Boots shook my hand and asked me to take a seat. I took off my marine corps hat and folded it into my pocket. He asked me why I wanted to sign up again and I said I had need of the money and hadn't really got straight since I'd left. I didn't see any point in telling about Effa.

"It'd take me a time to get your record. It ain't kept here." He picked up a pencil and paper. Bright yellow pencil, sharpened that morning, and paper that was such a stock that it didn't bend at all when he dragged it from the pile. He licked the point of the pencil which I knew meant nothing but showed him to be some farmer's boy or such.

"Were you on more than one class during action?"

20

"No, sir," I replied. "I trained right here in '43. Just about nineteen. Then the Pacific and Guam on the *Indianapolis*. I was on the Indy when we destroyed the *Akagane Maru*. And at Saipan."

He had not yet written and now his forehead creased as his eyes took me in and the pencil rolled between his fingers.

"The *Indianapolis*?" He looked me up and down. I must've looked like a long streak of nothing and he leaned back like a Monday morning judge when he's looking at all the weekend drunks. There was the sound of his fan clattering on the filing cabinet, the only sound. I always liked sounds like that. Motors, engines. Something off-kilter. Needing some adjustment. Guess that irritates some folks. Me, I get lulled to sleep.

I realized it was a question he was asking. The *Indianapolis*.

"Yes, sir," I said. "CA-35."

I didn't know what else to say 'cept her tag. He rolled that pencil like a cigar.

"How old are you?" His head was almost on his shoulder, still looking me up and down, taking in my unlaced boots.

Told him flat. Guess he figured I should be older. Not fine to think of someone near your age going through what I had. He must have thought us all fathers. Not kids.

I was holding up a mirror to him, shaving mirror size; close and magnified. Showing what might happen when you put on a uniform so young. Shit, it was only eight years ago. I still thought of it when I shaved and looked in the mirror. Close and magnified. Thought about it every time out night-fishing and something bumps against the boat and reminds that you shouldn't be there.

"And you want to go out again?"

"Yes, sir," I said. "I got nothing here 'cept my truck. And I'll sell that tonight if you take me on."

He put his pencil down. Smiled at me like he meant it.

"Shouldn't be a problem, sailor. But it ain't gonna happen

right away. I gotta get your record. That'll take a few days. Though you can take a physical. Tomorrow. Eleven hundred." He got a form from a drawer and pushed it to me. "Fill that out for the doc. You remember where that is, right? Probably the same goddamn sawbones!"

I leaned in and took the paper and he looked hard at the tattoo on my left.

I tapped at it under his eye. Bought me a drink or two that ink.

"I got that after Okinawa," I said. It was just the Indy written in a horse-shoe garland and an image of her coming out of my forearm. "Jap pilot crashed into our deck. Kamikaze. Thought we were going down then. Took three months to fix her up. The ship. Not the tattoo. Got it here. While waiting on repair. Should get rid. Proud to be on my first ship. Stupid kid thing to do."

He looked carefully at me then. "You boys get a pension? After . . . you know . . . what with your captain's court martial and all?"

"Nothing to do with us," I said and thought that it was time I stood and he shifted a little as I got up.

"I get some cash for it. I got my truck and rifles here," I said. "I'll sell them tonight. I got reels that I'd like to take with."

"Get your A1 done first, sailor. Then see. You might have something wrong with. Didn't a lot of you boys . . . get sick? You know? I mean . . . after?"

"Reckon so," I said and put back my cap. "I'll fill this over some coffee." I didn't have to salute him yet and I made for the door.

"Sailor?" His voice lilted up like a boy. I knew what he was gonna say. I stopped in the door.

"What was it *like*?" A sheen on his forehead and leaning forward all excited. Like all of 'em. "I mean with the sharks and all?"

22

I sniffed. Straightened up like they expected. Tried to look noble. I stopped telling a long time ago. That's why I bought a marine corps cap. Stop people asking. The Indy one I kept in my bunk on my boat or right now in my truck with the map and flashlight.

"Well," I said, and let that hang for a while. "Five days in the water. Reckon it takes five days to tell it. But I'll tell you something. Them life jackets you gets to wear, them kapoks, they get all watered up after a couple of days. They'll drown you after. They don't tell you that. Hard to get 'em off. Like a straitjacket. Your fingers don't work too good after a coupla days. They get all white and lumpy. Dead man's fingers. Can't wipe your eyes for the salt in 'em. Cut like razors. You tied a good knot when you jumped in the water. Weighs like another body after two days. Pulls you down." I tried to smile but it kinda winced and was gone. "Don't tie a knot."

I saw him swallow.

I winked back at him. "Like they say," tipped my cap. "Can't drown a man that's set to hang." I slipped out before he said anything else. I'd done on that talk.

"These three pears were for my breakfast, but I give them to you gladly. Eat them and stop weeping."

"If you want me to eat them, please peel them for me."

"Peel them?" asked Geppetto, very much surprised. "I should never have thought, dear boy of mine, that you were so dainty and fussy about your food. Bad, very bad! In this world, even as children, we must accustom ourselves to eat of everything, for we never know what life may hold in store for us."

3

San Francisco

That talking stuck in my craw. I put my head down until I got off the Mare. I went to my truck in the lot, yanked the door almost off then slammed it shut without getting in. I went to the back, under the tarp, and felt at the carbines through the gunny-sack to their lambskins. Then I felt my Penn reels through their wrappings. I kept 'em separate from the poles in case someone lifted 'em. I opened out one of them Senators, clicked it a few times as I leaned on the side of the truck, my hands below so no one could see.

That sound calmed, settled. For a moment I slowed it down, gave it two clicks, then two more, real gentle like. I imagined a tiger shark tickling at my butterfish. Dumb and fat, not knowing what was there. Tigers. Blowflies of the sea. Rat fish. No one wants a tiger. *Click-click, click-click.* I can feel him about to jerk then he goes away. Then back. Always comes back. Dumb fish. *Click-click, click-click.* I drop it back to the truck before he runs, before the whir and smoke of the reel, before I see the bitten wrists and the

25

elbows white and raw, a hand gone, forearm ragged like a torn sheet of paper, the tattoo almost all that's left. The bodies not yet bit kicking away the boy, kicking him from the raft as he screams for help, for his buddies to help him.

I cover everything up and look for a drink.

It's still morning so I takes a bus down to San Fran. I figure if I leave the truck and get drunk out of town I won't get in too much easy trouble. Besides, I like the Okie beer in San Fran, and you can't get the 'Gansett out here.

November, so crab season. You can smell it when you get off the bus. Follow your nose to Fisherman's Wharf, right at the end of the Embarcadero, *the end of the line*. Fisherman's Wharf. Corny, happy horse-shit name.

Pier-45 and all you can see and smell are the cauldrons on the dock and boardwalk. Dozens of 'em, like a conclave of witches. Wood smoke, hot iron, crab shell. Dungeness crab. Best in the world. That's a bold statement I know but once you tasted it you don't need to try any different.

The wooden street carts look like they made 'em at home, like kids with their soapbox cars, some of 'em just crates turned upside down with the cauldron right behind. Thirty-five cents for a cooked crab handed over in newspaper with a wooden fork, twenty-five cents raw, to take home. Get a slice of lemon for free to flavor and clean up after; lemons as fruitful as oranges here, pluck 'em from trees if you want. If they'd let you. But that's all business now. All fenced off. Kids don't eat for free.

Some folks don't eat crab. Crab's a bottom feeder, three hundred feet down. They eat the dead and the shit. In Chicago and New York when them gangsters got the notion of dumping their rivals in the river or out to sea no respectful person ate crab.

You never knew what them crabs might have been sliding into their jaws.

I watch the boats as I sit on a gull-shit-dashed bench and eat. Hundreds of masts. I get the itch again. The itch to go out. The itch to be lonely. The men all look busy and right serious but I know they're supremely happy, religious happy. This is God's work. That's no romantic happy horse-shit. You know it to be just that. The land's a tool for the sea. Somewhere to broom your keel and sell your work. The real Earth is the sea, and she claims more of the land back every year. And more of us when she can. Turning us back to the sea, from where we came. She wants us back. We deny her. Too much. Think we control her. Build houses on her shore. She laps at us slow. Takes her time. But she has all the time. That's the sound of her tides. It's the deep laughing at us.

I've picked up a friend in a black mutt watching me eat. A terrier with a Labrador for a father. He's sitting with his head cocked and those pleading brows. He's surrounded by smells. Torturous for him. Like a shark caught in a slick, cruising the blood. I give him over my shell and he takes it real gentle, white teeth trying not to pinch me, and taps away over the boardwalk with his tail lolling like he's outsmarted me.

I stand and breathe it in, pick a boat that I wish mine. I got my own rods and reels, my own oilers. I could pick for a crew job. But I got the navy tomorrow. And I ain't no one's mate I guess. So why am I signing up to be yelled out every morning? There ain't a man alive who can tell me what to do today. Give that up tomorrow. I brush my hands free of the crab, rub the lemon through my palms and I smell a lot better than I did that morning and figure I'll head behind Jefferson Street for a drink.

Everyone is moving faster than me. I'm in their way all the time. Lot of women working with their men, scowling at me. All the folks in white aprons and plain faces. Hard to tell man or woman; they all dress the same. I weave through them excusing myself all the way. I'm slow 'cause I keep looking back at the masts, chewing on a toothpick like thinking on a pipe.

I have to drink something out of me.

Pick the bar with the smallest front. Take four steps to pass it by. Wood blinds closed on the windows. Perfect. Guarantee it's long inside. Deep dark booths. An Irishman at the bar to ask me where I'm from back home.

"Boston," I'll say with a grin and put my cap on the bar. "Brandy and Jameson. I'm for the navy tomorrow."

"War's over, Bub." He'll wipe a spot clean for me.

Maybe I won't say any of that. Two in the afternoon bartenders don't expect much from wharf-rats. It ain't society that he or I wants.

I sneak in, like you're supposed to during the day, close the door quick like the sunlight will kill the vampires within. Bar manners. Drinking rules. Good bars don't want their customers to see the passage of the day, that's what the blinds are for. It's all dull low bulbs in here. Perpetual twilight or dawn for those that drink at twilight or dawn.

He doesn't wipe a spot for me but I put my cap on the bar and my coat on the stool to show I mean business. He's not Irish. He's in his twenties like me, but he looks softer. No service back there. I half get on the stool.

"What'll it be?" he says, keeps the bar towel over his shoulder.

"Brandy and Jameson. Bottle Regal pale."

He gives me the beer on its branded tray and I slap him a five and we're done with the tray as I pick up the beer and he whips the tray away and goes about something else along from me.

I turn, my elbows on the bar, survey my fellow flies. They ain't worth recalling. Blue tobacco smoke over all their heads like waves, waves pushing 'em down, their heads to their glass. They are already drowned. All sitting alone in their own booths. All alone together. Ain't no friends here. Too early for friends. I put my back to 'em but there's the mirror behind the bar that makes all the booze seem twice as bountiful and shows the bums like a painting when someone wants to show the dirty America that they never knew but always suspected. I could point out how different I am from them to the crew-cut pouring, smile and shake my head at the pitiful horror of 'em. I ain't them. I'm shipping out tomorrow. Besides, I'm at a wake ain't I?

"Here's to swimming with bow-legged women." I raise my glass to my fine blond barman. He could be of German blood. What do I know? Never saw a German 'cept the ones that run the bait stores. Never saw a Jap. Never saw my supposed enemy, the man who would kill me. They were wrapped in steel like me or just the glint of wings across the sun. Might have been no one in those planes. Get sunk by a Japanese sub, do I? Could be a goddamn giant squid for all of that, or something ancient, miles down, suddenly drawn up by all the hulls crisscrossing the waters, thinking all them swimming dinosaurs have come back. Finally come back. Lot of ships got lost all of a sudden. We all heard them stories. No radio. No survivors. Never seen again. I hear a lot of subs picked up noises that couldn't have come from no whale. They'd be deep down, near the pole, at the bottom of the earth, and something would come "gulping" into their headsets. A volcano underwater they'd tell themselves. But then people had never been down that deep before. Underwater quake. We had to develop the technology to become prehistoric, to hear the old Earth underneath. But I bet that "gulp" from the dark kept 'em awake in their bunks sometimes. "We shouldn't be here," they'd think. "We don't belong here." Hundreds of years ago we were inches of wood between them and us, them being the deep ones.

Now it was inches of steel. And we still don't belong. Not our planet. Still the dinosaurs' world. We're the ants upon it. And ants don't belong in the water. Could have been one of our own that done for us; thinking we were Japs. That must have happened sometimes. Friendly fire. Who thought up that horse-shit? Friendly fire. Jesus H. Christ. I know it was the Japs that done for us now. The Jap captain was at the court martial for our Captain McVay. We were just boys on a steel giant's back or hiding in its belly. The sharks waiting all around, following our white keel, matching our white keel. Following like they used to shadow the slave ships. Waiting, gliding. Waiting as they once did, sure that one Black man will make the leap from his slaver. The black eye of the Negro looking down into the black eye of the monster. Hypnotizing him. Sharks stayed around the slave dories until the cargo reached the "blackbirder" that would take them to America. That's why they didn't chain 'em together, not 'til they were on the ships. Always one who rolls over the side. Not good if they're all linked together. Makos still hang around them African slave castles. Might be the same ones. Just waiting for the time to return. Like the ones in the real deep, in the trenches. Waiting. They got all the time. You punch 'em on the snout, in the eye, and they swim away like you're already forgotten. Then the dorsal remembers something. It goes full profile as she turns, that triangle cutting through the water. It's a she because she's got a chunk ripped out of her dorsal. Mature female. That's where some bull latched onto her with his jaws while he ravished her. Then that dorsal goes narrow as she turns back, then it slips below the water as she goes slower and she has to roll to get a good bite. And you never heard a thing. All the worst deaths are silent. They come out of the dark, or far away, and you never hear the bodies fall or the car crash, and you wish you had, never being able to say why hearing it would have made it easier, why being there when it happens is better, instead of the telegram, the policeman at your door, the sorry neighbor when you get home.

It will never make a sound. It will come and the water will run red and black and the screams wake you every hour of the night. Always the night. Sharks come at night.

"You should get out, buddy. I thinks you had enough."

I lift my head to Blondie. He mistakes my somnambulism for drunkenness. He has made me a corned beef sandwich and I give such a grin and plant my cap to my head and put my toothpick behind my ear. Great sandwich. Every sandwich is great when you're drunk and someone else surprises you with it. Other people's food always tastes better. Excepting eggs. No one can make you a good egg. Don't know why. Eggs are personal somehow. I tap my bottle for another brew, he shakes his head and gets me a Regal and I take a look around at a different bar. The place is crowded now, rowdy. Fort Mason is just around the corner and Hunter's Point—where they shipped us out to Pearl on the Indy—only a bus down the road so a lot of these could be service. I hazard it to be about nine because I have napped a little and always wake up about that time for my second wind. I have only ever heard half of Jack Benny and never seen a movie all the way through. I used to fall asleep during the intermission and my wife—that one be Carole—would elbow me so that I woke up with bruises. I'd managed to stay awake for *Pinocchio* mind, coupla years before. That was with Amanda, my first wife. I liked that cartoon. *Pinocchio* was the only book anyone had ever given me. I was eight I reckon and the book was battered old even then. I was on the stoop of Nolan's bar in Boston with a Dr Pepper and a split straw waiting for my old man to come out. That ain't so bad; that was the way then for kids. Nolan himself comes out to the stoop in his beer-stinking apron and hands me the book that I guess someone had left behind some time. He leans down, ruffles my hair and says something about the puppet on the front is as long and skinny as me, reminds him of me.

It was in Nolan's ten years later, St. Paddy's Day, that I got an iron bar over my head. Old Nolan picks me up from the floor himself, not a day older.

"Jesus, boy! You still that puppet? Ain't you ever growing up?"

I don't read much. Dime-novels for myself on the boat. The Saint and The Shadow mostly.

Good Carole. She didn't warrant contending me but any man was thin on the ground then. You may think me hard for talking less about Carole than Amanda but she knew me as a fisherman. That meant that between the water and the war I maybe spent one hundred days with her. Now I know that Napoleon nearly took back Europe in that time but still that's a short time for man and wife. Don't judge what you don't know. I still carry torches for all my women. And I don't respect men that don't.

There's a big commotion down at the end of the saloon. It's well-lit and clouded in a cigar fug, and even from here I can see the flash of green. There's gambling going on, a contest. I'm in a bad enough mood to be up for that.

"What's the game?" I ask.

"Monday," he says. "Arm wrestling. Big money."

"Do you have to buy your way in?" says I.

"Nope. But you're a little skinny, Bub. I'd sit it out."

I get off the stool and pick up my beer.

"Good and skinny," I pull down my cap and wink. "Get better odds that way."

I'm powerful drunk and that's a good thing. That half-hour

where you feel more than what you are. A foot taller, fifty pounds of muscle heavier. You're Popeye, the beer your spinach, and you push through the crowd. Effa wouldn't like this. Be a good way to remember her passing and better than fighting. But I shouldn't do it at all. Got a date with a doc in the morning but that Quint is another man, can't talk to him now, can't hear him.

"Who'll spot me for this duel!" I yell, pulling off my shirt so I'm standing in vest, figuring that's the way of it but I can't see anyone else undressed. I need spotting, only rattling with small change, Blondie had my last folding money.

I feel their eyes on me. I'm skinny but lean and hard, like I always thought the Saint looked. God knows who thought George Sanders could pull that off. The ship had bundles of all those RKO pictures. That Saint really ticked me off.

"That ain't the Saint," I said in the dark. "The Saint's vital! Vital it says in the books!"

Herbie Robinson, young boots from Cleveland, baseball player, yells over to me from the blackest part of the room.

"What's 'vital' mean, Irish?"

"I know it don't mean he wears a damn girdle," I said back to the cock.

Sharks got Herbie. He was younger than me. Bitten in half. Take that to a priest and see what he says. Maybe the Lord don't have dominion over the sea. Jonah and the whale? Look again. It was a fish. Can't get an arm down a whale's throat let alone a man. He'll chew you up but he won't swallow you whole. It was a shark. Look it up.

"There's an Irishman wants to wrastle here!" I slapped my chest. That would do it. A drunk Mick, good entertainment. The guys started roaring and the green was flying now.

"What's your name, pal?" A cigar is by my cheek and I see a blackboard.

"Quint," says I, and up it goes in white scrawl. Eight names.

"Have a beer, Mick," says another cigar and I now have two beers in my hands. I finish one as I takes my stool.

"Put ten on me," I says to the guy who looks like he has the biggest book, then I sees my opponent. He rolls himself out of the crowd. He looks like an Italian butcher and thirty years and thirty pounds too late.

"Make it twenty," I says to the book.

That Italian thought his weight would count. I was too fast for him and my wrist is a fisherman's. All my strength is in front of me and deep in my back and shoulders. I hoped his wife weren't watching. We didn't have anything to grip save the edge of the table. On the Indy we used C-clamps and your table was bolted to the steel deck so this was harder but I got used to it right fast and he didn't. I slapped his back to apologize and put my arms in the air as he rubbed his shoulder and slunk away.

I was 8–1 when I set down. Eight men in the pot so fair enough. The book raised his pencil at me with a shake of his head and I nodded. He wasn't giving me anything for 8–1 when he was spotting me, not after I'd slammed the Italian like a bottle. No matter. If he gave me twenty that was more than I came in with. I'd have to make my next lot look harder though.

I went to the head. My piss was orange and hot. I was drinking too much, eating too little. A fat guy came next to me. San Francisco must be full of fat men.

"You laid that guy out, Irish. And you're drunk. I'll put my dough on you next round."

"You do that," I said. "And I ain't drunk till the morning."

He saw my tattoo.

"Geez! You were on the *Indianapolis*?"

"Is that what it says?" I buttoned myself up.

"Shit, Mick!" He was smiling and whispering like I was his secret. "*What was it like?*"

He was asking me this in the john in the back of a bar. Docs had asked me this. Admirals had spoke about it in a courtroom at my captain's court martial. He didn't deserve nothing.

"It was good," I said. "I'm signing up to do it again. Don't bet on me this time. I'm gonna make it look hard." I patted his fat face. "Wait for the next round."

"You're gonna have to beat Liu," he said. "Liu only comes down once a month. Takes four hundred dollars home when he does."

"I don't see any Chinese out there."

"He's there now," he says, then we both hear the cheering and look to the ceiling like the noise is flying around our heads. "That's Liu. Winning. He don't drink and he's as strong as a bull."

"That's a good fact," I say and walk out of there. I got a full Regal left and that's all I care about.

I see Liu then. He must be sixty but hard to tell 'cause he's a big man, naked chest and head shaved like the Chinese do. I could fit inside him. I drink my beer high. A pale ale ruined by all the smoke. I like smoke. But I like it out on the sea. Indoors it's like burning hair, ain't no pleasure in it. Used to come out of the movies with Carole and your whole suit stunk of it, even your tie. You used to dress up to go to the movies. Effa didn't like to smoke and hated me doing it so I saved it for the sea. I didn't mind, that's where I wanted to do it, that's where I leave it. Ain't nothing like smoking on the sea once your lines are set and the sun is watching you as it dies, lulling you as it melts into the sea like iron into a cast mold, and the tide is pushing you out, away from men and their horse-shit. Think about everything then. All the world passing through your head, all your past. Every memory comes back to you. Every good day and every bad. Almost a shame when the reel starts to run and snaps you back into the here and now.

I ain't fighting Liu yet. I got a Polish to beat. I'm noticing that this is a fight of races. There ain't no naturals at the table. They're betting on us. Polish and Irish. Italian and Chinese, Greek and God knows. The only natural that Americans like to bet on are horses. That's it.

Me and Polish are about the same age. Same build too. I reckon he's got navy in him. We sit at the same time, nod to each other. He ain't got any ink on him but he measures mine. He knows I'm service now and I can see he's bringing his big game. This be tough. Polacks don't know to quit. They do a day's work before breakfast, and breakfast is potato vodka.

Still, Effa wouldn't want me to wrestle, and more she wouldn't want me to lose so I gotta beat him. I'm not heartless about Effa and you might think my mourning odd but I've been through the Depression and I've been through war and more than that. I've been through a working week that no one could believe even when they saw the newsreels before the mouse cartoons. I've been through something that fat men think they can ask me about in restrooms. The largest naval disaster in American history they say, maybe any history, I don't know. But I know that death circles me. And literally at that. I have looked into his black eyes. The only thing he doesn't like is disrespect. It's like that crying clown at the opera that visited us in Saipan. That clown ain't pale because of the make-up. He's pale because of the shame. Had to have an Italian translate that for me. Happy little guy from New York, real ladies man. He had slicked-back hair with a razorbill parting almost right down the center just like George Raft. I think he was taken on the third day. Hard to tell who we were with them oil masks all over us but I could make out his hair and guessed it was him. Screamed like that clown. Could hear him screaming under the water. Don't let anyone tell you that you can't hear sound under the water. They scream like they're from another world, like standing in the lobby of a movie theater waiting for your girl and hearing the show off the walls. In the deep you just make your distance from the dying, from the shame, and hide your head.

I clasp hands with the Polack. I won't have to make this look hard as I feel the littlest bones grind in my hand.

Speed ain't gonna do it. He's as lean as me. Our hands are spliced, each trying to get our knuckles over the top, only we don't have no knuckles, we're both worn. Ham-fisted lumps of men. We're dead-locked, still in the center. I'm guessing my face is as red as his, and the table is fit to break. Our feet are touching, pushing against each other. He's got flat rubber soles though, I noticed that. I got heavy cleats. Boots for a slippery deck, petroleum soles. If the whole bar upended I'd be the last to fall. Like when I walked up an eight-inch gun turret to jump to the deep. Good friction. He might beat me in a run in the street but I can see in his eyes that I've got the leverage.

So I got to sink him easy, like a porbeagle, like when you plant your feet in the chair and it's line and hook and I begin to push like I'm planting a gaff in him.

He does what he only can and pulls his arm in 'til it's almost under his chin, stops pushing over and tries to pull me behind his left shoulder, shifts on his seat. That's a damn amateur. There's just a big space over his right shoulder now, a cavern, and I don't go for the table, I go for the belly of the crowd over his right, some fat guy pumping his dollars in his fists and chanting my name. The Polack's lost his lever. It's just physics now. Poundage and line. Reel and line. Fish don't run 'cause you're weak. You were carrying the wrong wire. You brought a cheap reel and a thirty-pound line to a monster fight.

I don't push to the table, table don't exist, I push into that fat man's belly in the crowd and pivot when I feel the Polack gasp, like when the shark turns when he feels it, feels the line that he didn't even know was there, when he takes the bait that he thought was free. Dumb fish. And you gaff him like a piñata as he rubs along the side of the boat.

The Polack's hand cracks on the table, my fist my gaff, and I see his teeth gape in surprise just like a porker when he knows I got him.

The crowd cheers and I drop the Polack. I thank him but he can't hear me over the roar. He nods and stands up. He doesn't rub his arm. He just keeps nodding respect and backs away.

My back gets slapped by a dozen hands but I gotta get up for the next combatants. The table's wet with sweat now. A beer pushed into my hand. I stand with the crowd. Think about all the guys I beat on the Indy. All dead. Didn't matter how strong they were in the steel. You ain't nothing in the water.

My arm is my rod, as the prophets say. My sinews are the line, my past is my bait, my chum. Skinny Irishman. Gonna beat you all. Surrounded again by sharks. I'm beginning to hate this room with my drunkenness. Bets on who will lose, who will fall. Worse than sharks.

Liu brushes past me like I'm not there and the seat creaks beneath him. He's sweating a river like he's oiled up and maybe he is. Slippery devil.

He's got a big Greek to fight but he don't look like a fighting Greek. He looks nervous. I met Greek soldiers in Tinian. They think they're all Spartans and that ain't a bad heritage to have; better than an American anyhow. We ain't got nothing.

They had this script on their arms, on their badges, with a Spartan helm. "Come and take them." Should have seen the grin on the young buck that told me that. He ran his finger across it like it was the navel of his first girl. This was what them Spartans said to the Persians when they told 'em to lay down their arms. "Come and take them." Thousands of years before we even dreamed of a flag. Didn't have to draft Greeks into the war. But this guy ain't one of them. He's got too much American in him.

Everyone is cheering for Liu and I lean back into the crowd to enjoy it. This will get me good odds. I sidle up to my book.

"I'll take that twenty now," I shout over the howls, "and I'll give you a show. Else I'll keel over at his first push." He slips it to me. He knows he can take bets on me as we wrestle. And I ain't gonna win.

"Liu will break your arm, Irish," he says and we're watching the Greek pile over to the floor like a sack of shit and the place erupts around us.

"I might win," I says, right in his ear now over the ruckus. "And be walking out of here with four hundred dollars and just your twenty."

"He's got a hundred pounds on you, Mick," he sneers. "You got thirty seconds to hold him. I might take a hundred before he takes you. Twenty buys you to hold 'til your arm busts." He chomps on his cigar. "You don't give me thirty seconds and I got some boys that will see you outside."

I pull my cap down. "You ever take a five-hundred-pound bluefin? I done that twice a week, Fatman. I'm champeen of a ship of dead men." I grin. "Don't tell me my business."

I wheel away from him. Liu's in my seat, least the seat I was in for my winning that is. You ever fight over a seat? That's my Saturday night.

He ain't got up after flooring the Greek. He's sitting there like Buddha. He don't have to move. He is the mountain that prophets come to. The names get rubbed off the board. Just three of us left clear. I never even see the other guy. Me and Liu the semifinal. But he's in my sit and that might rile up the crowd.

I stand in front of him and he takes a few seconds to flip his eyes up at me.

"I'm there," I says, pointing at the chair his bulk is squashing.

He don't say nothing, looks right through me. I don't know if he can speak English. Maybe this is what he does for work. He goes home to some tenement in San Fran's Chinatown and slaps hundreds of dollars in front of his wife and goes to sleep for a month. Then he rolls off his mattress one Monday and comes here again and beats all. Month in, month out. I don't care. I got my twenty so I ain't lost a dime for my drinking and I have my bus transfer home. If I can land a five-hundred-pound tuna I could hold up a fat Chinaman for thirty seconds.

"My seat," I says again. "Liu, is it?" I lift my cap and give my white smile. I got good teeth. No sweet tooth and I always uses a pick. I like the little pain at my gums, the smell of blood on the wood. My own juices. Like when you wipes your finger in your ear and takes a sniff. Your body your own little putrid world. Ain't nothing clean in keeping teeth white. Just little acts of pleasurable torture.

Liu wants to keep his seat and points a finger down to the opposite chair. A big whoop comes up from the sheep around us, glad they came out for this. I'm smelling fish and bloodied salt and ice from some of them. Fishermen have come in late. Now seeing one of their own setting down.

I rock my head and take the seat.

"Well, Liu, I guess I'm gonna have to take you off that seat. Ain't I, 'Little Boy'?"

Little Boy. Private joke.

I spit in my hand and put my elbow down. The spit runs down my wrist and Liu watches it, grimaces. He's got thin lips, don't think he knows how to smile, just those down-turned lips framing his round chin.

He puts his hand in mine like he's an emperor sealing a peace treaty. Don't know if he looks like a Jap, never seen one. I think Chinese have different eyes.

We had a kid from Ohio with us on the Indy. Toby Wanaka. He was adopted by a Jap couple as a baby. His real mom a prostitute—which was pretty much the only children Japs could get. He signed up after Pearl Harbor and his family was interred in Granada, Colorado, a month later. His dad ran a photo store so that was doubly risky I guess. Toby was mad as hell. He couldn't even write home in case he was helping the enemy. We had a Jap-American battalion in the war, when all those newspapers were calling for Japs to be ousted. Like I said: nothing more segregated than an American army.

That Jap battalion was the most decorated of the whole war for the number of men it had. Any American war in fact. Their wives and children, their parents and grandparents in camps, for that's how long we go back with Japan, their grandparents coming over with the Irish. Not that those San Fran newspapers would have it. Every Jap was just all invaders. The only good thing a newspaper is for is for putting a sheet of it on the sea to check which way you're drifting when your engine's off 'cause the fish don't like your engines. The paper ain't got no windage, see? It lays flat and goes with the water.

Don't know how Toby felt when a Jap sub sunk us in the night and he leaped to the water in his shorts. Don't know how his parents would have felt if he'd have got killed by a Jap. Guess the sharks saved them that thought at least. Mighty hospitable of 'em.

Taking Liu's hand is like kneading dough and wraps around mine like the same, like when you push your fists into it. His tits are resting on the table like two heads looking at me with their brown cyclops eye on each. San Fran is a fat city.

Let's at it.

Well, that fat Chinese sure had his gods standing behind him, and Irishmen ain't got no gods 'cept the one beat into him, and that one only wants you to die being scared of him. I swear there was a sound like a hand-clap and my right arm was keeling over like it wasn't even mine. I got solemn real quick.

I pushed back and, Jesus H. Christ didn't I hold him and see that Chinese widen his eyes at this skinny Mick holding him like a wall. Thirty seconds I said I would hold.

I couldn't do nothing but grind my teeth and hang on but that Liu hadn't landed no bluefin with a thirty-pound twist rope, and that's all we had before nylon, which was war surplus but sure did change fishing. I was landing five-hundred-pound fish with wooden and Bakelite reels and male Calcutta rods with hose-clips holding the rope to the bamboo. And that's what Liu was up against. He was just tuna to me, and even at his most hulking he weren't no five hundred pounds. And I would show him that, and show him that drunk to boot.

I don't know if no thirty seconds went by but I know there was a roar building. This was new to Liu and he showed it. His face was surely animated now. I gave nothing in my face, but I had muscles in my neck that hadn't worked for a long time that were just about ready to pop. I think I'd earned my twenty and my arm was at an angle that wasn't about to pull off no miracle.

Then Liu dropped the prison rules we were playing.

I guess his fat was a good hideout, for he started pulling more than push. But you couldn't see that with his arm like a leg of beef. He was pulling me across the table so my ass would rise and then he could push my arm down like he was correcting a clock.

That's how he did it.

His arm so fat you couldn't see it shift if you were in the circle around but he was pulling me up. So I was done. I didn't have the weight for it, to plant back down. My arm was going.

I pulled back and my good teeth were grinding and Liu's eyes closed. I looked over his head to my book. He nodded and I'd sweated enough, the brandy pouring out of me and back into my mouth. I licked my lips. I had a day's mustache. That wouldn't go well with the navy tomorrow and my blood left my arm as I thought on that. One flinch of distraction. Don't deviate when a fat Chinaman has your hand for a puppet. He got a mite of self-respect all of a sudden and my muscles must have blinked because my boots left the floor. There was the cheer, which covered all the pain I was in, and I was on my back with the chair wrapped round me. I kicked it loose, its legs giggling as it rattled away.

Lot of laughter now and I scrambled up, my arm burning. I slapped my muscle and it was getting bigger and redder. It was ringing on me something bad but I couldn't feel it yet. Good to be drunk when harm comes. But I was regretting the morning to come.

I don't know if there are statues of a standing Buddha but there Liu was with his belly gaping at me with its button like a surprised mouth and his tits a-flapping, his nipples like amazed eyes. I reckon he had his challenge for the month. He was saluting the crowd, his sweat spraying the front row and they just wiped it off their mouths still cheering.

My arm was blowing up like a boat fender and them drunks were playing my back like I'd won. I guess no one had taken Liu so far. My book was handing out green and taking it in and paid me no mind.

But I'd got my twenty and went back to my jacket on my stool. I took one beer, a Regal I called for when it was offered, and that cooled my sweat, someone pleased to buy it me. In my jacket, my arm squalling me as I pulled it on, I remembered the doc's form and pulled it out. I had yet to fill it. Over coffee I had said. That seemed like yesterday. And I didn't have a pencil. I called for one at the bar and Blondie didn't have one either but I think he was holding out on me. How else did he tally up his bar? He'd just got used to Irishmen not handing things back. Fair enough.

All the noise around me and all I could do was stare at that paper and think how I was gonna fill it. I was gonna sleep in my truck as usual. I'd go into a hotel and ask the Irish at the porter for a loan. Aye that would do.

I looked up for Liu to thank him for my burning arm but didn't see him with all the bodies around and setting him up for the final. Didn't see or care who against. I saw the Polack and gave him a tip of my cap. Might see him at Mare tomorrow. You never know with Polacks.

I'd done Effa proud, disapproval proud like when a woman shakes her head but has to pinch her sly smile, and that was all that mattered, and maybe a little profit which wouldn't hurt. Another day's food and drink and then the navy for my mash and beans from now on.

I became sullen again and kept my eye to my paper as I went out the door, reluctant, like I was going to work. The only way to leave a bar.

It was night, San Fran still had gaslight then and it was like walking back a hundred year, the fog rolling in so you couldn't see the water or half the street. Still there were girls hanging under the lights, only the red draw of their huddled cigarettes marking 'em out as they clung together. The front wasn't so gentrified then. These were not like Hook Street New York girls with their flesh all out. These girls wore their boyfriend's pea-coats and wool hats.

I put my form back and headed for where my bus might be,

maybe have to get a streetcar to the depot. It was only about ten I guessed and I'd just got past the bar when my book comes out of the fog beside me. I stopped, just to see if I had to make way around him or through him and played my toothpick in my jaws.

"Weren't no thirty seconds, Mick," he said. He blew his cigar into the fog and I noticed then how much I stunk of him and the rest. Took me a second of straightening out of my booze to hear he was talking to me.

"You got a pencil?" I said, and then my arms were behind me from two guys at my back. I didn't struggle. So OK. And I went along.

An alley, so garbage cans and a caged twenty-watt bulb outside the delivery door of a Chinese. Two boys pushing me along and the book just asking for my twenty.

"I spotted you, Mick," he said. "Give it back. Or I take it." They were scraping me along the wall and my arm was hurting now. I shook free and made drunker. Rubbed my head under my cap and waved 'em down.

"All right, all right," I said. "Just a minute."

They stepped back. Two salty boys in oilers and caps. He'd have to do better than that but I was thinking of my arm. It wasn't broke but it wasn't going to help so I needed a corner and I stumbled further down the alley past the garbage and found the brickwork.

"What if I give you five for the twenty? That do?"

"Gimme the twenty and the five, Mick," the book said. He offered out his cigar. "Take this for your walk. Be happy. You got a busted arm, Mick. Don't make it your legs."

"Quint," I said. "Not Mick." I looked at 'em and grinned. "Quint." They'd remember that.

They laughed at my Irish braggadocio. I was Pagliacci now. I thought of that George Raft hair. A shark biting.

That book must have made a hundred out of me. I would've if I had my own twenty. Must have been paying these boys twenty just to stand there. Like I said, fighting over a chair was my Saturday night. This was Monday. So I'd have to go easy.

I told you I once got an iron bar laid up my head. St. Paddy's Day in Boston. Almost got a rhino horn there now where the bone grew over. Skull like a rock. Reckon it will fox a few in a thousand years when they finds it. That's if I'm not in the deep come Judgment.

Don't think they had no iron bars, would've shown 'em by now. Reckon the book just bought 'em in the bar. I might have stalled if they'd have brought an empty bottle at least. I ain't a fool to go against tools but prepare if you're going up against an Irishman or a short one. Irish and short men fight like demons. I had a jockey as a mate once. Drink done him for racing and he could only swallow egg sandwiches twice a week, all he could stomach, but he could lay out an entire bar. Tall guys just think they have to be tall. Real surprised when you lay 'em down. They hold out their jaws like prizes.

"All right," I said, "let me gets ready."

I don't think they thought they were gonna hear that.

I threw my cap down so they looked at that and I took my toothpick and put it in my top pocket so that they looked at that and not my truck keys in my fist.

"I can't take my jacket off," I giggled drunk. "My arm's bust." And I slammed the keys into the first fella's eye. I pulled the keys back. Needed them. His howl like a light coming on.

I let that howl and sight sink in and then grabbed the other kid by his wrist and elbow and followed him through to the corner at my back. He slapped the wall with his head and I felt him go light through my hand and his legs near tripped me as they splayed.

46

The keyed one wasn't coming back. His hands were about his head and he was running into the fog, and the book went to run after but I took his collar and he melted on my hand like a kitten lifted.

"I know you got a pencil." I went inside his jacket and stood on his cigar as he squirmed. I dug past his dollars and found the book, a three-inch pencil stub in the middle. That would do. I left his dollars. I ain't no thief if I don't need it. I had the wall allying still so I threw him against and onto his pal and picked up my cap.

I went on, but quicker because I remembered what San Fran cops are like. And now my right arm was like someone else's. Getting worse.

Got me a pencil though.

At first he made a wry face, but, one after another, the skins and the cores disappeared.

"Ah! Now I feel fine!" he said after eating the last one.

"You see," observed Geppetto, "that I was right when I told you that one must not be too fussy and too dainty about food. My dear, we never know what life may have in store for us!"

4

Strange for a man like me to ride on a bus. I need to be in charge, need to be the pilot in front, feels dangerous else. I'm wide-eyed, drunk as I am, with my arm ringing. I don't know how people can just sit. They look out the window or sleep or make out when there's this guy at the front in control of tons of steel and our lives who doesn't even look like he can spell bus.

I guess WWII and Korea had spent a lot of good men. We now had a lot of guys with bulbous eyes and lips and their guts straining their shirt buttons doing good jobs when they should have been shining bingo chairs or staying at home with their mothers. I spend the whole time staring forward through the windshield looking ahead for him. Not even sure he's awake.

Korea went by me. I was down in Florida. No one wrote me a telegram to come.

Them of us who came out of the water from the Indy were let quietly go. Hid us 'til the end of the war so the press couldn't get hold. Fade away was what they wanted. The Indy just a big embarrassment, a big shame. They kept it from the papers till late August. They'd let us down, them admirals and chiefs let us

49

down, but our captain, Captain McVay, got convicted for it. Americans always gotta have a scapegoat.

The bomb was secret. We didn't know that mind. Not 'til we'd spent days in the water and no one came. We'd delivered the uranium and parts to Tinian, to make up "Little Boy". The bomb. The Hiroshima bomb. Supposed to end all wars. Now we were testing H-bombs in the waters I almost died in and we had rockets going up from the army base at Canaveral all the time over our heads on Merritt. After just coming out of another war. And so were the Russians. The papers lauded our tests, damned the Russians'. Like I said, only one use for newspaper.

The reds were coming now. Reckon they'd decided that after WW they'd had enough of people tramping over their yard. We'd seen the German's V2 and liked it so we gave haven to a lot of Nazi scientists and started building our own, right out on the Cape, where no one but us hicks could see. And a baboon was driving my bus and a guy my age was the officer in charge at Mare Island. We didn't stand a chance.

I guess every president just wants to build something bigger and louder than the last. To leave his mark, leave it burned in the dust that follows. Can't be a president if you don't have some war. Always gotta have an enemy. It's in our blood. We invade and call it defense. And claim all as victories. Get your painting in the White House, not standing on a battlefield but sitting at a desk with pen in hand. And a nice fat war memorial to lay a wreath on. The dead won't be able to vote you out. Salute 'em for just that.

With some fumbling of his mitts the bus driver manages to stop. He's sweating like he just landed a plane with one wing. I get back to my truck. It's been raining here. I had spent my day only forty-five minutes away and it was bone-dry until the fog came in. Mind you I had been in a blacked-out bar. It could have snowed and I wouldn't have known.

There were cars around me when I got here in the morning. Now I'm the only one. Looks like the truck dropped out of the sky. I wonder, a drunk's melancholy wonder, who those people were who parked around me. Where they've gone. Did they sit in an office and see the rain and curse for their automobile getting wet, their wax-job wasted. Did they run in the rain and jump in their car and shut the door with a fat sigh like they were home already and then back to cursing again as the car steamed up.

There are square dry patches all around where a car protected the cement, then wet ones where Bob went home early, before the rain. Did he look at my old girl all rusty and beat and think on the bum that must belong to her. Could he make him in a crowd. He bets he could. He'll put his paper and his lunch pail on the seat beside him and thank God he's got a real job.

I put my hands back under the tarp, feel my Penns. They rattle and giggle at me. They have felt the rain, anticipated the sea again, imagined that the rain was the spray and they were not in the bed of a truck but on my *Akron* again, gleeful again, of use again. Everything has to be of use. No point in existing otherwise.

I cover 'em up. Can't sleep with 'em tonight. Too wet. I pick up my gunnysack with the rifles and take it into the cab. I'll fill out my form and sleep if I can. I'm starting to think off the drink and I ain't got no more. I'm guessing it to be near midnight. My windshield is looking out that way, to the black water, so I got something to look at instead of the human world behind me, the tenements and the stores. The other world. The one for spending the money you earned in the real one, the one that has no use for it.

You can only see the water from the street through the occasional break in the wood. A glimpse as your car flies by and then gone like the flash of a camera's bulb that for one second lit up the world. They build towns like that to stop folks dreaming.

Hide the sea. Keep 'em blinkered like working horses. Stop the sea trapping their young men with its bait. They forget it's there. Until it roars and reminds and climbs up their walls.

I got no radio so I roll down my window and listen to the water. We only ever hear the serene surface, that music them happy horse-shit poets dream of. Beneath, especially now, most especially in the dark, is fury. Frenzy.

The surface, a door, the fine-painted door to an asylum. The worst slaughterhouse. We don't call it the sea. Call it the deep. Has to be a four-letter word for something like that.

Sometimes, in the dark, you haul up *things* in nets. Things that don't belong in any world. They're just jaws and teeth, spiked teeth, long as knives. Nightmares. They're always an ugly brown, a shit brown. Covered in barbs, a screaming face, screaming as if its whole life is just terror and it exists solely to inflict its terror, and it inflicts and inflicts and saws through everything that swims in front of it. Ain't no happiness down there, not in the fathomless trenches, not in the pitch of the deep. It is close to Hell. Its creatures know it.

I think I dream of learning to swim. My arm and the deep are churning up vivid sights. Normally I dream of nothing—nothing that I remember anyhow. I might dream of the dull stuff. Dream of eating, seeing folks that I knew, taking a piss—which means I need to get up and take a piss. But now I'm eight years old and in the sea and my drunk father is taking me for a swim. He's laughing and swearing at the coldness of the water as it is around his waist and the water is lapping around my chest and neck and I'm scared.

Do they still say charabanc now? This was like a bus or a long shooting brake. A truck where the owner would have an open coach built to put on his wheelbase for summer rides down to the water. You sat opposite people you didn't know and you weren't indoors like on a train or a bus so you spoke to people because you were riding along in the world and not looking at it out a window where you all concentrate on it like a movie screen. You duck under branches together and share sandwiches and choc beer. I guess it was more an immigrant thing. Anyhow, we had taken the charabanc that we Irish all pooled together to ride as we couldn't afford the narrow gauge that ran then to Revere beach. My father had gone down to his vest and took me naked out into the water. This was June but still the Boston water was frosty. The swimming didn't get very far.

We all have the same times. We've all been in water before. For the first time. Deep water that is. Deep for a kid, leastways. And it's all deep for a kid.

You ain't wading no more. She is lifting you like a mother with every push and then you're moving away from the spot you were standing and you don't notice that she's pulling you away from the human world. Inch by inch. But you can feel it in your belly. But your toes still touch the sand, still attached to the streets and houses. And then you step down and there ain't nothing there. And your father lets go your hand.

And she has you.

She goes over your head, like a blanket smothering, and you beat against it. Sound and light still, but now dim and rheumy. Your breath and blood in your ears. You can hear your insides. You feel the pressure of a million miles of water running against, running through, and you can feel for the first time that you are water and only too much air, but that will change soon enough. You will return.

Your feet seek the earth, you try to sit because your rear always finds ground, that always works, until right now. New laws around you.

You panic to grab the walls, the floor, because they've never let you down when you're falling. But you ain't falling and nothing is happening except that moment when she pulls the blanket and the sky and the beach comes back and you can hear the laughing and the screams off the roller-coaster. She teases you with this vision of your old life with every wave and then you're gone again, into her blue, and the sounds are snuffed and you're flailing for a rail or a tree or the sidewalk and there's nothing there, nothing to catch. You've been snatched from the street. A raggedy-man has muffled you into his coat with his wicked laugh, the folds of his heavy cloth muffling your cries, squeezing the life from you, and no one will ever see you again.

I'm in the water with other young men. It's hot now. Boiling hot.

I'm dying.

I look down, down to my feet through the broiling soup. There is no bottom. I'm falling from a plane, but not falling. I'm a stranger to the earth. There is a million miles of sky above, and my head is swallowed to the neck by a garrote of water a million miles around and below, strangling me. I'm nothing. I'm holding onto an empty potato crate. I have read the word "potatoes" one thousand times. I have pictured the word being made months ago by some prisoner in Folsom just for me. It's branded in. He did this a thousand times.

At night I see the stars, the milk of galaxies, but it's like that on the land. But from there you don't see the planets rise from out of the sea. On land, back there, with those still of the earth, you feel small. But you can touch a wall, lean on a fence or the hood of a car with your girl and you are as big as these objects that we made. They fill the space of the world and you are not alone.

Here you're nothing. Less than existing. Your cries die just past your face when you call for the other boys. Your cries are flattened by the water, by the deep. You can barely hear 'em leave your mouth. A child's squeal.

Some boys have swum near me, their faces chapped and dappled with oil but their eyes gleam with secrets.

"C'mon, Quint," they whisper, "the Indy's just down there." They point through the water as if it is a hole in a circus tent we can sneak through. "She's just there. You can see her. We can swim down. Air traps. Some of the doors would be closed. Didn't they lock the canteen up every night? I shut doors behind me. The water will be working. We can get a drink. Get some ice cream. Get food for the boys. Don't you want to help the boys? Don't you want to live? She's got tons of water. Don't you want to live? Don't you want to help us? She's just down there. Take off your jacket. Can't swim with that."

They throw off their hoops from their neck. Start taking orders for what to bring back and guys are shouting out their wants with tight throats. Others want to go down with 'em. It makes sense they say. We're dying of thirst. The ship was made to hold air. Food. Water. I grab 'em as they pass, tell 'em to be quiet. They push me away. I'm the crazy. I must want 'em to die. They are young, immortal. They saw a ship of fire sink beside 'em. It is just below. It was huge, colossal steel. Too big to be gone. Did we not build and know her? A plane hit her and bounced off. Water can't take that away. She is larger and stronger than us and if we're here than she surely cannot be taken away. She is a real thing to touch, not this nothing all around, this netherworld. You can walk it, they say. You just gotta hold your breath. You can walk down the water like steps. The officers have been dipping down in the night. They know it's there. They want us to die. Save all the food for themselves. You don't see them crying for water. They don't drink the seawater like us. What are they hiding?

"Come on. It's all down there. It can't be that deep. Come on. You scared? Don't you want to help?"

You can't stop 'em. These are city boys. They're used to ice cream on every corner. Coke in their refrigerators. They never had to eat clay biscuits. In the mess they would leave their potatoes if they weren't mashed.

They go below and never come back. Others think they are holding out on 'em. They see 'em, can hear 'em down below, laughing and drinking and eating steaks and listening to the radio for the ships to come. For the ships to come. Thousands of ships out here. There is one coming. There is one coming. We should go down and eat with the others. Might not get fed straightaway when they pick us up. Don't want to be too weak when they come, won't be strong enough to climb the ladder. Come on. Let's go down. Don't you want to live? What kind of coward are you?

Something brushes against my leg.

My father picks me up from the water. He is laughing and wipes my face but I cry right back. He laughs more, the beer breathes in my face and he drags me back to the beach. Something brushes against my leg and I scream.

They all scream. I scream, you scream, we all scream for ice cream.

"What kind of coward are you, boy?" he laughs and I splutter the foul water from my lungs and the roller-coaster rattles as it climbs and I splutter awake and look out at the dawn on the water, on the deep.

I am clutching my burlap sack of guns.

"What does it matter, after all?" cried Geppetto all at once, as he jumped up from his chair. Putting on his old coat, full of darns and patches, he ran out of the house without another word.

After a while he returned. In his hands he had the A-B-C book for his son, but the old coat was gone. The poor fellow was in his shirt sleeves and the day was cold.

"Where's your coat, Father?"

"I have sold it."

"Why did you sell your coat?"

"It was too warm."

5

I don't know the sawbones. He could be twice my age, my father's age I guess. He has a bald strip down the center of his head like that Italian kid trying to look like George Raft but the parting is now beyond any stretch of handsomeness. He's just being tidy. He has round glasses with frames the size of silver dollars. I could see him doing nothing else but this trade. And that's good. Good to have work forever.

I'm down to my vest and wish I could've showered. He is tapping my back, as they do, and listening with his scope. The plugs in his ears don't affect his voice.

"You were a seaman, Mister Quint?"

"Aye. A booter. Aimed to apprentice to be a fireman."

"Why?" He changes sides with his tapping. Sounds like I'm made of wood.

"I'm good with engines, pumps. Not too smart for anything else."

"Well, I don't know about that. I can't even lube my own car. Turn around."

I turn to a light already in my eye and I cannot see him past the glare.

"Did you have any problems after? Any recovery problems?"

I shake my head, he asks me to stay still as he switches eyes. "Did you drink any salt water?"

"No. Rinsed my mouth a few times. Hard not to. Like a kid at a beach."

"And your mouth swelled up like cotton."

"You know it."

"Did you get ulcers?"

"Not in my mouth. My rear didn't look too pretty though. Not that it did before."

He shuts off the light, watches me blink.

"You saw what happened to guys that did? The ones that drank the water?"

My eyes take some seconds to come back. I got sun-blind when they took us back to Guam. Took three days to see again. All that time I knew I was lying in a bed, knew everything was OK. But I couldn't see it. I thought I was dead or—worse—still in the water, just hallucinating like the rest, like those guys who walked down the steps to the Indy below. Waving for me to follow. You'd swear they did walk down as well, like the salt formed 'em a stair.

"Sailor?"

The doc had asked me something.

"Yeah, I seen it. That ain't pretty either."

He looks away to put his pen-light down. "Touch your toes."

He watched that real careful. I couldn't see him looking but I could tell 'cause I could see his legs and he was statue still. I had to push my shoulder to get my right to touch. I came up and I could feel my face was red. That was the drink. He'd be used to that. But my arm had a red stain on it, down the muscle like a birthmark.

"Hold out your arms. Like this." He makes like Karloff.

I do the same and he sees me wince. I put my arms down as he watches.

"Doc. There was a little fun last night. A little sport. You know?" I rub my arm, relieved that I don't have to pretend it's not on fire. "Pulled a muscle." I said it like it was him that done it, like we were just tussling brothers and I give him a pal's wink.

He comes forward and takes my arm, cups my elbow and pushes it up and pulls down my wrist like a pump. A red-hot flash goes up my arm and I'm biting down to stop crying out.

He pats my shoulder and takes a sit on the front of his metal desk.

"Why now? What do you want to get back in for, sailor?"

He says this like Santa to the boy on his knee. Want. What do you want?

I think of telling him about Effa, that I got no reason to have a home on the land no more but docs love to hear that. In war they have to stamp through as many as they can, that's their higher orders. Out of war their oaths come back. They're back to saving lives. They want to save young men.

"I ain't got no job, Doc. This I can do." I shrug. "I ain't got nothing else."

He is studying me, judging what he can say like a cautious pitcher measuring the heavy hitter.

"What group were you in? In the water?"

I scratch my head, I can't stop my face from grinning. "You want to know if I had it hard don't you, Doc? Why I ain't scared to go back?"

"You all had it hard. I can't imagine. But I know some of you had rafts. Some of you had those useless preservers you had to keep inflating. Some of you had kapoks . . . And . . . some of you had sharks. I know that much. We're still writing papers on it. Learned a lot from you boys."

60

"I'm alive ain't I? I want to go back don't I?"

"Do you want to go back *there*?"

That hit me. Docs like to throw them curveballs.

"I ain't afraid," I said. "I know what I'd do."

"And what's that?"

"I wouldn't be wearing no life jacket."

He comes off his desk, takes the scope off his neck and squeezes its rubber.

"What did you do after the war?"

"I fixed up a boat. I ran charters out of Merritt Island. Well, you gotta get out into the bight first of course. Only trout and tarpon around Merritt."

"*Charters?*"

"Fishing charters. Weekends for rich boys."

"What do rich boys fish for?"

"Sharks."

I say it fast, like I'm swearing at him and he stiffens like I've slapped him. He recovers quick like good docs do, like service docs do when the droves of gurneys come wheeling in.

"Could you not go back to that again?"

"I can't go . . . I ain't got no boat." That was a lie. "I want to serve my country again."

He nods and goes behind his desk to his metal seat, hides his eyes, putting them to his forms.

"You have not pulled a muscle, Mister Quint—put your shirt back on—you have ripped it. Oh, it will heal. In a fashion. And you'll get used to it. But I cannot permit you to sign up again. Not in this navy."

I have my shirt half on. "What's my arm got to do with anything? It ain't broke."

"Mister Quint. You cannot extend your arm." He tosses down his scope. "Suppose I need you to pull me out of the water. From your right side. You could not reach me. You would not have sufficient muscle strength to pull me out. You would be a liability to your crewmates. It is them I have to concern—"

I snatch on the rest of my shirt and I'm at his desk and there's the scrape of metal on the linoleum floor as he pushes himself back.

"I would get you out." I inform him plain and straighten up.

He pulls his chair back to his desk, doesn't flinch.

"I would get you out," I repeat. I'm buttoning my shirt.

He settles real quick.

"Maybe you should consider the merchant service, Mister Quint."

"Is that it? Is that where we go, Doc? Like that poster? Like that, 'You bet I'm going back to sea' shit?" I make for the door.

He calls as I open it.

"Mister Quint?"

I lift my chin as I put on my cap. I'm already thinking of gas money I do not have. My navy checks waiting for me in a post office box back in Merritt.

"Don't be sorry to be alive, Mister Quint," he says. And I let it pass because he means it. He had service in him.

I tip my cap as I leave. Close the navy behind me.

"I'll give you four pennies for your A-B-C book," said a ragpicker who stood by.

Then and there, the book changed hands.

And to think that poor old Geppetto sat at home in his shirt sleeves, shivering with cold, having sold his coat to buy that little book for his son.

6

No money. Pockets rattling. One note. I'm luckier than most. Least I ain't got no children staring up at me. I got guns with full clips, I got rods and reels and I can find me a crab for bait. Box of matches and three dollars of gas and a truck to sleep in. I am King Solomon with riches. For one day at least. I was in water with nothing to eat or drink for five days and I still lived. Let me hear how poor you are.

A sergeant shows you the fishing survival kit that comes with the raft. It comes with a knife to gut the fish that you'll catch. He doesn't tell you about the guy who'll curse you away from the raft with that knife or that the matches and most of the kit are in cardboard. Not much good in the water.

That sergeant will stand in front of the slide image projected in your mess and preach, "Three minutes! Three days! Three weeks! You know what that is, soldier?" We ain't soldiers but his speech is spittle and practiced. He yells at us.

"Three minutes without OX-Y-GEN! Three days without H-2-O! Three weeks without I-D-HO!"

Three minutes without air. Three days without water. Three weeks without potatoes.

That's all you have to live. That's the measure of a man's life. Three, three, three. *Click, click, click.* Nothing else matters when it comes down. And you'll always want that three to become four. And we had thousands of potatoes. They had floated up. Temptation from the Devil below. His apples. Poisonous with salt. Can't think that all of us resisted.

November night in Vallejo. I've been thinking. Thinking slow and watching the sun go down just as slow from the lot. My lot now. The office jocks have given my truck a wide berth. I have been there two days in a row. That makes me a suspicious character in the real world. A man not at work. Staring at the sea, like the sea can mean anything. No one likes sunsets that much. No one has nothing to do. Only the dead have nothing to do. *He wants to steal my car. He's watching my pattern. He wants something. He knows something.*

They all gun it out of the lot. Sparks off their fenders as they hit the ramp.

Innocent men think you want to take something from 'em. Guilty men think someone wants to take *them*. They don't think about the car, the wallet, the wife. Someone just wants *them*. They dread to not hear the word "please" when someone calls their name.

"Bill, will you come in here, please." "Please, buddy. Old pal. Pal of mine." Don't want to hear, "Bill. Come in here." "Come with me, Mister Johnson."

They're always waiting for that day. And when it gets to six and it didn't happen and no strangers are waiting on the doorstep when they pull into their drive, that's another win. Another day they got away with it.

I know I don't have gas to get me far and I know the doc ain't gonna hunt me down and say he's changed his mind. Go back. That's what he was saying. A Chinaman has changed your plans.

Here is one ocean, the one you left before. The one that almost had you. And behind you is the other. That one you ran from. How many oceans do you think there are, boy? How many backs do you think you have, boy?

I got beer. I drink fast, watch the sun die and the waves rolling away from me. Have to earn my way back the same route I got here. And anything could happen getting there. Get a real job. Find somewhere. Go see Amanda again. All that would only be something if I had to. If I had to stay somewhere. I know that. I know being locked by dirt ain't gonna last.

I gotta turn the wheel. Tick over what gas I got. Just to hear an engine again would soothe. Head east. To the other ocean. The *Akron* waiting along the Indian River. I planted it, I can get her back.

Don't do anything you can't undo, and don't start anything you can't finish yourself.

I can go see what they did with Effa. No, not that. Something else. Florida done now. Pick up my checks and the boat, that's all.

The Hamptons. That's it. Lot of rich boys up there. Montauk. That town breathes with gills.

In the thirties they ran a train from Jamaica Station in Queens to Fort Pond, Montauk. The "Fisherman's Special". It left at 3.30 a.m. all over the weekend for the desk jocks to escape from the city for the fantasy of returning to the real earth for a time. The "reel" earth for a time. A train leaving the city at 3.30 in the morning and packed to the windows and packed to the end of the line. The "reel" earth. The "end of the line".

Charter captains had to have those click-counters like doormen at nightclubs, counting heads so they weren't overloaded.

Hundreds of guys would run, *run* from the station at dawn to the dock with their rods up in the air like kids running to a fair with balloons dancing over their shoulders.

Just this year a boat got sunk. Fifty desk jockeys on board. Fifty empty desks Monday morning. Fifty picture frames sitting on desks with smiling wives and kids who would take years to smile again. Some secretary moving round the offices and flipping the picture frames down, putting 'em in boxes. Friday morning three hundred and more guys would pack the special again. They used to leave the windows open so guys could squeeze through to stop 'em crushing each other in the doorways. Madmen desperate to get to the real earth.

That'll be it. The Hamptons, Martha's Vineyard, Montauk, Amity. That's what I need now.

I'm the age of my father when he had me. That is a startling thought, a roiling thought as I turn my engine and the truck grumbles awake. My age, and he had a wife, a son, a job. A job working a press at a paper but a job at least. His son has three wives behind and no work. Can't even work in the navy and that work I know better than the living doing it now. A big Chinaman who is snoring on a mattress in a tenement surrounded by children is oblivious of what he has snatched from me with his fat hide.

I listen to the engine. She growls and whines like a boat engine, the hood rattles. It is the most pleasing row.

Gear and reverse, squeal the tires a little and slam her into first like I'm punching that doc on the jaw. I make the rear end spark as I gun out of there and up the ramp, spark fireflies just like the desk jockeys that fled. I imagine the cars we leave behind sigh in relief.

Even in the cab I can hear my Penns and rods rattling with excitement under their tarp. It might be false spring when I get back or I might sell the truck and catch a train, suffer people for a while. Think on that later. Plenty of time and road. Plenty of ocean. Plenty of fish.

Plenty of sharks.

A few minutes later they returned, carrying poor Pinocchio, who was wriggling and squirming like an eel and crying pitifully:
"Father, save me! I don't want to die! I don't want to die!"

7

It was that man Mundus in '51 that started the whole sharking thing. No one wanted sharks. No one ate 'em then so you couldn't sell 'em. They were trash, they ate the real fish, often right off your line. But Frank Mundus, out of Montauk, saw all those city boys coming off the special and he figured them guys could go out and catch a hundred-pound fish if they were lucky, otherwise it would be just scup and blackfish. He'd wander up and down the dock and whisper in their ears like a pimp.

"Hey, Mister? You wanna go *Monster* fishing?"

That's what he called it. Monster fishing. He became the Monster Man. How else could a guy who was only coming out for one day hook a fish over eight hundred pounds? Even if you couldn't take it home you had a guy on the dock who would take a photograph and mail it to you and you had a story for the rest of your life. For the rest of your life. Think about that. Even if it got away.

For the rest of your life.

If you hook an eleven-hundred-pound tuna you earned it like a day's work, it could take the day to find it. But a Great White—the man in the gray suit, the Landlord—or any shark, those guys would follow the boat. They had their memories, their memories scored into their cells. Memories of the ships and the slaves and the wars. Man went to war at sea as soon as he built a boat, and, like on land when the vultures followed the legions, the sharks followed the ships.

I remember reading about Tecumseh when he was down in Florida, before the civil war, at St. Augustine, and the sharks would swarm the inlets like flies. They sent a whaleboat out to pick up some soldiers from a steamer that couldn't get in. Well, the weather came up, as she does when soldiers are coming to shore, and broke up that whaleboat.

A boy made it back by clambering on the capsized boat as it drifted in and told what he saw. Told that the sharks came.

The next day Tecumseh went down to the shore and found a couple of bodies on the beach torn apart. They almost made it. From then on they told the steamers to anchor further down, to not come into the inlets, they would sail out to them.

Here be monsters.

Memories, see? Wood, boats, war, slaves, men. Sharks following below, buzzards above. Other fish avoid boats, you have to make it attractive to 'em. But the man in the gray suit will come with. The attraction, the make-up paint, is why we have the rods at the back of the boat. The tuna or marlin looks up and sees your keel. But that ain't what *he* sees. He don't. He sees a school of mackerel. The new boots you got on the boat complain that it stinks down in the stern. Stinks of gas and is noisy as hell when the engine's rolling and the bait buckets of old peach cans filled with chum are stinking more than the gas. Ain't no Cadillac on the water. You tell 'em they don't have to stand with their rods, just sit back anywhere and wait for 'em to tell. They stand there holding their rod like their presence is doing the fishing, drawing the fish in. Happy assholes.

The fish thinks your bait is stragglers from the school. Fish hunt the weak. That's why con artists, grifters, are called sharks and his victims are fish. The weak, the vulnerable. Shark comes from the old German. It means "villain". All slang has merit.

So the fish, if he's dumb enough and don't notice the engine, comes up and takes a bite. That's a good reason to go out when the water's white and the rain's hammering. Get the old ones then, the smart ones. They can't hear the engine under the waves and the rain. That's when you get the fourteen-hundred-pound tuna. He is forty years old. He's survived longer than the boots that landed him. He gasps on the deck. He has sired thousands of children, he has survived two steel wars, looked up and seen hundreds of schools of mackerel crossing the ocean. He has seen torpedoes silently boil past him. He has seen the lights in the sky and the metal giants sink below him into the trenches where the other fleshy giants lie and where the wooden ones fell long before. Now he's on your deck with his blood running thin like cheap wine and some boots is cutting out his guts and organs so the urine and shit don't spoil the meat. You can count his rings like a tree. He is ancient and he fell to trickery. But he did fight in his throes. More than we do. He raged. We whimper and ask for more blankets. That's why I never understood the shooters and the archers. Don't you want to fight? You could go down an alley and shoot a dog, and maybe they do, that's their mind I guess. I'll tell you one thing and this might be the only thing I ever tell and it might be worthless.

I can remember every fish I brought in.

And when I catch the next one, the last one is in the memory of my arms as the memory of hooks he has slipped is in his battle against. He has taught me how to do better and laughs at me when I fail. And I'm never gonna win. That's why those desk jockeys ran down the pier from the special.

Every fish is your first fish. Leave it at that. I've known lots of
professional sportsmen and they all say the same thing. Quietly.
They say it to me because they are on the ocean and she won't
tell and I do not exist off the dock and the beer is just cold
enough and their feet are resting, crossed on the stern, and the
wind carries their words as it thrums at their line and the sun is
just at that hour when you can look at it.

They hate their tennis. They hate golf. They hate their football.

They do not run down their pier. And so they come to men
like me.

"*Poor Blackbird!*" *said Pinocchio to the Cat.* "*Why did you kill him?*"

"*I killed him to teach him a lesson. He talks too much. Next time he will keep his words to himself.*"

8

Brevard County

There is something about the sky in the east that the west coast don't know about. The west have the sun they feel. They think they do. They think us all a-shivering.

It is warmer in the west, granted. It is the sun. But ours is the weather. The sun and the sum of the oceans. We know the seasons. Our calendars are the parades of fish that mark the months, mark the seasons.

The fish have their "columns", an image of the deep as pillars of cold and black and blue leading to the light. The Greeks named 'em. They named everything to do with the deep, and the sky above it. They knew what was important.

Each layer, each column, is a different world, a different smorgasbord of flesh. Layered. And we that sail the bights and the ledges ride the columns. Doric columns holding us up. They don't have that in the west. In the east the Atlantic holds up our little boats like kites on the wind. Miles are beneath us. The drop-offs. Like our drunk fathers leading us out to make us swim. The

75

ground drops beneath our feet. We are looking down from a mountain and don't even know it.

The New York bights.

Decades of junk, military junk, human junk. Artificial reefs of torpedoes, keels, tires and bricks that have created a new breeding ground for deep-sea fish. Bleeding hearts would argue that we were polluting the seas. The fish said otherwise. They bred in the junk like flies and rats on any landfill. Eels gulping out of discarded gun shells, tarpon making homes in mountains of bricks like any New York brownstone. And the Landlord, the shark, muscling among, drawn by the tenants. Getting his rent.

Screw your LA. We got the Gulf Stream. We got the bluefin, we got the bights. We got the deep. We got the real game. We got all the fishing, got all the hard trade, all the ports to Europe. All the rockets screaming to the Reds, screaming to space.

We shouldn't be looking up. Should be looking down. Should send rockets screaming to the deep. We aim to know more about the stars than we do the dark below. We think the deep is the past, is the historical, the prehistorical. It'll be our future. Any fisherman will tell you that. Jesus tried to tell you that. Ask the fisherman about the future. Life began there. The fish and the birds. That's your Genesis. Life will end there. Her gasses and the ice will come for us. Like I said, we had to go technological to know the prehistoric. We heard the "gulps" from the Earth when we put microphones into the sea. We ain't racing to the stars.

We're running to 'em.

I'm drunk again. I have a Shell map that shows me the way home. It has a man and a woman on the front cover. He has a red jacket and black hair. She has a white dress that don't belong on the road and is leaning into his shoulder as he points to a Shell sign that surely don't mean nothing.

"We go this way," he is saying. "We will do well." He don't say it. It's only a drawing. It's in his smile and his pointing arm.

The routes are numbered with shields. Security. Safe passage. Toll roads. The government will protect you here. The shield is a badge. Don't you like badges? Otherwise there is just a circle and a number. A highway. Lines and numbers like a cross-stitch. Sew your engine this way and you might do OK, but follow the Shell route and you will survive, I guarantee it. And your wife will lean into your shoulder. There will be hamburgers here, a Coke any way you like it, a vanilla ice-cream float. We all scream for ice cream. Here there be someone to wipe the bugs from your windshield.

I'm parked at the side of the road at night with my flashlight and this map. I have my engine off, planning to sleep, to take my boots off. Headlights come in my mirror, then red lights from his grill and that one rolling red eye high above, whirling slow like on an amusement park's ghost train. I curse, like we all do when you see 'em, even if they only mean to help. And they don't want to help after dark. After the deep dark.

Cops.

Only women and the infirm like to see cops. They love to find a single man on the road. If you got kids and a wife they will become the friendly old uncle. Officer Fair-weather. Help you on your way with a wave and a ruffle of your son's hair and a wink to your daughter.

But his headlights have already picked you out in your seat alone. He has plucked free the snap of his holster. Lowered his gear to chumming speed, come up in your slick. He is eight cups of morning-old coffee too much. His dried chicken sandwich from that waitress he sees more than his wife is repeating on him. He is night-fishing. And his fat black-and-white patrol rolls to a stop in front you, covers your door in dust, leaves his rear lights on to blind you.

You are in his slick. His butterfish. He's the Landlord. Fishing. Fishing for you. He is looking for a bad time to go with his indigestion that has become his common state.

He rolls out the car and his suspension goes up a notch, but you knew that. Knew he'd be fat. Only see the big ones at night, like the sharks. The thin guys on the motorcycles, and the beat cops all thin. The fat guys with their skin-mags under their seats take the night shift. They are avoiding their teenage kids and their chiding wives that married a guy in uniform when he quit the school football field and put on a gun-belt when she was hot every morning. That was twenty years gone and she don't get dressed anymore for when he comes home. She gets dressed for shopping. He only sees the slippers and house-coat that he left her in. They are done. And I gotta take his shit for that. I gotta take the shit for his belly and his night-sweats.

I take the window down before he gets there but I don't smile at cops. I wait until he speaks. They like that. His chest is at my window, he smells like a car. All gas and smoking brakes. Guess I don't smell much better; I have only two changes of the same clothes and wash 'em in gas-station restrooms.

He has those glasses with the flip-down sunshades under that off-white cowboy hat like they do it in Brevard. I'm almost home. It's late February and I am more beaten and road-worn than the end of last year. I saw my Christmas along the road and lived it through the fairy lights of other people's houses that I could see deep off the highway. The lights have gone, back in the attic, back in the basement along with the spirit. It's a mild time of year, still good for shirtsleeves. Gotta get out on the water to get cold. Do not let your eyes look down to a cop's gun.

"Where you going, son? Late to be out."

No hello. Not looking at me; he is shining his flashlight into my cab all around, uninvited. It's about eleven o'clock. Not late for anything.

"I'm just checking my road," I say and tap the map beside me. "I'm to Merritt. Didn't come this way. Came out on the Bloody 520. It ain't on this map. This is 50 though, ain't it?"

He puts his flashlight straight at my chest. "We don't like that name, son."

"Meant nothing by it." I tip my cap, my Indy cap. Don't know why I was wearing it.

The "Bloody" 520 is a marshy two-lane. It has trees overhanging and when you go down it at night them branches are like green arms overhead threatening to come down and swoop you up. It's a tunnel of trees. It feels like going down to something, something dark, even in daylight, the road diminishing around you. The nickname comes from its number of automobile accidents. Fatal accidents that is. Some see spook-lights along it. Balls of light dancing in the trees. I ain't ever seen 'em. I can't believe in ghosts. Don't believe any serviceman can. Go mad else.

He sees the cap and the stitched badge as bold as his star.

"You were on the *Indianapolis*?" He's chewing something. "Your father? You're mighty young?" The average of us was nineteen. "You didn't steal it did you, son? Swap-meet?"

I play my toothpick and show him my white teeth. "You think an Indy man would put his cap in a swap-meet?"

All cops hate servicemen. They didn't get to go, see? They spend their Saturdays sweeping us up or rolling up to our houses when we fight with our wives. They see the ones that didn't die—or didn't die yet—and it always seems to them that all the assholes made it back. And now they had killed men in the war and were bigger assholes. Can't blame the cops for that.

The flashlight swings with his head. "What's in the back?"

Ain't no point in hiding anything. "My rods and reels. Some empty bottles and clothes. Two rifles."

The flashlight steadies. "You want to show me them guns, boy?"

Boy now, is it? He steps back as I open the door and I shouldn't find that cute. Threat am I? His spine is rigid, his hand near his .38 and maybe I should drop finding him cute. But it's night and I've had a six-pack and he don't care about the beer on my breath. He's fishing. The man in the gray suit. The Landlord.

I'm taller than him and his jaw goes tense at that. I switch the toothpick to the other side and flip back the tarp.

"Step away," he barks. The yellow light goes over the bed of my truck. He picks up my big Senator 16 and drops it back like a dead beer can. "Jeez, boy! What you fish with that? Other boats?"

"Tuna. Marlin. Shark."

I can only see the back of him now and he shouldn't do that. He is too confident. That don't work in service.

"*Shark*? Can't eat shark." He has found my rifles.

"You can kill 'em," I say.

"You got a permit for these?" He holds up my Enfield. "English gun? What's that for?"

"I got a permit. Not on me. Shoot sharks with it. The boys like it."

"You shoot sharks?" He is studying the gun like it's a phony twenty.

"I don't. The charters do that. I hook and line."

He snorts, still weighing the gun.

"Don't you like American guns, boy?"

I point. "I got my Garand. My M1. She's a Springfield arm."

He peers over the gunwale of the truck. The M1 is wrapped up in her cloth.

"That's more like it." He drops the Enfield to the truck bed and wrestles out the M1. He has forgotten about permits. "Lot

of these cheap guns around. I should get me one." He holds it
to his eye and shoulder and lets the sling hang. He is not a shooter.
The sling should be under control. It's part of the gun. Seen lotsa
guys get tangled up when they had to shoot and run. I take the
sling off on the boat; some idiot will get it wrapped round a cleat
else if he don't mind it. You gotta keep the sling tense. Wrap it
round your arm when shooting or keep it tight against your
elbow with the gun in front when walking so you can get it into
business real quick. Shoulder it when it's quiet, when you're in
your ground. That's when they take pictures of soldier boys,
walking in their own ground, so everyone thinks that's how you
carry a rifle.

He wheels it across imaginary targets and then right across
my face. He holds it there where he watches me not change my
look and wheels it on over the horizon.

"What say that British gun can do against this American beauty,
boy?"

"Garand was Canadian," I tell him. He lowers the gun.

"You wise-mouthing me, boy?"

"No, sir," I say. "I'm just trying to get home."

"To Merritt? Who the hell would want to get back to that
shit-hole?"

"That's where the ocean is."

He sneers and pulls back the bolt, sees the brass. Locked.

"Loaded too. You think there's fish out here, boy?"

"Fish everywhere."

I ain't doing too good now. But, told you, there ain't a man
alive that will tell me what to say, badge or not. Just tin. My father
would punch the shit out every bailiff that came to the door and
take their hat. No one ever came back for their hat. He used to
joke about what their wives and children would say when they
went home without it. He only owed 'em money. They owed him

shame. He'd walk to the bar wearing that hat. Every time the street saw him in a new hat they knew what had occurred and the cops pulled down their hat brims and were out when the bailiff called.

The fat man has my gun.

"What say we do a little target practice, boy? My American here against your English." They are both mine and I'm getting the sense of it. He rummages in my truck; rifle and flashlight in one hand. He'll shoot me or his foot like that. He pulls out two of my wine bottles with his fingers in the necks. He clacks 'em together like he's a milkman collecting. He shoulders the M1 and seeks out a fence post with the flashlight. I don't say anything. He has the gun so I will follow.

"There," he says and I can't see him from the glare as the light goes over me. "Fifty yards behind. Take the bottles, boy." He holds 'em out to me, the glass giggling. "You ain't burning to get anywhere are you? I wanna see a service boy shoot."

I walk up, he has my gun at his hip, and I take the bottles. I step to the truck to get the Enfield.

He whistles.

"Whoa now. Set those bottles up, boy. Get your gun when you come back."

I still don't speak. I turn to take the walk. My back to him and my gun, and I'm beginning to think of it. He could shoot me now. I'm a drifter. He has come across me in the night and found me troublesome. Drunk and armed. I'm already a typewritten sheet and a toe-tag. A hole in my back as I ran. Another crazy serviceman dealing bad with the free world. And I'm an Indy man. I got a lot to be crazy about. So I say nothing and his beam lights the fence for me. Six feet between posts. It's sixty yards from the road, not fifty. I'm treading down. This could be the ditch of my grave.

I set up one bottle, expecting I don't know what to come from behind me. Nothing happens. My feet and up to my knees are wet as I clomp to the next post. These are my wine bottles for my homemade. I guess he don't care about that. I don't know if I'm avoiding a ticket for shit or if he is my new best friend. There will never come a day when cops don't do this shit. Price we pay for having cops. Gotta have cops, so bite it.

I don't shield my eyes from the flashlight, I just walk straight toward it. He might prefer to shoot me from the front. That would go better in his eyes, in his report. I hope it has not been more than a month since his wife let him climb on her. Hope he has some sense or has jerked off in his patrol car at least and he is only playing with me. But I always hold the attitude that death is coming; that it is always just one wrong word away.

Death is little more than the wrong look, the wrong side of the street. The wrong place. The wrong water. The bump against your leg. So I look down his flashlight as I climb back so he can see my face. See that I ain't minding.

"That-a-boy," he says. He balances the flashlight on my truck and I'm back with him, the bottles glinting under the light. "I'll go first, boy. Show you an American gun."

He wraps the sling around his arm, looks like a soldier now. I can hear him breathing over the stock of the gun, his breath in the air, his mouth snarling, belly pumping.

He pulls and the crack echoes against the steel of my truck.

A bottle chimes like a bell and vanishes.

"Hoo!" he yells. "Look-ee there!" He puts up the gun. "I gotta get me one of these guns, boy!" He leans on his hip. "Say now," he spits. "Ain't I got it already? What say we gamble for this one, boy? See if you make your shot." There is no crime here. I was by the side of the road looking at a map, a day from home. He's not even taken my name and I won't remind him.

"What's the bet?" I say and reach over into the truck for the Enfield.

"Well," he spits again. "You hit that other and I don't take you in for that six-pack on your breath and your no abode." He sucks his cheek. Puts back his hat. "You miss. I keep your gun and you don't stink up my cells."

I know the draw of it now. That's all I needed. Needed to know where I stood.

"I got a home," I say. Not sure of that as I say it.

"Not in my county," he says. "Don't care where you think your island is. I'll hold you for thirty days for tramping on my road."

I grip the Enfield. She's oiled and greased, like it was yesterday. It is yesterday.

I move the toothpick to my left side, move the gun to my shoulder. All is black, the flashlight just lighting enough. He slides the bolt again on the M1, don't need to do that to fire, he's just making sure I hear it. I roll my head to him just for a second and roll my toothpick back again and put my eye to the shot.

I squeeze her trigger and I can feel the pin hit the case and the jolt like a jump of static and there is the smell and the leap and the bottle is still standing.

He slaps his leg.

"Hoo-ee! You missed, soldier! You damn shit missed, you sonofabitch! Ain't I always said the same about you soldier boys!"

I put the gun to the truck so I ain't got no gun against. "Navy," I says. "Never was a soldier."

"Then you navy boys can't shoot for shit! Ain't I right?" He picks up his flashlight, turns it off. There is only his car's reds painting us like firelight.

"Reckon so," I says and smile along with. "You got yourself a gun."

"Damn right I do, you sonofabitch!" He rubs my M1. "Now get the shit out of here, boy."

He moves first. Puts my gun to his backseat.

"*Indianapolis* my dick!" He slams the door. "I'll be back around this road at six. I find your piece of junk on my road I'll pull you in for a month, boy. You better be on that island tomorrow."

"I'll do that," I say. I lean on the truck and watch him squeal out and back where he came and he smirks at me like satisfied cops do.

He's going uphill, miles of straight road, heading west, west where the horizon is still just blue enough and the moon lights him and his path. I watch his dust.

And I pick up the Enfield from the truck.

I climb on the hood, the sling tight around my arm, and I lean over my cab. The gun set atop.

He is a third of a mile from me already. My Enfield is an American Savage. I would have to return to my shack on Merritt to pick up the scope. But I can make do. And I ain't ever that drunk.

An American Enfield adapted to be a sniper. Make do with my eye, and that sure is a pretty red light under the moon that a fat man is too hot and horned-up to turn off.

I follow his light up the road, almost half a mile now, almost too much.

Almost.

I stroke the trigger like I'm brushing an eyelash from my cheek, and I can't even hear the shot for I've removed it from the air with the slide and pull of the bolt and I'm back again behind the sight and the car is all I see, its grasp of the light like a beacon, his headlights cough into the sky as he hits the brakes. I can almost hear his cursing as the shards of his red light tumble down his windshield and I wait for what I know he will do.

The car turns, long-side against my sights as he has slammed in reverse and gone hand over fist to turn.

Sonofabitch, he is saying, is spitting. *Sonofabitch.* His chicken sandwich hard in his chest, his feet pumping gas and his palm grinding the gears. And my Enfield sees his hubcaps and I pass my toothpick back and forth and bite down.

I sew him again, deft, like cotton through a needle, straight as making a hook down in the bucking stern where fishermen hold their breath.

I see him bump and jerk to the side of the road as his tire blows. He doesn't give up straightaway but no matter. I come off the hood and put back the gun. He ain't coming back anytime soon.

I start slow, knowing he can see my rear lights as I crawl out. I am my father knocking off hats. I always was. I am. My inheritance.

I go slow down the road. It ain't quite worth the gun but it'll do. It'll do until I can get back on the sea.

He didn't even take my name.

Dumb damn cop.

"Listen to me and go home."

"But I want to go on!"

"The hour is late!"

"I want to go on."

"The night is very dark."

"I want to go on."

"The road is dangerous."

"I want to go on."

"Remember that boys who insist on having their own way, sooner or later come to grief."

"The same nonsense. Goodbye, Cricket."

"Good night, Pinocchio, and may Heaven preserve you from the Assassins."

9

Merritt

Charlie Hawt had a little store on Myrtice Road. He sold gear but too far in from the water to bother with bait but being off the water meant he didn't fleece you for his line. His store adapted to the season. So summer was lawn chairs and umbrellas and white-painted cane hand fans and shit like that and then autumn and Halloween junk and lawn Santas.

I would sell him my bleached shark jaws. Easy work. Customer catches a blue shark or porbeagle, which nobody wanted, and I'd elbow 'em that it was good practice to land him; that we could cut him for bait.

I'd cut out the jaw on the deck and start steeping 'em in an empty bait peach-tin. You can't boil 'em clean because the teeth fall out. I cut off squares from the Styrofoam chum-markers to keep his jaw wide. See, a shark's jaw ain't part of its skull; it comes out like false teeth. Nature made 'em like that so they can bite off more than they can chew. Like us happy assholes.

I'd bleach the jaws when I got home and mount 'em on Pecky Cyprus off-cuts and Charlie would give me five bucks for every one. That was after Mundus made shark-fishing a common-man thing. Every kid wanted a shark jaw on their wall. Whether it was a thresher or a blue, Charlie would put a little tin-plate on the wood saying "Mako", "Whitetip", "Great White", and he'd make up some year it was caught and the kid's faces would light up like he'd handed 'em free ice cream and their dads would be ten bucks lighter when they'd only stopped by for directions. Ain't nothing better for a store-keep than a car with screaming kids and a man walking up your path with a map.

I walked into Charlie's like it was my first day and he looked at me like I was a ghost on the last.

"*Quint!*" he gasped and put down his pencil then picked it up and put it behind his ear and put his hands to his counter. "Well I'll be . . . I thought you was dead for sure, son!"

I looked around, chewed on my pick. February, so some Santas going cheap and whitewash and paintbrushes for spring-cleaning. Anytime of the year Charlie's store always smells of white spirit.

"No, Charlie. They ain't got me yet."

"Where you been? You cleared off right after Effa passed. Where you been?"

"I went off. California. Tried to join up again. They'd had enough of me they said."

He looked out his fly-screen to my truck. "In your *Dodge*? You get dogs to drag it?"

"She'll see you out, Charlie. Want to buy her?"

"Shit, son, I already got a broken car. And a hen-house. You came back again in *that*? You want me to phone a hospital for your back?"

Charlie was always the place for news; that's why I come here first.

89

"I paid Tom to look after Effa. That go OK?" I was picking up brushes, idling along to the reels and lines.

"Sure did. You gonna say hi to Tom?"

The back of my head nods.

"You been home yet?" His voice was sweating a little.

"Not yet. I gotta go to the post. Pick up half-a-years checks I reckon."

"Well, you better pick up a gun, son."

"Well, why's that, Charlie?" I wasn't really asking. I'd guessed as much.

"Effa's brothers have taken up your shack. They say they're doing it for honor. Waiting for you to come back. I say they're just living rent free and drinking and roaring up the place. Folks sick of 'em. Damn you for marrying Indian."

Chule and Po. Effa's brothers. Chule older than me, Po younger. Both bigger, and bastards, which is why Effa swayed to whites when her father died and her mother ran off. They came looking for Effa once and I greeted 'em with my carbine out a window and Effa with a kitchen knife on the porch. People will direct folks to your home if they know a fight and gossip will come of it. No way they would have found us else. I hate town-folk. Ain't got much time for any society. Always pretend I can't hear over the engine on the water until a fish bites and I gotta yell what they're doing wrong. Can't leave any of 'em alone when a fish is on. They become as dumb as dogs when the line runs. The fish are smarter and your evolution goes out the window.

"I figured that," I say.

I'm at the lines. Not a lot of twist lines left. All nylon now. Army surplus. Parachute stock. God knows what the government thought it was going to do with all that nylon. Must have made somebody rich. Now they're giving it away. Good for fishing though and nobody saw that coming. Like those glass rods. Where did they come from? Japs probably. With them rods and the nylon you could add five hundred pound to a man's arm. Shooting rockets from the Cape and fishing with glass rods. Planning to kill from out of sight and pulling more fish than ever before or had a right to. People were gonna regret all that one day.

"I gotta go back, Charlie. Got some boxes and lines out there. Gotta get my boat."

"Get your checks and I can sell you some line and hooks, son. Don't go messing with Indians."

"Gotta mess with something, Charlie. And your hooks ain't worth a damn. Thanks for the heads-up. You look well." I tip my cap and I'm on the door.

"Spend a couple of checks on a gun. Your Dodge won't scare 'em that much."

I'm on the path.

"I got a gun, Charlie."

The Dodge starts first time; just to show him. Seeing Tom Gelmas could wait.

The dyed redhead hag at the post manages to make her lips even thinner as she counts out my money, worse than when she had to get off her ass to go to my box. I ain't never seen her before. I lean on her bar like I'm waiting for a drink, cap way back on my head humming Beethoven's Ninth as she licks her thumb. My father played that record every Sunday morning until you could almost see through it by the time I left home. Said it was an Irish rebel tune. Full of shit my old man.

I thank her for my two hundred and forty dollars with my cap.

"Know that I earned this," I say, rolling my pine in my jaw, and she almost tries to smile.

"Young man with a pension don't seem right. Not when you got all your arms and legs. My son died. What you do? Shoot yourself in the foot?"

I pull the cap down. "They got rid of me, lady. Wouldn't have me again. I delivered the bomb."

"What bomb?" she sneers.

I fire out my hands like a firework, blow her a big blasting noise and she jumps.

"*The* bomb, lady. *The* bomb. Look it up." I touch my cap. "Respect to your son." The whole place watches me in silence. Damn town-folk.

Well, I gotta get it over with. I buy a bottle of J&B—can't get Irish down here—a quart of apricot brandy and a tin of corned beef. Don't want to risk going to get some eats just in case Effa's brothers are doing the same. Don't want to do anything in town that sends black and white cars, and if Chule and Po are here in town I could get my stuff before they get back. With luck. If I ain't spent it all yet. Cat running out of lives. Catfish running out of line.

The next two hours, even before the sun goes down, will be rough. I gotta drink some. I open the truck just as something clouds and screams through the air from the Canaveral base. The whole street of people stops, their shadows stuck to the ground, and I look up with the shadows at the pulsing smoke-tail. Guess you don't get used to it.

I slam the cab door. I got thirty miles to go. I break the paper seal on the whiskey with my thumbnail.

I've gone past all the shotgun houses now; those wooden homes built on pillars with the rooms off one corridor so that you can open the front and the back door and let what breeze there is down here trickle through. Now we're down to the trailers and the shacks and the cook-outs where folks don't have kitchens. Pine island. And it ain't an island. I built my shack here and I had to walk my own trail to get to my jetty and boat, but I'll drive round to get it when I get my gear.

The asphalt runs out, like the machine just gave up and puked its last bit of road. Can't even get mail. There's a gate but hell knows what for; no fence attached.

My truck recognizes the road and settles down into the nicest she's been for two thousand miles. I start to see the slick of bottles and trash before I can see the house. I don't know Chule and Po to tell about 'em but the trash and my broken screen-door tells me enough.

I keep the truck in gear when I shut the engine, like telling a guy behind you to watch your back, or to keep your neck up while you sleep to stop you from drowning.

I think a lot about how some of us must have kept in touch after the war, after the deep. They were guys with good parents, good girls waiting. Normal guys. Then there were the ones like me, the ones that didn't tan on deck, that didn't meet up and write after, the ones that in the mess cleaned off the others leftovers as they smirked and passed over their plates. I ate what they didn't 'cause I knew hungry and I was staving it off. I even squirreled food. Hid crackers and cheese and sausage in my gear. Always fearing it would end. Knowing it would end. I knew the dust clouds that hit Boston in '34 when I was a kid. All those farmers quitting their fields and heading to California leaving nothing but dust, and didn't it blow to Washington and the East as punishment for their abandonment by their elected. The Indians told us not to plow up the grass. Greed was what it was. Price of wheat goes up. Government needs it. Dig up the grass. Government don't need it no more. Screw you. It snowed red dust in New England that year.

I heard at the court martial that the Father, the ship's priest, had a raft in his group that came with a fishing kit and rations. One of the few. He would share that out, send a swimmer to the other groups with a handful to take a bite and pass it on. And didn't some of those boys not pass it on. The same guys who would let me lick their plates, who wouldn't eat potatoes lest they were mashed and creamed, now held onto Hormel spam and crackers like dollars. They beat and pushed away the swimmers the Father sent, and the other groups hollered and splashed but them boys just cursed and wouldn't give it up. This was not the story of the feeding of the five thousand. You may misunderstand this story. That was no Jesus miracle. It was a miracle of human nature. See, Jesus and his disciples had the loaves and fish but Jesus knew that the folks that had food were keeping it to themselves. No one goes out to a Sunday meeting without a picnic. By passing round the pitiful basket it gave them hoarders the opportunity to drop something in and pass it on. That's how the multitude got fed. But these good Christian boys in the water forgot all that or thought that Jesus made the food, and wouldn't he always? They were used to full bellies. They held onto their spam to wait for a miracle that was surely coming. They didn't have to spare food. They'd be eating pork chops for dinner like always. Guess that's why Jesus sent the sharks. Those boys didn't learn anything he'd told 'em. So the sharks came. That's the fairest simplicity of it that I can think of.

I'm still sitting in the truck. Nothing has moved so I'm figuring maybe Chule and Po were in town after all. I don't deserve that much luck. If I just get some of my lines, my boxes, I can replace everything else. I gotta fish. Gotta get my boat. Gotta have some work.

I'm out of the truck and walking through all the crap to the porch I made. Jesus H. Christ. Even the white walls I painted are shit stained. I'm not quiet but I ain't dancing up there either. I hear movement, then a shout, and I slow up. Knew I didn't deserve no luck. But then my father never needed to buy a hat either.

Chule appears in my door, fills the door, Po looking over his shoulder. Can't imagine 'em sleeping in my and Effa's bed. Must be like Laurel and Hardy. They always shared beds. No one ever thought anything of that.

There's no vehicle so I guess they walk to town when they're sober, just to get wet again. I see Chule's eyes on my truck and I break his stare.

"I don't want no trouble." I keep my voice plain. "I just want to get my stuff. Then I'm gone."

Chule holds in his gut. "This is our sister's house. There is nothing of yours here." They both come out on the porch. "And that is our sister's truck that is promised. To me."

Don't Indians ever buy nothing?

"I built that house. And I don't want it. And that's the only reason you're still standing there. And I'm coming in."

I'm at least thirty feet from my truck, from my rifle, but to get its confidence would mean turning my back. I know they're too cheap for guns but they were born slinging knives. Besides I don't like too much gun trouble; that tends to follow you around if you get too comfortable with it. Only consider guns for hunting and no wrong or bloody end will be yours. Don't point fingers or guns. If I had children that's what I would say. But that ain't gonna happen. I have married for the last time. I know that because I am just about to fight with my in-laws over some line and two tackle-boxes.

They separate as I put my foot to the first step and I hold. I ain't about to walk up with 'em aside me. My arm's better but smarts if I push it. So I'll push.

"You know what messes you boys?" I roll my toothpick. You know me by now for what that means. My grin follows and my cap goes back.

"Effa loved me. You ain't ever got close to her. 'Cept when you spied her in the bath."

They blew then. What I counted on.

I backed the step and they came down like bulls but I needed that against their weight. I grabbed Chule's shirt and dragged, let him carry himself to the mud, and Po was surprised enough to not see my fist plow into his gut like a gaff. But his head came up and caught my front teeth and I lost part of one and saw my cashed checks flying away to get it capped. I pulled his shirt like a hook and let him follow his brother.

I was on my porch. Looking down on 'em. They were both up together, not hurt enough to drop steam. They were coming up but my navy cleats kicked 'em down in their faces.

Like all big men they were shocked that they tumbled so easy by a little guy. I've seen that look dozens of times. They think themselves walls and they don't understand how it happened and that cools 'em real quick.

"Settle down," I said, and I was whistling through my tooth, spitting blood. Damn that. "I'll be in and out," and I was already through the door and they didn't come after.

Nothing of Effa remained in there. They'd been shitting in buckets and not down to the water and the outhouse. I couldn't even piss out the window when it was raining with Effa around. Ain't no plumbing out here.

I don't pull any memories, just my good gear stuffed in a pillowcase. Don't see my scope for the Enfield. Guess it's in the empty bottles rolling across the floor. My hands will be full when I get out so I'll take it easy and go out the back so I can come around nearer my truck while they're still looking at the door.

I curse when I come out and by. They are at my truck, at its bed with their heads in, where my gun is. Damn.

I shout. A roar only, like to scare dogs, and they start and turn, my boot-marks on their faces, their cheeks swelling, hands empty, so good.

"Away! Get!" I yell, but I feel lonely now. I make to appease, just to remove 'em from my gun. "You can have the truck. For Effa's sake. I don't need it. I'm for my boat. Clear away and let me to my stuff."

Chule fronts me.

"Go. And leave it all. You are not welcome here." He speaks like a chief in a Tom Mix comic.

I walk toward 'em.

"Let me to my gear."

They back away, and in truth I didn't expect that and I wouldn't be ready if they rushed me, so I move quick before they decide different. I drop the boxes in the bed and my arm comes out with the Enfield, the sling wrapped tight. Their muscles twitch to come on but they choke when the slide goes back. They ain't that dumb.

"I know your aunts are your sisters and I swear to God I'll make sheaths out of your guts and screw your mothers with 'em if you don't get in that house right now!"

I save up insults.

"I'm to Moore creek. You pick up the truck there. I don't want it after that."

I get in one-handed, the rifle out the window, and start one-handed, that's why I left it in gear, and I gas toward 'em and they beat their feet as I circle round and run out of there. Gone from there. I won't have time to see Tom Gelmas; Chule and Po will drink up a nerve and come hunting and I'm all out of luck, good or bad. I'm to my boat.

I run my tongue over my cracked tooth. I'll make a stop in town about that.

And then I'll plot where I'm gonna be.

There was silence for a minute and the light of the Talking Cricket disappeared suddenly, just as if someone had snuffed it out.
Once again the road was plunged in darkness.

10

Boats aren't natural things. I don't mean 'cause a man built 'em, I mean that they ain't natural for the water. But what is? What really is? Hell, turtles don't even look like they belong. Most sea creatures have the look that they should fly, and maybe they did. At one time. And the ones that ain't fish crawl, and they look mighty uncomfortable doing it. It's like the ocean came up awful sudden and a lot of lizards and crawlers that shouldn't be under the water got swept over. The sea off the East Coast was once land, the trenches were once waterfalls and lush grass and mountains where men before the Indians once prayed. We shrug and accept it as past because our time is short and we can't conceive the ages, and they dig up fossils of mammals all the time from the tops of the deep and sell 'em as key-chains. Think Spain brought the horse? They find their ancestors in the tops. Horses all over the earth. The Indians must have done for 'em and the Conquistadors just brought 'em back.

The tops, the bights, a Grand Canyon just off our cities. Deserts swallowed up by water, by the Great Flood maybe, and maybe the Unicorns didn't get on the Ark, became narwhals and swordfish instead and the octopus lived in deserts after all. They lived in crevices of stone, like they do now beneath, and they slid across the sand like you see snakes do; them snakes that didn't get caught by the water. Get an octopus on your deck and he's right comfortable checking out the place, eye on you all the time, moving around the boat like he don't even need water, like a Carolina senator walking the town and pretending he enjoys a warm Coke and the apple pies of middle-aged waitresses in starched pink aprons. And then senator octopus stretches up and climbs to the transom and over he goes. He slides back to the water like you didn't catch him in the first place and he was only coming up for a look-see, checking if the deserts had come back, like a recon for the others in the dark.

"No world yet, fellas," he'll report. "One more epoch yet. They're still there. Still up there."

The boat. She is there. Boats are constant. Even after hurricanes and you see people's houses all smashed to bits you'll see a boat half across the highway or leaning against a broken-up store.

Her bow points almost to the sky, like those rockets a few miles away, like no months have passed. She has waited frozen on the boards that I set around her. My Ark. Whoever built her made her to last his life and mine, and, as I said, boats are not natural. A little less alien than us on the water, shielding us, but still, wood upon the water. Wood and water. Natural enemies. Fighting all the time. Wave comes up and tries to push you to the stars, wave comes down, changes its mind and tries to take you down to the crabs.

Forty-two feet long, including the pulpit, and built out of yellow-leaf pine hearts. The deck-house all pine. One wheel on the flybridge and another in the galley. The keel is yellow-leaf also, ten by twelve inches thick, cut from the hearts and no knots

101

allowed. That's a lot of wood to find without knots. Not cheap. I thank the lobster-man that paid for her. I found her. I guess he must be dead. Boats always outlive. People buy 'em when they're too old, and there's always that saying:

"The best day of your life is when you buy a boat. The second-best day of your life is when you sell it."

I stroke her hull. Black below, red just above, everywhere a human might go painted white, friendly white, although now it all looks tobacco or piss stained from years of blood swabbing the boards. I drag off the tarp.

I'm the first to touch her since I left her; I can feel that. She has two-inch oak over her ribs and another two on top of that. This before fiberglass so she has half-inch ply strakes as a skin. I climb all this like a boy climbing tree. I'm on the deck.

Deck.

Fine word in any language.

My petroleum cleats are home and they stick. I think of those college boys sliding and squeaking across her in the fancy rubbers they bought the day before. Happy assholes.

She had a gas four-stroke when I found her; more bird's nest than engine. Me and Howie Turnbull landed us a Superior four-cylinder diesel from a wreck yard and we drove that engine to her in the back of a Model-A and heaved it aboard and wrenched it in ourselves. That was just after the war when peace meant blue-collar types had hobbies again and sport-fishing was no longer a rich man's game. Howie was a genius. He could fix an engine over the phone. You could stretch the receiver from the phone on the dock and point it at the engine and mash it over and he'd listen and tell you what was wrong. Mostly it was a lump-hammer to the alternator but you get the model of the man. Oil pressure was his thing. Fishermen don't care about oil pressure. Just as long as there's water and gas pumping out the back everything's fine. Until a piston blows one day and then Howie tells you that you should have minded the oil pressure. We're fishermen not mechanics. That's land-work. I was different. I worked on engines in the navy. I knew that if you looked after your hoses, belts and batteries the engine just needed oil. It's the little things that go wrong. A hose-clip can ruin a five-day out. Keep tape and a hammer and an oilcan close and you'll get home somehow. Six gallons of oil will get a busted engine home when you're out sixty miles. Always keep a gallon of oil for every ten miles or shrug and wait for someone to tow you in. Your charters will not love that and bully for a refund. I came in once just on the tide but because they could hear the engine they didn't know no better.

It takes me two hours to get her into the water, barging and warping her in with my Dodge, and when she's in the Indian River doesn't my old girl Dodge give up the ghost. She waits until I hit the red rubber starter of the boat, after I've checked the oil in deference to Howie Turnbull. Night now, and the headlamps of the Dodge that light-housed my getting the boat to the water, like a buddy holding a torch, dim like a candle waning.

I jump to land, take up her hood and pluck out her giblets of hose and belts that might live again. The lamps go out. That's pretty fitting. She's done her time. Thousands upon thousands of time. She and me. A thousand years old.

Last from her cab I pick up my Indy cap, after my gun, after rod and reels. I pat the hood with a lorn thanks, because that's what you do to the right machines when you leave 'em the last time. Sometimes you don't get that chance with people but some cars and motorcycles will wait like dogs for the last goodbye. Or maybe you don't care that much. Maybe you never needed a machine to live or a dog trotting ahead or behind depending on his requirement for the day. I know that she'll never work for Chule and Po. And that will do.

The *chow-chow-chow* of the engine has me and echoes back from the banks. Even her searchlight is working and leather shapes slap and slide from the grasses under her glare. I tap the battery gauge until the needle nestles just under the red where it flits like a trapped moth under the glass.

She coughs and the flap over the flue sputters but then she remembers and the pistons churn and settle down into that *thum-thum-thum-thum* heartbeat that is under the command of my hand on her throttle.

And the river opens.

And the sea is coming.

"No one lives in this house. Everyone is dead."

"Won't you, at least, open the door for me?" cried Pinocchio in a beseeching voice.

"I also am dead."

"Dead? What are you doing at the window, then?"

"I am waiting for the coffin to take me away."

11

I pull in to sleep before I reach the Cape. I need a dentist so in the morning I'm walking to town again and hoping that Chule and Po are still measuring what to do with me and cursing my broken Dodge; she'll hate 'em for that.

I find a street tap and wash my face. The only place open is the post so that will do and good enough that the red-hag ain't there. I know Potter behind the counter and he's an old man who don't care what you ask or say and won't give comment. He don't even notice that I've been gone.

"*Dentist?*" he says it like I'm crazy and has to look at the ceiling to think. "No orthodontist. Have to get over t'mainland for a cap, I reckon. You got a bad whistle there."

I don't want back on the main, not when there's a cop with a busted Mars light which he blushed just as red about when he explained what happened to it. He'll be looking for my Dodge like he's looking for Dillinger.

I go to the wall that lists all the post offices from here to Montauk. Amagansett first. Sounds too much like my beer so that won't do. Don't want to be thinking of drink all day. After

Amagansett comes Amity. An island. A real island. not a peninsula like Merritt. Don't bother with the rest of the alphabet.

"They got a post on Amity?" I ask Potter.

"Surely do."

"I can get my checks sent there?"

"Yep. Dentist too I'll bet."

"That's where I'll be," I say. "Forward me on."

And it was done, with a stroke of pen from us both.

"Mighty rich folks on Amity. Holiday place." He grimaces like the words "rich" and "holiday" are dirty words.

"I got my boat. Sea's free."

"They don't like strangers."

"That suits. Same here." I shift my pine pick and lift my cap back. "You forward my checks now, Potter. And don't tell where I'm gone."

He folds our dual-signed paper like a conspiracy.

"Reckon they'll find out soon enough, son."

It is the last grin I see on Merritt.

Amity. An island. Can't think why I didn't think of it before. Water all around yet land always in my eyeline. Gunwale to land. No blank horizon. Not an island like Merritt; shaped like a flank steak and more archipelago than island. Amity is good and small, adrift between the Hamptons and Montauk. Good place to charter. Ferry twice a day. An island.

Islands.

Islands was the notion that started to appear after the third day. The Pacific full of 'em. Like pebbles in a river. And some of the boys began to whisper, and not so whisper, holler that there was an island nearby.

We were well apart from each other, some of our groups like a checkerboard, like squares on a battlefield, like you see on a calendar about the Battle of Waterloo. Them creamed mashed potato boys swore there was an island not far, that the officers had swum there because they had the maps and knew it and were letting us drown, saving paradise and the food for themselves. Always the tanned football boys against the officers. Us grease-monkeys paid no mind; used to bosses. Those boys thought there was always cards held against 'em. Swim to an island? You think so? With the whitetips all around, circling us like Indians on a wagon-train in those cheap RKO's they sent us?

The worst that happened was that they went off, swam away with any saps they could persuade, and because we never saw 'em again others thought that they had made it; that the officers had been holding out on us and so they tried too. That was the common thought. Someone was always holding out on someone else. Someone had water, someone had Spam. That was the way. Even the Father couldn't provide us with Jesus in the water once the thirst and the hunger comes, and he tried; he screamed his prayers through the nights. But someone was always holding out. That's just the way people think about each other. That priest ranted all night.

"You shall not be afraid for the terror by night. Nor for the pestilence that walks in darkness. Nor for the destruction that wastes at noonday.

"A thousand shall fall at your side, and ten thousand at your right hand. But it shall not come near you. There shall no evil befall you, neither shall any plague come near your dwelling. The young lion and the serpent shall you trample under feet."

He didn't say nothing about them sharks.

When you're bobbing about just above your neck you can't even recognize your friends; all covered in oil. Sea-creatures, that's what we were, wearing our kapoks and preservers like hermit-crabs.

Nothing but a set of heads. Not even human. Circling around like rubber ducks at a fair where your kid hooks 'em to win a prize you already paid for.

I got no kids but I imagine there must come a day when they grow old enough to realize that you never paid for 'em to hook a duck. You paid for 'em to buy a piece of crap. Ain't no skill in hooking the duck. It's the dime for the crap and only you and the carny knows it. It is a secret between you both.

Does the kid ever realize? Or do you just walk past the stall one day and your kid never asks to have a go no more? Tell me, I don't know. Or does he believe there's an island just over the horizon and he swims with 'em that tells 'em so. And none of 'em ever comes back, like those that walked down the salt steps to the battleship below. And the others follow. All of 'em holding out against each other. And they all never come back. And others follow because they're all holding out against each other. And only days before we were in a war together. Excepting now we were our own enemy.

You can do me a favor—if you got kids that is—and now I'm talking to you across the void here, between you and me and this scrap paper you might pick up. I ain't got kids so I need you to do it for me. Get yourself a *National Geographic* or something, get a picture of a whale, an octopus and a shark, any shark. Put 'em in front of your kid. Ask him which one's the bad guy.

He'll pick the shark. And ask him why.

"Because he looks like the bad guy," he'll say. Or something like that, I don't know how kids talk. And you know you don't have to cut out any pictures from no magazine either. That's me talking to you from across these pages. And you know.

Pay me no mind. I have found myself finishing my whiskey. Best don't listen to me now. Pay no attention. I'm throttling to the sea with my right hand and my left around my J&B. I look behind me and see the lights of Canaveral, and fore, the light-houses of the coast waving me to 'em a sweep of light like a siren and me with enough diesel to pass 'em, to go on, to leave. Good oil pressure. Howie Turnbull's catechism. That will do. I can feel the deep opening beneath as the black folds around the hull.

And I can hook that duck.

Death was creeping nearer and nearer, and the Marionette still hoped for some good soul to come to his rescue, but no one appeared.

As he was about to die, he thought of his poor old father, and hardly conscious of what he was saying, murmured to himself:

"Oh, Father, dear Father! If you were only here!"

These were his last words. He closed his eyes, opened his mouth, stretched out his legs, and hung there, as if he were dead.

12

Amity

It is near nine hundred sea miles from Merritt to Amity. A bad drive. A good boat-ride. Distance is a different thing on a boat. You need to look at the sky more, see the hours in your past, the hours of your future. Can't do that through a windshield. Best you can do is see the next ten minutes. On the water you can see the journey whole. You got the ocean and the sun on your right, the land on your left. Just a bird soaring over the country and not part of it. Every hour it changes and there is always something to do. Check this, check that, coaxing and fixing as you fly, walk about, eat, piss over the side, throttle back and fish for supper. Got your boat to talk to and thank. Just you and your god and the whole weather mapped out above you, changing as you power along at little more pace than a stroll through a park.

I look to the shore. There, in the white-faced towns looking back at me are the tax-men, the bosses, the cops, all of 'em getting paid out of picking our pockets. Me, I'm free, and the ocean is free. All I need is gas money, and I can catch two tuna that will pay for that for months and it won't be a hard-sell either. I wonder why I ever stopped doing this and then nod that I didn't. I was only waiting out for the new season after Effa died. I ground her out of me that's all. Busted my arm, popped a guy's eye, cracked a tooth and drank it all away. Now I'm back doing what I can do. What I can only do that's legal and worth something. Navy won't have me and most of them are nothing but jailbirds of another name. Nothing more criminal than the service. Any service. Folsom is full of old service. We are destined for hobos and prison. And we accept it too. Someone should study that.

Winter is slow for boating and I want to get to Amity for the season so I take my time to save gas and money and to spot the deep where the monsters might lurk come June. I map and plan. I go to shore for apples and eggs and speak as less as I can to people I ain't ever going to see again.

I have tracked my waters ten miles out, introducing my keel to her so they can get to know each other. I spin the wheel to point my bow toward the land again. It is the end of May. Three months on the water, over the deep. I'm the seaman again. More salt than flesh. Fully back now. Don't care what has happened in the country afore me. Maybe another war. But they'll all need fish. To eat or to kill. All happy assholes gotta kill something. Fishermen eat what they need or what they can sell for other's need. Assholes get pleasure in the kill. And everyone wants to kill sharks. The codmen will give applause when you bring in a shark. Whites bite through their catch as they haul up the net, they like to jump to use their weight to carry their prey down. Ruin a net and the catch.

I don't have a dinghy to row into harbor so I got to pay two dollars to a pipe-smoking retard called Frank Silva to moor up at the Point. I have, without thinking, checked the other boats that are clearly charters. A mustached guy in camo jacket and cap has pegged me the same. Charter men are like cowboys tying up their horse outside a saloon. Eyeballing each other. We hate and respect in the same thought. There are only so many herds and horses to work and each new one is dollars taken. And are you better? Do you go out on Fridays? Do you charge less?

My *Akron* don't draw no respect. She's older than me and all the others but larger for all that. The trees she came from might have had children that are probably now boats themselves.

I walk the streets, Water Street and Main, with my hands in my jeans and my toothpick back and fro. Amity is the whitest town I've ever seen and all of it uphill. I don't mean white by the color of the folks—although that is a fact and you see the same overweight woman everywhere and they all dress alike—by white I mean the whitewash of the houses and the picket fences. Sometimes a blue and pink clad home stands out or a dark red with white window-frames, which I reckon belongs to the working men, but mostly these are rich folk's places who only come here in the summer. Not a lot of kids but plenty of teen-agers. Wealthy middle-agers retiring I guess and dragging their kids to an old-folks home. Lot of vandalism on Amity in the summer. All those hormones trying to get out. Very young and very old, that's what they got here. I tip my cap to the ladies which marks me out as a stranger I guess judging by the grim looks in return.

Post office. I give in my form to a man who looks just like old Potter back in Merritt—the Postmaster must breed 'em—and I ask him for a bar. Dentist later.

He tells me there is the Randy Bear out on Old Mill Road and Saxons in town if you want to eat something. Saxon's I can walk to so that will do. I don't want to eat.

*

There are ducks outside on the tables and complaining around the chairs Saxons puts out for those who want to eat outside. I pass a duck in the doorway and inform the barman that there are plenty more outside shitting on his tables.

"Is that so?" he says, and the barflies laugh into their highballs. I guess I'm telling a local joke. I find a long empty space at the bar and take off my cap.

I have seen one man already straighten at my coming in. It's the guy with the mustache and camo jacket or his twin. It's as if he's followed me or I him, cowboys sizing each other up. I move my toothpick and order a 'Gansett which I know they have from the neon over the bar. It's a fine dark-wood place, real clean and with those green-shade lamps like they have in billiard halls and I spy a pool table at the back with some checkered shirts playing back and forth, so playing badly.

The cold gas is barely out of my beer neck when the mustache comes along and I see he has peeled the label off his bottle; thinking on something.

I lift my eyes to him before he reaches me and he stops at that and leans his bulk on the bar. He's a few years older and we could be brothers in the way we dress and look and that's all we got going for us.

"That's a real shitty-looking boat you came in on today," he says.

Going straight for it. Fair enough.

"She needs a clean," I say. "You got a broom? Want to earn ten bucks whiting her up?" I sup my bottle. "Or your wife? She want ten bucks for anything? She good on her knees?"

Ain't no man I won't screw with. Not if you're gonna come up and call me out in your first breath. I see him flush and I lift my bottle as the barman chuckles into his chest. It'll take five sips to end this.

"You planning on chartering out here?" he growls.

"I am. I'll take two squares. Ten miles out. North and east. That will do me. For now."

He rears up then, knows I know my business. See, when you charter you mark out your area in squares, four smaller squares to a square. Coupla miles each. Ain't nothing official but you gotta do something. Something to keep out of the way of the fisherman that work to sell fish and something to keep your lines away from each other. Work your squares and no one argues. Fish your squares and no harm done and the squares gives you space to move on if nothing's biting in one of 'em. I think of them squares of rafts and linked hands, the sharks circling outside. I'm still checker-boarding the ocean.

"I got all the North," he says. "You ask anyone. That's Ben Gardner's lot. And I'm Ben Gardner." He says this like I'm supposed to blow a bugle.

"Quint," I say and tip my bottle. I delay rolling my toothpick. I hope he notices this as my measure of respect. "What you fishing for?"

"I got the tuna," he says. "And the marlin. I'm the man for that. That's my hand."

"Well, I guess even a fucked-up monkey finds a banana now and then."

He goes stern. He is figuring my mouth when he has a corner-booth of buddies to back him up.

"I got the whole east and north," he says.

I squint and lean back. "Ten miles out? I don't think so, 'Ben'. I only want tuna for gas." I drink again. "If you get short I can sell 'em to you. Any day you want. Any hour. If you can't handle it."

He smiles like a burping baby.

"You ain't fishing for tuna?"

"No," I says. "Just for gas. I can't afford no five-day fish. I'm sharking."

His laugh blows up the bar and everyone turns.

"*Sharking?*" he convulses. "*Shark-fishing?* What kind of shit is that?"

They come at night. They stay outside the group. They pluck at the drowned like chickens at corn. Hyenas of the sea, foxes through the trash, the drowned trash that you push away when they give up and sink below and you take off their dog-tags and add 'em to the collection around your neck. You push 'em away to keep 'em from you. And you can hear the teeth coming.

"Monster fishing," I drink again. My third sup. Five to finish it; to finish his shit. "Going for whites."

"Trash after trash!" he laughs. "*Shit!* I don't even need to speak to you!" He takes his beer and walks back to his laughing buddies.

So it didn't take five sups and it didn't end like I thought. Civilized town. Shit. I might not be happy here. There's a moment of red that runs through me with the beer.

Should I leave it at that? Have I done talking? I disparaged his trade and he mine. But I stuck a wife note in there and he didn't mind. He might not be one I have to grudge against. Early days Quint. Ben Gardner don't have to lose his head yet.

He and his buddies are still laughing in their corner and I take my fourth drink and find the bottle done. Not five at all. I should ignore the laughter. I don't aim to settle anywhere but I don't want too many foes the first day. Effa was sick of me for the folks that wouldn't speak to us.

I rap my bottle on the counter to the barman. "You got a dentist here?"

"Southampton hospital," he says and points out the door. "Quarter-mile south. Dollar-fifty for the beer."

Dollar-fifty! I gotta get rich for this town. Ben Gardner swivels his head to watch me leave and I dip him my cap. Not my Indy cap; town don't deserve that yet. I leave to their laughter behind me.

I got plenty of days to silence that.

I notice that they like to give their roads names to attach themselves to the mainland. We are past the East Hamptons and three miles out but they name the hospital Southampton and it sits along what they call Montauk Highway, although if you tried to drive it to Montauk you'd slam your hood into the sea.

I pay for a porcelain jacket crown and that's half my checks done but at least I ain't whistling no more and look a little less like a hobo. Can't keep my tongue off it and it feels like I got a stone in my mouth. I'd got used to the gap.

Got no car but I gotta get diesel for the *Akron* so I stop at the Gulf station—it's a Mobil now, same gas I guess—and I buy a red can and drag it back to the harbor to find that they have gas there. The fishermen are laughing at me like crows and shaking their heads as they go about their business. I'm drawing their interest like a virgin cheerleader in a frat house. I'd trouble myself but I just paid for a tooth and I wouldn't have my full mind on the game for guarding it.

I set to work.

I got my rods and Penns. I can take ten, maybe twelve guys out at a time. That's not a lot but for a weekender that's a hundred dollars at least. There's a music store on Main and I pick up four spools of No.12 piano wire for the leader. Use that to tire the fish, bring him to the side of the boat when he's done his proud fight and gaff him. Lose a lot of line and wire if you let amateurs loose on sharks. Can't afford that. The piano wire keeps down cost. I can't afford to buy chum so I get a couple cans of dog-food. If you punch some holes in it and put it in the water on a line you can net pounds of butterfish. Not great but it'll do. Keep 'em alive and squirming in buckets till we mash 'em up on a block and scrape 'em into the peach tins.

I introduce myself to the boss at Cy's Diner, the closest diner to the Point. There's a "Bob Smith's" seafood place along Avril beach but that looks like he can't even feed himself. I give the busboys at Cy's five bucks to know my name to the fishermen that might come in. I don't do this very friendly. I scare 'em into remembering my name. I shake their hands too long like I'm trying to guess their weight and never take my eyes off theirs and stand real close. I repeat their names over and over with every line like I knew their mothers in a bad way before their fathers. I smile with my mouth only and they're trembling when I leave. I don't know how to elicit favor any other way. I'm a born bastard. My father's son. I act like this to my charters. If you play like a jolly asshole and tip your hat and wipe their asses they don't think you mean business. If you're a hard-ass they think you don't need 'em and they want to impress. Men become like little boys when they leave the land. You've gotta be in charge, they want you to lead 'em, you gotta treat their fun like it's a serious business. You can curse 'em and yell and they always come back as long as you get 'em fish. Otherwise you're just a miserable sonofabitch who owns a boat and they'll go elsewhere.

I get back to the harbor at dusk. I'm the only one there. The boats all sat there like they're sleeping. Ben Gardner and his assholes gone back to their fat wives and pork chops. I'm the only one to sleep here. Me and my boat the only ones to sleep here. Nowhere else to go. My kerosene lamp the only light. I turn it down and watch the moon and the falling stars while the others sit at home watching Perry Como. I can sleep four in the bow where the pump-head is, where my charters nap for their two-dayers. But I like it up here.

In the bow you are sleeping close to the water, you can hear it lapping at the boat right beside your ear and only inches beside you, your head inches from the deck above, like being on a battleship again. I've had my head just above water for long enough I reckon.

I have my two-plate burner and my Campbells condensed and my Pepperidge crackers. Eating cheap until I'm earning. It is June tomorrow. The season. And the ferries will come in. I could maybe get a dozen in the stern I'm sure. I forgot to buy drink and I ain't forgot to do that in a long time. I wrap myself in my old field jacket that my boat has kept for me along with the life jackets I'll never wear. Green field jackets for sailors. Someone probably got rich on that shit as well.

I don't sleep.

"When the dead weep, they are beginning to recover," said the Crow solemnly.

"I am sorry to contradict my famous friend and colleague," said the Owl, "but as far as I'm concerned, I think that when the dead weep, it means they do not want to die."

13

Morning to the harbor master is about ten o'clock. I have made up my rods by the time he comes to me. He is smoking his stinking pipe and pointing it at me to get off my boat.

"What's the problem, Frank," I say, real friendly like.

He points at my wheelhouse-window with his pipe's stalk. "Your tag is for Florida," he says. "You ain't got no license to fish here."

I swing off the boat. I catch Ben Gardner and his buddies elbowing each other. I think I've been ratted upon. I act friendly-surprised like Brer Rabbit or Tom Sawyer. Never mind my new capped tooth; I might have to sort something anyways.

The ferry is coming in over their shoulders. She is three decks high, cars full on her front, their chrome glistening. It's a fine day. The bike rental place is polishing their wares just yards in front of the dock. The ferry blasts her horn.

"Well, Frank," I say, and push the peak of my cap far back, "written on the red there," I pull him to look at the paint, pull him a little too roughly, "it says, 'MS 15 LF'. You look that up and you'll find this is an ocean vessel. And down in the bow her lobster heritage is burned into the overhead. It says, '281413. Net 13'. Deep-sea lobster. I can fish the ocean. Don't need no license for that. And I plan to fish ten miles and more out. I'd be real surprised to find that Amity has more than five miles '*mare-clausem*' to restrict me."

I watch his thin eyebrows crinkle over my Latin. I give him my shark smile, my eyes dull.

"But I don't object to buying a tag if it'll keep you or that asshole Gardner happy and off your back. What is it? Fifty?"

"Hundred to fish in Amity," he says.

I don't smart at that though it busts me down to twenty-five bucks. Instead I make like a high-roller because I'm already paying him two bucks a week to moor here and all I need is one good Saturday and I'm back in funds.

"Well, Frank, why don't we go in your office and get this sorted?" I give him my best empty grin.

I'm in his white paint office. It smells of fish and pipe-smoke. On his walls he's got some prints behind glass stained with tobacco film. I smile and tip a thumb to 'em all as I pass.

One is *Watson and the Shark*. This is an Apollo-looking young boy being attacked by a shark that is purely out of imagination; painted by a man who'd never seen one. That shark took that boy's leg below the knee. True story. He survived and become a British politician, for London, I think. Fearless sonofabitch by all accounts. Shark attacked him three times before his shipmates saved him. Have to be fearless after that. Boy becomes a man overnight after that. Brook Watson. Look it up.

The other is *The Gulf Stream* as told by the brass plate. I don't know this one but I pretend to Frank otherwise.

"Four porkers around that little Black fella. Trying to eat his boat. He don't seem too bothered. Lost his mast and sprit. He's looking at the promise of the swells. That's the way to play it. You like porkers, Frank?"

"Porkers?"

I roll my toothpick. "Whites, Frank. Great Whites. You like 'em?"

He only then sees that I'm speaking of his paintings.

"Oh, the pictures? Hell, they were here before me."

"That they were," I beam and push back my cap again like I'm admiring him. "Can we get this license sorted? I'd like to catch some of those guys off the boat."

"Not today. I ain't working today. Monday I can get you stamped."

"Not working today?" I get close, like I do. He forgets to sit at his desk. "So why we talking?"

"The other guys", he jerks his head to the outside, "don't like you working without a license."

I shift my toothpick. "But you ain't working today. Are you, Frank?"

My toes are at his toes. My shadow over him.

"I . . . well . . . there's the concerns of the fishermen. The . . . other fishermen." He steps back, fumbles some paper and chews on his pipe. "But . . . well I guess I can't do anything today. Not 'til Monday. I guess."

"Rules is rules," I smile cold. "And we'll get that pink slip on Monday, Frank. I'll date it from today. Not a problem. Pay up then. Excuse me, Frank. I gotta get to work." I dip my cap before the door and give him a fine wink. "I like your pictures."

I'm done with him, slam his door and get back aboard. I can feel Ben Gardner's look burning. Screw 'em. Fuck 'em all. They're afraid of me and I like that. I ain't gonna harm your business. I'm only plying a little trade and you just wait and see what I bring in. I'll have all the kids and tourists around my boat when I hang a white on your dock. Kids don't care about sport. I'll hang 'em a monster that they'll tell their grandchildren about. They like to see teeth and jaws and blood, not pretty rainbow skin and fins for a pot. They want to end monsters. Like them villagers raising torches against the Monster. Frankenstein's monster that is. I was seven when I saw that. They didn't have ratings for movies in those days. I nearly ate my hand I was going through the popcorn so fast. In the player's card the Monster gets a question-mark for his actor. Keep the mystery. Everyone enjoys a monster. Because everyone knows what a monster should look like. They don't want to think him human, don't want to see him swimming and alive and vital, doing only what he does. They just like to see 'em dead. Dead in their world, as if you saved 'em from him, as if he was going to come out of the sea and get 'em while they slept, toes first, under the covers. Under the cover of night and water.

And you hang the Monsters by the tail rope that landed 'em, and pull their jaws wide and bloody and show 'em what you saved 'em from. And you have to put out a cardboard sign on the dock to say that you've counted the teeth. Everyone wants a piece of the Monster. A cheap piece. Everyone waving a flaming torch wants a piece, a photograph of 'em standing beside the dead like they used to do in those old cowboy shots. Coffins against the wall.

"*Shot in the breast and know I must die.*"

Linen gloves on the desperado. Assholes all around his shame.

The only life on my deck is the butterfish writhing in my buckets. I had put out a chalkboard with my day rates on a lawn-chair but came back from the head to find it gone. Screw 'em.

The others, Ben Gardner and his pups, have gone out. I suspect that they don't stay out; their charters liking to get back to their boarding-houses, and I suppose they have made a book for the season already so I have to wait for stragglers and chancers or frat boys on a run. I sit. I got time. It takes a while to make a name. If I wanted to waste the gas I'd go out and get me a shark, a Monster to swab the dock and draw a crowd. The whites will be coming up from Mexico now, following the breeding of the rays and the tuna and the Gulf Stream. Take a week or two yet to meet the big tuna and shark. The old boys with the rings like redwoods. The smart ones. I will check the catches that come in. If I see any commercial asshole with any game fish under seventy-three inches, under regulation, I'll speak my mind to their jaw. See, you gotta leave breeding stock, let the young ones complete their journey. Otherwise the world is doomed. And I mean that. The day-boaters can catch pretty much what they want, for their own eating, but as we go on, as this becomes the working stiff's sport of choice, I say even that's wrong. Just take a photograph on the boat and let the fish go. He'll make more fish. He'll feed the world tomorrow. Dead he won't do nothing for nobody 'cept make your dick bigger.

I reckon the other boys have sniggered to their charters that the *Akron* only hunts for trash. Chum belittling the shark. You find one of 'em who wouldn't paddle like a dog and clamber up their own prop, cutting their hands, if they found themselves in the water when the Landlord stalks. I been in the water with him for five days. It's more than fear. It's the primordial jelly still hanging on your cortex, the jelly of the prehistoric, the "gulp" from the deep. And I've seen it all.

I'll catch what they're afraid of in those moments when their feet have no purchase and the water is running in their mouths as they claw for the ladder or their father. I'll show it to 'em. That which the Japs and the Hawaiians think are gods and that they think garbage. Old gods. When the world was young, before our God was written.

The predator.

You have guys with glasses and long hair and papers tell you that more people get killed by bees and peas than sharks. That's a fact. Be a different fact if sharks had wings or grew in your garden. I guess Oppenheimer told us that more people get killed by bullets every year than by one of his bombs. Not if there were more bombs than bullets. But we did try.

Thirty-eight years ago, along these very waters, a shark attacked five swimmers over twelve days. One survived. He only lost a leg. But I bet he didn't see it like that. Bet he didn't see it as "only". Bet he sweats every night even now; worse since he read about us.

See, what happened was that the summer of '16 was a heatwave and the polio had become endemic. Lot of folks went to the shores for the cool and the thinner towns where the polio might be thinner also, and the sea has always been known to heal, to be pure; for those who don't know no better. So what you got was a hell of a lot of people taking to the water all of a sudden. And that's all it takes to make you interesting. I know that. Five people in twelve days. All because more people came. All because more people got in the water. I know nine hundred and more men who got in the water. I know three hundred or so that got out. I ain't got no papers but I'll stack my figuring against theirs. I got all I need to know.

So I have a bad first day. I know I've gotta do something about that. Round about six, when Ben Gardner and his lot are coming in and I don't want to see their pride I head over to Cy's Diner. Head over to glower at the busboys for not sending me any, and to sink a few.

There's a small crowd there and it takes me a minute or two to needle out the excited conversation. I drink my beer slow.

"There's a black whale out there." This from one of the tourists I reckon from his new boots and jacket and one day of no shave. "Dead whale drawing all the fish. Gulls everywhere. Eating him and the bait. Sonofabitch."

Another announces the same, adding that which I already know.

"That will bring sharks. By tomorrow the tide will bring it in. Then we'll have trouble. Sharks at the shore. Keep your kids in."

He talks like he's fished all his life instead of just weekends. He ducks from my eye.

"Where is this whale?" I say, and say it loud so the bar hushes and looks at me and glasses go down.

"I don't know, mister," the first guy says. "Ruined my day, I know that."

"So I don't want to talk to you so stop yammering." I clamp him down and he blushes. I slam my bottle and the room breathes.

"Where's this whale? She'll draw monsters. Bring the deep up. You all want some fishing? Some real fishing? That blubber will draw eleven-hundred-pound porkers by morning. Nothing a porker likes better than whale. That's his Fourth of July. His Thanksgiving. Any of you want to draw a thousand-pound fish to tell your women about, that's your chance. That's what I fish for." My Boston-Irish brogue is lulling 'em like a song.

"Can't eat a shark," some asshole hides his voice from me as he says it.

I answer him anyways. "Can't get a five-hundred-pound bluefin in your trunk either. But you could catch a monster. Save some lives. Go bad for you all if sharks come in. You could reel in a thousand-pound shark like picking cotton with a dead whale as bait. Two an hour I'd say. Maybe more."

I see 'em think. Think on their photograph on the dock. Think on the kisses of them fat women.

"So who here knows where it is? You don't want it coming up and stinking the shore. Have makos and whites swarming like flies. Not a good stench for summer."

Ben Gardner pushes his gut through the door. He checks to the crowd and holds the door to block his buddies behind.

"Not in your waters, little fella," he chuckles like Santa. Everything about him is cute. He thinks himself a man, and around here I guess he might be. He's as daunting as a cherub on a Christmas candleholder. "She's ten miles north," he goes on. "That makes her mine. I might go sharking tomorrow." He walks in and I've lost the crowd. "Gotta make it safe before that blubber comes floating in."

He's right on that. Shore-folks tend to let dead whales wash up and then try to bury 'em like something noble. That's a beach ruined. It'll be covered with crabs and blowflies come July. What you gotta do is burst 'em and break 'em up. And that's good bait. All game fish want to eat what's hard to get. They love squid, they love dolphin, and they love whale. Most people think bait is just fish, and for poor givings it is, but if you want the good stuff and not the middling you gotta use steak not meatballs. Same as us. Man wants to come home to steak cooking in the air not hash.

I nod to Ben. "You giving up on tuna? Not good for you today? Sun in your eye?"

He stomps toward me but slows when I only shift to lift my beer and now it's empty and I reverse the bottle quicker than his fat feet. I hold it like a rolled-up newspaper against a fly.

"You're a mighty wise-ass for being here a day, little fella." He shakes a finger at me.

Screw him and his fat ass.

"I've been here all my life, you fat-fuck. Every ocean." I put the bottle down, roll my left sleeve, and I don't ever do that.

Rolled it not for fighting. For the ink. I shouldn't lower myself like that but sometimes the ignorant only understand pictures.

He sees the ship, sees the name, and he gets that eye like all of 'em do and everyone strains to see what he sees.

I roll my toothpick.

"Don't be telling me my business."

I give him the look that nigh on six hundred men taught me when they died. He pales and stiffens up, and you can hear the walls in the silence and a car radio from the lot playing Joni James.

I look around the room. Through 'em all.

"I know sharks. You want to be a hero and catch a monster, you come to me. Tomorrow. The *Akron*'s my boat. The one that don't look like a doll's house. Looks like it works for a living." I barge Gardner and he spins from my shoulder. His cronies step aside on the step and I'd give myself a wink if it weren't for the planning grinding in my head.

Gotta get to work. Get a bottle and get to work.

I'm a couple of miles out of the Point and bearing north out of Cape Scott—where I saw Ben Gardner make his turn that morning—before I even have a plan. Flashlight on my compass; luminescence died long ago, probably before I was born.

It's a rough plan, just a hunch, and it might come to nothing but it's been done before and by lesser arms than mine.

Get the whale.

Get the whale and gaff it, line it, drag it. Black whale. That's what people call 'em when they don't know better. It's a Right. Gotta be. He'd have died and fell to the bottom, maybe to the very deep, to the trenches and the giant squids had a piece and the other things we ain't found or remembered yet.

He'd have rolled with the tides and been belched back up when his gasses got to work. Now he's chowder, now he's bait, now he's shark food. He might come up with a good chunk of his belly already gone but the whites and makos that were homing on the breeding have sniffed him out. Sniffed out their steak.

It ain't so crazy; not with the J&B. It's dark but that don't mean nothing. I'm a thief now, the dark my friend. There's the Amity lighthouse from South Beach and you can see the lighthouse blink from Montauk Point like a diamond, and that's a north run. Keep one light over my stern and the other over my bow, and me spliced between, and the whale somewhere between.

I aim to drag. Drag the whale to my quarter, take her ten miles out. Might take me till dawn but it'll be worth it. I'll be the only boat on the Point that knows where the whale is, where the playground is, and Ben Gardner and those other assholes will be turning their wheels wondering where it's gone.

I'm going into the Atlantic nearing midnight. Going to a feeding frenzy most likely. Sharks feed at night. Met a thousand of 'em once, counted 'em to pass the time like reading the word "potatoes" on them crates. Nicknamed some based on their scars and bitten hides and shouted out their names as warnings. The boys that didn't know no better pounded the water and hollered when they came on.

Sometimes the shark went away.

Sometimes he wouldn't go away.

God never turns up. The Devil tips his hat to you, walks right beside you. God sits on a throne, keeps you beneath. You can get to know the Devil on first-name terms. He'll come to dinner if you ask him. God sent his son and angels. The Devil comes in person. Gotta respect that a little.

Thum-thum-thum-thum-thum-thum. The engine chants. Counts the hours like a clock.

The searchlight picks out a white glow, an island sitting in the

131

sea. A dead island. There are gulls upon, waves upon. I'm on the flybridge. I throttle back and drift toward, turning to port to swing my stern around. The exhaust flap above the water sputters to a stop and I have finished my sounds on the sea. I listen, I drink. A brume over the water like the mist of a dawn field before a battle. And it is there. In the black. From the deep. Again.

The teeth. The sound of the teeth. The water. The water detonating as the tails thrash.

Again.

Nine years later. Nine years and hundreds of souls in my arms that not even a fat Chinaman could stall.

"What do you want from me?" asked Pinocchio.
"We have come for you," said the largest Rabbit.
"For me? But I'm not dead yet!"
"No, not dead. Yet."

14

Me and Amanda lived in Mission Hill, Boston. One room above an ice store. She was the first woman I screwed. Took about ten times to make her pregnant. I remember laughing the first time when she took my virginity, and she sure took it. Rode me like a calliope carousel pony with no choice or saying from me. She got mad and slapped me at my laughing through it. It seemed a hilarious act to me and not lustful at all. It was like playing.

I was sixteen and she was eighteen. Lied about my age to get married and I've been the same height since I was eleven so it weren't no problem. I don't think we were set for a long time. A day after getting hitched I had to get my silver wedding ring cut off because my finger had swelled and I couldn't afford another or to get it fixed. Not a good omen. When I married Carole and Effa I found out that the groom don't even need a wedding band so I didn't bother. That's a jeweler's trick.

None of our family were at our joining. Truth be told we were running away. Me from my drunk father and her from indifference as she was not her father's daughter but a dalliance of her mother's when her father was at the first war. So he hit her more than hugged I guess. She escaped to me. Takes a strong man to clothe another man's child. Not sure I could do it.

I was selling newspapers and day-old fruit that I would buy from the market just to keep us in bread and eggs. I was almost grateful when she lost the baby. I still think bad about that when I wake up in the dark and can't get back to sleep. But I was a boy living like a man. That never goes well.

Pinocchio was the movie that year. It played for six months from February. Think about that. A movie playing for six months. A damn cartoon playing for six months. I took Amanda to cheer her up when she finally got out of bed.

Color movies were still a magic, and movie cartoons after *Snow White* were like a miracle. They were truly marvelous. Comic books come to life, and even they had only four colors so this was better.

No one spoke; we were mesmerized in the dark and people even forgot to smoke. And I didn't fall asleep like I usually do. But it wasn't like the book old Nolan had given me on his stoop. I didn't pay attention then that they had changed the shark to be a whale. That was an appeasement. They knew you couldn't show a shark eating a boy and his father. Nothing cartoon about a shark. Whales are slow and friendly, like a moose or a hippo and Disney could see that, even if all them animals are deadly when it comes down to it. Can't cartoon sharks without cartooning fear and that's hard to do, maybe even wrong. And if people gasped at the whale a giant shark would've made 'em shit. And it was a shark. Like Jonah. Like I said. Look it up.

Amanda went back to her mother soon after that. I couldn't make rent or babies so clearly I was still a boy. I ran out on my owed rent and went to the Boston shore which was forever in your ears. Another world behind the wooden-fronted buildings. I found work in the fisheries, always dirty work to be had no matter how poor the country. Always shit to pick up, and this was the great home of "The Sacred Cod".

That's where I found the boats and the sea and found a life that don't need rents or taxes and where men laughed at their work and your day smelled of it and you could measure your success, your worth, because of it.

I caught my first tuna. Four hundred pounds. By tradition the fat heart was cut out for me to eat raw. I refused and the house laughed at me and the man who cut it tossed it to a corner and I looked at it shamefully.

It was perfectly in the corner, joined at the walls, blood against each wall. It might have been as old as me. Bigger than my own heart, bigger than mine and Amanda's combined.

I stayed on the sea.

I went to Merritt in '42, just before they changed the draft down from twenty-one to eighteen but they still missed me 'cause I was a fisherman now. I was part of the war effort.

Carole was my second wife. The second woman I slept with. I met her in a bar, which is never a good way to find a good girl. She was pretty and plump and just wanted to be kissed and married. I had money then. I was first mate on a lobster and had more money than I'd ever known. Hundred years ago prisoners would riot if they were fed lobster. Slave food. When rich folks started to build country homes near the sea to spend their summers shellfish became billet-of-fare and the price went up. We were at war and we all became closeted and savored our home-grown food. We laughed at the war then. Our newsreels showed tango-dancing dogs and a gray-haired Chaplin playing golf and tickling some girl who should have been at home with her parents. Lobster filled every restaurant from New York to Maine. Europe ate corned beef and Spam. That changed when we started to meet Germans and the coffins started coming back.

Carole stopped giggling at my kisses and left me by the time I was conscripted in '43. That's because the money ran out as the government took our catch for the army and paid us 25 cents when we got a dollar before. Carole went back to her parents. They always go back to their parents. There ain't no prospecting woman who should dream of marrying a fisherman.

I saw *Pinocchio* again in Guam, after the bomb, after the shark, and my ulcers were healing. RKO had sent it us before it was properly re-released in October, re-released after the war. They were always good to us for movies, even if they had screwed up the Saint.

I'd been through two marriages, one war and five days with the shark. And I couldn't stand to see that whale again.

I threw down my crutches that kept me from chaffing my salt-ulcers that made my shits like sandpaper.

"It wasn't a whale!" I yelled. "It was a shark!" I kicked chairs and the others cursed me to sit the fuck down. I stormed. "It was a shark that swallowed the boy! A shark that swallowed Jonah. That's the whole fucking point! Screw you all!"

The MPs dragged me out and took me to their cell. I had water for supper sitting in my surgery robes. That much respect. Not a whale. Not a cartoon whale. I was Jonah. Screaming from history against a King James translation. I was him. It was a shark.

Look it up.

I'm at the gunwale with my Enfield, engine off, the searchlight on the whale. The beam picks out the eyes flashing back green, and there's my bead. I slide the bolt and steady myself against the wood.

One. Into the black flesh. The meat pops like a boil bursting; the same disgusting satisfaction.

Two. They don't even notice the crack of the rifle; don't know if they can hear or not. Dumb fish. The birds have more sense; have moved away.

Three. A fat one taking a bite of only water. I'm trying for their brains. They are taking turns at the whale blubber, polite like. One comes in to the balloon gut swollen with gas, takes his turn, his jaws opening like some giant bear-trap, bigger than his head.

Four. Just above his eye and he rolls away as another takes his place. They don't show no pain. Never do. Only disinterest and placid indolence until they bite like they're in orgasm, thrashing to tear the flesh.

Five, and my deck and head is full of gun-smoke and the explosion is flattened by the water. No one around to hear. No one to see.

Six. A porker who took two bites and was shoved away by another for his rudeness.

Seven. Into the diner who shoved. He sinks away. I'm giddy now, can't even hear the thrashing.

Eight. A black hole where I've hit this one already; coming back for more with a .303 twisting toward his dumb brain. One rolls as he bites, his white belly like a fat puppy, looks just as soft, his remoras clinging like babies.

Nine, into his heart I hope, and the hole drips slow but he don't notice and takes his meat.

"You wanna see something?" I yell at my college charter boys. We'd got nothing but blues all day and the assholes were annoying the shit out of me.

We had nine blue-sharks hanging from the gin poles and one with a tail rope on him just coming up the side, not more than three-feet long. I took my knife and slit his guts and shook his insides to the water and put him down in his own innards. He starts bucking and thrashing at his own self, chomping through 'em like a starved dog. His guts come out of the wide hole and he eats 'em all over again, and out they come again and he keeps going at it, running in a circle to eat himself over and over. The college boys are laughing and pointing their beer at the spectacle. The sea a circus. A circus of freaks. He will not die as long as there's food. Them boys would die at the cut. They should admire not laugh. Every one I ever met was an idiot. The blue is contorting and spinning, eating, gorging. He's like some Chinese symbol. Infinite life. A dragon eating his own tail.

Ten. Right in the eye and still he don't care. The last casing chimes to tell me I'm done and I'm breathing hard.

I've got another stripper clip and feed it in. The loading of the mag has calmed me. The thrashing goes on. I put down the gun. I'm sweating and take off my jacket and cap. Work. Enough revenge. None of 'em dead. Too dumb to feel pain, too innocent to deliberately inflict. They just bite to live. They inflict innocently. Existing before the world knew pain. Just their work. And I gotta get to mine. I say that a lot.

So to it.

The Marionette could have told, then and there, all he knew about the shameful contract between the dog and the Weasels, but thinking of the dead dog, he said to himself:

"Melampo is dead. What is the use of accusing him? The dead are gone and they cannot defend themselves. The best thing to do is to leave them in peace."

15

The night makes things slower. I've turned the light to the stern but I'm now the shadow blocking it, blocking it over the ropes and the gaffs so I work careful and slow. The sharks go at the meat in order, they fight very little. They do not care that I'm there, did not notice the rounds I put into their heads. They can eat almost a third of their body-weight to get full. They show pleasure in eating, eat swift as dogs. No. More. More than that.

It is rapture. It's their God.

I lean over the transom and spike a fly gaff into the whale. My face is only feet from 'em. I've entered their world and I think they see me now. I look into a black eye watching me as I drive a stake into his meal. But I'm not meat yet. I'm like the gulls. Not interesting enough yet. I'm a fly near his dinner-plate that's all. His jaw rips wide, expands in a gulp of white, his layers of teeth glow in the lamplight and he rolls away with another chunk.

I'm gonna gaff the flesh, pitch it like a tent and tie it to the cleats, then start up and drag it away with the sharks trailing behind, following my breadcrumbs or the pied piper leading the rats away, taking the children of those who knew me before.

This will be the only hard part. Once the whale is on it'll be a slow drag. A tail rope would be good but I can't see his tail, or his head. He's just a white island, like I said, a featureless shape twice the size of my stern. His head and tail might be below the surface; no air in 'em to stay afloat. Just a lump of fat on the water. He trembles as they bite, as if he's still alive and this excites 'em every time, every bite.

I tie the first cleat but the gaff slides out. Not enough weight in it to hold on. I pull up the rope. I figured this might be the way of it.

I drink and think on. I'd hoped I could gaff it as is, just from leaning over the transom, but the rot has already set and the flesh comes away like ice cream. I got two things to do:

Find the tail, rope it and hope I don't tear it from its spine as I pull away, or gaff it in the center of the island, where the flesh is more. But that will mean stepping out onto the beast. Over the transom and walking it, like a good whaler would. But normally I'd have a rope tied around myself and a mate to pull me back should I fall through the blubber like quicksand. Ain't got one of those.

Could fish all night and never find the tail. So walking it is. By morning I'll be rich with fishermen if I can bring her in. Think on that. I've walked whale before but in daylight. There were sharks then, but they are more subdued in the light, like vampires, like Lugosi. Now they are exploding like depth charges around the corpse. I count about twenty, mostly tigers and threshers. Can only guess their size by their jaws. Twelve foot at worse. Less than five hundred pounds at best.

Screw it.

I take two roped gaffs and climb over the transom.

*

I was in the brig when the torpedoes hit. Three decks down. We had made a record crossing the Pacific to Tinian—guess maybe because they took off our two planes to make room for the crates that carried the bomb parts—and we'd had shore leave in Guam and me and two Irish cooks got in a brawl with some local boys just because. We got a ten-day captain's court martial and had to suffer marine assholes guarding us as we made our way to Leyte. That was supposedly in preparation for the invasion of Japan; so we thought. We had no idea we'd just dropped off the end of the war. The first atomic bomb to be used against man. To burn him into the earth. Burn him and his children. I guess if we knew we might have had conscience. I don't know if the pilots knew. Would you release that bomb? Could you do that? I say that if you built it you should be the one to drop it. Take it off your blackboard and shove it up 'em yourself. You might think twice then. You know why we dropped the second bomb a week later? The Japs doubted we had another. We had to show 'em we had 'em to spare, that we could bomb 'em faster than they could breed. There was a saying that went around:

"When we're done the only place they'll speak Japanese will be in Hell."

At Captain McVay's court martial we found out that the Jap sub had fired six torpedoes at us. Two of the spread hit. They had Kaitens on board which might have made up that six. You know what a Kaiten is? That's a suicide torpedo. Got a man or two on board, guiding by periscope. Hatches close and they got no opening on the inside. They used kids from poor families, eighteen years old, with the promise that their families would get a great pension. I know bad ways to die but that tops a lot. Fired out of a tube in the dark, into the night, into the black water, and if you don't hit, don't explode and burn, you'll sink to the deep and suffocate or blow up from the pressure, blow yourself out your own asshole. Got to give it to the Japs. They really wanted to win. I just wanted to eat.

I can feel sand underfoot, am confused by this for a second; as if he has already been to a beach, and I wonder where it has come from. I nod that this is the sand he has brought with him from the deep. He would have rolled for days and days and it has become embedded in the grooves of him like sawdust on a butcher's floor. He has brought up prehistoric sand which now meets my twentieth-century soles. I'm walking on sand probably met only by dinosaurs. It is a cold, lonely thought; ancient, and I don't like to think like that. It makes you feel small. And I have to be large now.

I tread slowly, use the gaffs like hiking sticks. It's like walking on Jello. I press down with one foot and my other rises behind me. His body is belching like an ogre but I can tell it can be done.

The sharks are stretching the flesh like they're straightening bed sheets, tearing at all sides. They know me now. They can see me as they bite and I look back at 'em. If I think they could wonder it would be at me. But I'm not hindering their feed so let me be, like the remoras on their bellies and their pilot fish I'm no significance. I have seen men walk on whales and stroke whites like dogs. And like dogs you might only rile 'em if you try and take the food-bowl from 'em before they're done. I've seen men feed 'em from the hand when they're like this. They see only the meat, only the grinding. You are invisible. But they're eyeing me. Sizing me up. I have become part of the whale.

I gaff deep, feel bone I hope, though it is probably just good meat. But it holds as I pull at it. One done, and now both arms free to drive home the other gaff deeper still. I can do this. It will happen. I will drag the whale to my quarter and have a full boat tomorrow, for Sunday, one day before all them jockeys have to get back to their Monday desks. My name on Amity.

And then I slip.

"And my father?"

"By this time, he must have been swallowed by the Terrible Shark, which, for the last few days, has been bringing terror to these waters."

"Is this Shark very big?" asked Pinocchio, who was beginning to tremble with fright.

"Is he big?" replied the Dolphin. "Just to give you an idea of his size, let me tell you that he is larger than a five-story building and that he has a mouth so big and so deep, that a whole train and engine could easily get into it."

16

The first torpedo took out the bow. That seemed impossible but it happened. It was right after midnight, Sunday into Monday morning. The crew had a chicken roast and strawberry shortcake. I had bread and water. I wouldn't eat or drink again for almost six days.

We began to list straightaway and the bunks above fell on top of us—I mean me and the two cooks locked in the brig. We were on our faces when the second hit us, amidships they told us later, and we'd just got our breath when the lights shivered out. I was flattened in the dark with other Irishmen on top of me but we knew what had happened.

It's a strange calm that comes. You know you've been hit, know you might die, but all you can think about is that you've got to get through a series of doors and you'll be out. Just one door at a time and you'll be out. You didn't die from the hit so now you just have to walk. But we were locked in the brig so that weren't good.

Our marine guard was straight enough not to run. He turned on a battery lantern and opened the door, which was already at an angle and he had it on his head while he pulled us out. We were three decks below, that meant we were already underwater. He led us out of there, clearing berths as we went and dragging fellas with us. We dragged 'em out in their shorts. That was part of the problem. Because it was night a lot of boys were undressed, in bed, and, as natural, you took off your belt-knife while you slept else it dug in you, and we were in the brig so had ours taken. Them knives might have been mighty handy when the sharks came. None of us had our knives. We could have fished with 'em. Could have stabbed the sharks. Could have cut our throats. At least I had clothes on. Better than most; though I might have preferred the roast chicken instead.

We made the first hatch and already the chiefs were calling down that they were closing 'em because we were listing badly now and our own shells had started going up, going up inside the ship, and you could hear and feel 'em rumbling along the steel. The chiefs were gonna tomb us in. You can only get through a hatch one man at a time. I elbowed the marine aside. He was only a detachment for the bomb that we didn't know about; we were crew. He came up right after, on our boots, and some asshole chief put the pin through the hatch when he was clear and dogged it even though there were yells coming up behind. Crew behind. Not marines. Men who had been sleeping. Hundreds of 'em.

We gave him shit but he pushed us along. The doors were burning hot, could cook your hands on 'em. Two more decks and now we're crawling along the walls like a fun-house. Running from the dead. Left 'em waiting in the most complete dark. Waiting for the water. I can't imagine what that was like. Don't try to.

I slide down the whale like slipping on an ice lake. Nothing to grip. I hold onto the gaff-rope but my waist is in the water. Again. Foam and fat and blood about me.

My feet land on a body beneath. I can see its gray hide in my mind's eye and my soles slide over him and he rises and I push off him and scramble up the rope, sand under my fingernails. There is a thrash of teeth at the water where my boots were.

I stand, pull myself up by the gaff. That much is right. I have lost the other gaff but I've got plenty more. The transom has started to drift. Should have tied myself to a cleat, should have put out a drift-anchor.

I picture myself lost on a whale's belly, surrounded as my boat floats away but I won't let that be. It is only three steps and a roll to get back to the boat and for a moment I think I'm done, that this has been close enough.

But it has only been ten minutes' work.

I scramble back aboard and tie the gaff-rope to the transom and it holds. I have the whale, and the sharks still pay my boat no mind. Some have gone, their bellies full now, but I know they circle out in the dark, waiting to digest. That's what they do. They stick around. As long as there's food they stick around.

I go to the wheelhouse for a towel and change into my other pants. My boots shrug off the water and I don't wear socks to worry about 'em. I'm sweating as well as wet. Don't mind wet; gonna get wet on a boat, but I hope the sweat ain't a sign of fear. Sure that I don't feel fear anymore. Only fear it coming back.

I take a drink and take my breath. One more gaff should do it. Then plain to home. My whale. My sharks. They bite and gnaw behind me. Not a care of me or my searchlight lighting 'em. The light the only unnatural thing among us. It flickers; coughs like an old man and they animate like a silent movie in its throw. Only not silent. Not when there's blood. And I have the stench of whale on me now.

*

We all got out alone. Near nine hundred men. All alone. It is pitch black, the moon clouded. All electrics gone. I'm walking an eight-inch gun turret that I used to clean and grease at a different angle and the water is rising to it, coming at me like I'm falling to the ground. The bow has gone and we were traveling at speed so she is scooping up water where the bow was, listing and plowing down as she goes, as she was, as she were.

I jump, I have a kapok at least. I jump weak, almost hit the rail and then I swim best I can, dragging the kapok behind. The ship is howling, the sea boiling with oil and the white rage of water erupting all about from the ship's fall to the deep. Men have been jumping for minutes and the ship is still plowing on. We'll be miles apart once she's done.

I roll and turn, struggling to get the kapok over my head. I can see the ship in the silver light through the clouds covering the moon. I'm too close. Immense, she is like a football stadium in her size. She cannot go down. The sea cannot do this, cannot *will* this.

She moans, a dying monster, welcoming the deep, calling to it, calling home. There are cries around me, boys calling for captains, whistles blowing as if there is a boat at their shoulders.

Her four screws rise up, still churning, pouring water, and there are boys on the fantail holding out for her to right and float because that's what ships do. Too close. She will drag me down with her. I kick away, go nowhere, and she's diving down fast and bodies jump from the rail, hit the ferocious screws and they become mist. And they do it again and again, and become mist, and I hope it is only water and oil that hits my face. I feel my legs pulled from me, pulled as if a raggedy-man who skulks below for boys is taking me at last with his bubbling laugh.

I scream, so I miss taking a breath.

"Mother mine!" cried the Marionette, scared to death; and dressing himself as fast as he could, he turned to the Dolphin and said:

"Farewell, Mr. Fish. Pardon the bother, and many thanks for your kindness."

This said, he took the path at so swift a gait that he seemed to fly, and at every small sound he heard, he turned in fear to see whether the Terrible Shark, five stories high and with a train in his mouth, was following him.

17

The water went around my head and I lost everything, like as a boy when your mother gets you out of the tin bath, covers your head in a towel and rubs the life out of you and you claw at it 'cause you can't breathe or hear anything 'cept the rough towel beating around your ears until you're dizzy.

I thought I was blind. I closed and opened my eyes and it was no different. I didn't know if I was upside down or not. I couldn't figure, and I knew that in three minutes it wouldn't matter. As that fat sergeant had told us.

"Three minutes, three days, three weeks."

But I hadn't taken a breath. Already my cheeks were blowing out. I would be spared. And I felt that calm come about me again. The towel stops chaffing. She wraps it around you, swaddles you close.

Something grabbed me around the waist, like arms, and then it moved to my chest in a rush and I could feel the water getting fat around me, viscous, solid, changing form, as I was, as I was returning to the deep. And then I was being pushed above. Snatched again. I could feel my guts and insides, feel the shape of 'em rolling inside me as the punch of the water echoed with the pressure from below.

It was an air-bubble; enormous gulps of air coming up from the Indy as she exploded below on her passage to the deep. She was descending three miles and the pressure was making sport of her. In her death she saved some of us, her final protection. Air we had breathed returning us to life.

I was thrown out, up, back among the cries. I landed in oil like most of us and my kapok righted me and then I was in the water for sure. At least alive. Kind of. A semblance of it.

I walk back to the stern with a new gaff and rope. I set out the drift-anchor—just a rope and a canvas cone that will drag the boat, slow it some against the tide. I loop a rope through my belt and tie it to a cleat. My mate. The feeding goes on and I look down to the rifle. I got plenty of time to shoot 'em. When it suits. Work now. Gaff the whale first. If I gaff her good maybe I can fish to put a tail rope on her and her spine might not rip as the other ropes take some of the strain. But I gotta be quick. She's got maybe twenty small threshers and tigers about her now. Thousands of teeth already shaving meat. And they'll be the Monsters soon. Taking their time coming, moving through the slick with all the patience, all the time in the world, letting the pups take their feed. All the time in the world. The ancient time. I want them ones to follow me. Bring them ones to my waters. Take a Monster to the dock and get the cameras popping and all the kids squealing and crying, all the fishermen knowing my name by Sunday night, all booking up with me for the next weekend. I climb over the transom again and I'm even grinning.

It's not so hard now. I've walked the whale once and know how to balance on her. Just a few feet on, that will do, get a good deep hook in her and away we go. Tails are moving away now.

They know I'm here. They're playing cautious. For the most sharks ain't interested in men. You might get bit out of confusion or curiosity but not malice. Still, a bad mistake with little apology when it happens. When.

If sharks wanted men we'd have all been dead by the first day. They took the drowned, took the ones that swam away, took the weak. Some of us got bit and didn't even know it 'til they took us out of the water 'cause we were so numb from the sea. That's a bad surprise.

I curse at the teeth and eyes that stay and bite and watch me as I tread. They are waiting for me to slip again. I'm talking to 'em to show I'm not afraid. I'm loud and cursing their shit for brains. Keeping 'em in their place, letting 'em know I'm their boss. Some of 'em bleed where I shot; puzzling over this strange feeling in their skulls which can't be related to this glorious flesh that has come.

I tell 'em just how many of their jaws, their fathers and mothers, that I have bleached and sold to Charlie Hawt to mount and sell to kids. That is what they will become. A trophy in a den. A show-and-tell for school.

I ram the gaff and the whale flesh rolls. They get excited again. All their mouths are just blood and strips of flesh as they rise to tear at the shivering meat. I move back slow, be a bad time to slip again, and then my soles are back on the boat and I tie the rope off and look at the gun. Time for that yet. I climb to the flybridge, pleased at them all. Their work has made me a great slick. A good chum-slick for the Monsters.

I push the starter, throttle forward, looking back over my shoulder. The ropes tighten as we creep forward and they watch the carcass move from 'em and I gain three knots and that will do. They fight among themselves, ram each other like rutting bulls, blaming each other for their loss.

154

I push harder, fog 'em with diesel fumes and serenade their supper wickedly, still with my eye and my flickering light on 'em.

"Farewell and adieu to you, fair Spanish ladies! Farewell and adieu, you ladies of Spain!"

I throttle more as the whale makes her own wake and dorsal fins start to turn, start to follow. The *Akron* the mother duck.

"For we've received orders for to sail back to Boston!" Fifteen fins or more trailing like knives through the spume. Fifteen men on the dead man's chest.

"And so never more shall we see you again!"

The world was a different design now. There were the yells and the whistles but around that din there was a new world. The crescent moon had come out from the clouds and the water was steaming and sparkling and little fires had broken out on the oil and drifted like Chinese lanterns. Potato crates and debris popped up like corks and the Indy had gone. In twelve minutes she had gone, and we had been almost asleep before, and was it a dream? Just minutes before we had been covered by steel and blankets and light and the smells of men, of piss, garbage and grease, and the still heat of a battleship that makes you hover by any vent you can as you pass. And then nothing. Miles of nothing below us, miles above, and a million miles of water about our necks. It was like something had hit the earth, like what killed the dinosaurs, and now we were the last of them and wondering what had happened and something new was going to rule. The world had been pulled away, yanked from us, pulled like a blanket to get us out of bed, to get us to school, and we shivered in water instead of on bed sheets and wondered how.

I reckon we were too shocked to die straightaway.

Something rubbed against the neck of my jacket and I jerked

round. A potato crate at my back and I grabbed hold. I was in oil and there were those little fires floating all around so that weren't good. I could hear lots of shouts but the swells were rough. Couldn't see anyone. Then someone came toward me, backward toward me, and I called out. He must have heard because he came at me like I was pulling him in. I took the neck of his kapok and dragged him to my crate. He was covered in oil, his face shiny and black. And he was dead. I tell myself he was dead.

I took off his jacket and hooked it on my arm and then I took his tags and put 'em between my teeth and tried to push him away. With the swells and the oil he just stuck to me. Each time I pushed him he buffeted back at me, nudged me with his head like a friendly horse. I had to lose him; he might take me down with him with his arms loose and all. I had to get out of the oil 'cause it was inches thick and it would make me heavy and the fumes would make me sick. I had already swallowed some in the panic of not being dead and every time a wave came I took in more. I puked over him and lost his tags.

"Sorry," I said.

I pushed him down under the surface, through the oil, and held him there. A long minute went by and I looked at the clouds scudding across the moon and then my hand went light as he left me, and he went home.

I puked more, worried some about the oil and the water in my lungs. Shame if that would be what killed me. I had a second jacket over my arm now and thought that was good to keep me up and I pushed the potato crate along in front of me and began to kick and float out of the oil.

A while, almost as long as it had taken to sink a battleship, and I had stopped hearing screams and knew I was alone. Alone with a crate of potatoes and two life jackets. I was the guy at the end of the market with the sorriest goods to sell but I was rich then in the water.

A call came. A friendly holler.

"Hey!"

I couldn't tell the direction, the water snapped every sound to its surface so I stopped swimming, floated and listened hard.

"Hey! We got a raft over here! Get over here!"

I saw them then, least I could see a body waving at me when a swell came up. He was sitting on the hard edge of a raft. I looked at the crate and then back at this savior waving at me. I left the crate and kicked toward.

The swells brought 'em to me. In the water you are like that newspaper sheet I lay to see the tide. You ain't got no windage. You just bob and float. But the raft has the Leeway Effect, above the waves, and can travel more, so they got close real quick.

Arms pulled me up and I was puking and someone snatched my other kapok and held it close. I said nothing but he called me a sonofabitch anyway.

I gripped the cords along the rigid sides and tried to put my feet down to the latticed floor but it wasn't there. The raft broken. These guys were just hanging onto the sides, weakening their arms all the time, and every wave that came it was like being punched in the chest.

"You got any food?" one of 'em said, his eyes staring white out of his black face. All their faces were black with oil and I guessed mine was too. The oil burning and blurring my eyes and acrid on my lips. *Food?* We had only eaten four hours ago, and I hadn't had no chicken dinner and strawberry shortcake.

"No," I choked. "I got nothing."

"Sonofabitch," he said. Everyone was wearing masks with that oil, and it was dark and we were all scared. People will be blunt if they are wearing a mask.

"You got any water?"

"Why the fuck would I have water?"

He slapped me then.

"You sonofabitch!" And he rolled away from me.

I looked about 'em. Ten guys in a broken raft. You could get twenty in one. In a good one. This was floating junk, two sides missing, no bottom. Several of 'em had burned faces, their hair smoking or half-gone. One of 'em had his eyes scorched out. He kept touching the holes like he was trying to find 'em. He didn't speak. Another was on his side and holding on with his legs and floating. His arms had been burned to the bone, tendons hanging, skeletal hands, and he was keeping his arms out of the water, his eyes staring up to the clouds, trying to concentrate on 'em, moving himself out of his body and away from his pain.

Ghouls, a detritus of ghouls. They could see I weren't in that bad a shape and one leaned over and started to pluck at my jacket with smoking fingers.

I punched his face, weak, just a kid's punch, and his nose came right off under my fist and he and I just stared at it as it got swallowed by the water and left him. Left to wait for him.

"Sonofabitch," he said to me, and his face bubbled out of where his nose had been. I couldn't say sorry. Don't know why. He slumped back, sobbing, turned away, and his back looked like he was wearing a set of wings, wings like a kid's Halloween angel costume. The wings lay on the water at his sides. It was the skin off his back. Blasted right off him.

This was a dead raft. I was better off with the crate. I had lost a life jacket. I wasn't going to lose anything more. I slipped out of the raft and they let me go, my crate still in sight. I was alive, and they let me go.

"Sonofabitch," I heard behind me and then more crying.

A few swells later and I saw the same waving again, heard the same call.

"Hey!" he yelled real urgent. "Hey! We got a raft over here! A good raft! Food! Come over here, Buddy!"

I kicked away. Aimed at the moon.

"But you can't grow," answered the Fairy.

"Why not?"

"Because Marionettes never grow. They are born Marionettes, they live Marionettes, and they die Marionettes."

"Oh, I'm tired of always being a Marionette!" cried Pinocchio disgustedly. "It's about time for me to grow into a man as everyone else does."

18

I'm still serenading. Don't know if I'm wooing or mocking the party at my stern. Doubt they can hear anyways. Ain't for them.

I look back at the thrashing behind the boat. Just when one of 'em thinks he has a hold the boat pulls the whale free and he shakes his head in frustration. Still they follow. Always. They'll stop when they're dead.

It's almost one. The Montauk light is on my port so if I head there now I will be going north to my quarter. Keep at five knots and I won't get there 'til three. I'd get back after five if I'm lucky. Against the tide on the way back. That's too slow. I throttle up and the exhaust splutters over the whale and spooks the sharks. Seven knots and the rev-needle twitches high but I only need to keep that up for a couple of hours. The searchlight dims as the alternator struggles at the extra strain. It'll hold. It'll outlive me that engine, that diesel Superior. Check my Rolls battery when I get in. With a full stern of happy assholes, maybe two outings, I could have me four hundred dollars by Monday night. Buy new clothes, a proper fishing cap, maybe one of them English harpoon guns the posh boats use. I am emboldened by my own prosperity, of the future mine. I push the throttle harder.

"And so never more shall we see you again!"

I was heading north, treading slow. By the clouded moon ahead and the tide across me I figured that was north and would be the best compass to head for. The ship had plowed north as she went and guys must have been jumping as she went so that's where they'd be. I needed company, and not dead company at that.

The potato crate was my buddy, my crutch. I climbed astride it to rest now and then but got cold right quick every time with the water on me. Sitting on her and taking a breath I hoped the vantage might help me spy a group. Not everyone could have burned. I couldn't be the only one left alive. Even Irishmen ain't that unlucky.

It was like riding a pony sitting on that crate. She rolled side to side, her saddle only inches above the surface whenever I got on her, my legs in the water. And I couldn't hear a sound. Just the play of water against my legs, the waves silent. That was strange. On a ship, on deck, it seems that all you can hear is the water. It roars against the ship, hates the steel breaking through her power and she spits at you all the time, cursing the engines that try to drown her out. Her trying to drown you and take you back.

But here, now, in the night, she was quiet and patient. She knew she could take me at any time. She had taken my giant ship, crushed that like a paper boat and swiped hundreds of us from her. Maybe she couldn't see me yet. The flea upon her back. Maybe that's how I could sneak away. Or she was watching me crawl across her table, her hand raised above, biding me to suffer before she slapped down across my back. Wiped me clean off her.

I got down off the crate, into the cold again, into the oil slick, and got back to trying to crawl through. And it was cold. The Pacific is a baking day in the sun but night in the water has a cutting chill. Not too bad for a lad used to Boston seas, but hours of it would tell. I hoped dawn would bring boats or planes. We must have got off a message. All we had to do was wait. But what "we"? Only me on the sea, and who would come to find just one boy?

I stop crawling to ride a swell and when it's gone I see a guy in dungarees riding a gunpowder can.

He looks clean, like he's just riding it for fun and has come from somewhere else and this is how he always travels.

He yells but can't wave 'cause the can is the only thing keeping him up and he ain't got no vest. I wave so as I don't take in no more oil or water by yelling and the sea brings him to me. I don't recognize him but that don't matter. We are best friends.

"You seen anyone else?" he asks, calm like we are at a high-school cook-out.

"No," I say. He don't need to hear about ghouls. "You all right?"

"I don't know," he says and looks to the sky as if he is looking to the moon for an answer. "Where is everybody?"

His can hits me, hits my potato crate, and we are together, and that much is right.

"I don't know. Might just be me and you."

"Where's the captain?" he says.

"I don't know," and it seems stupid to even ask it; we got lots of captains. Captain McVay could be on the moon for as much as it mattered.

I sup some more oil and water. Can't help it. The sea like a mother pushing soup on me.

A voice comes from the dark.

"Raft here!"

It comes from a throat not burned and it's followed by a friendly whistle. Not the sharp burst from a high-school coach or drill sergeant. The whistle of a school-crossing guard. The whistle of a dusk bird, the chirp of a cricket. The whistle of a voice running out of breath.

A swell brings 'em into sight. A dozen and more heads on the water.

"Hey!" I call, splutter water and wave. "We're here!"

I can see the raft in the moonlight but they are already moving north. If they had paddles they might have come toward us. As it happened we left Hunter's Point with plenty of jackets but our rafts were ill. We had the right number but lost a lot when the bow went up. Only a handful had the full team of kit. Some had paddles and survival kit, some kit and no paddles. Some nothing. This one had nothing I would find. But it was a raft. A golden fleece.

"We should make for 'em," I tell my gun-can boy.

"I can't do it," he says and shakes his head. "I'll wait here."

"What for?"

"The planes will come. I'm OK."

"What planes?"

"Shit, there's planes all the time. We just got to wait."

"You ain't got no jacket. We should go for the raft."

He looks across and the moon clears enough that I can see him. He ain't got no oil on him. With his dungarees he looks like he just stepped off a farm and he still has his white cap folded in his front pocket. Waiting for orders. He must be from a different ship.

"I ain't gonna make it. I'm beat tired. The planes will come in the morning."

"To hell with you!" I say and push away. But I can't swim through the oil with my jacket; she's drenched already, oil eating through her seams, and the raft is being carried away, the heads already like seeds on the water.

I shrug the jacket off and hold it up to him.

"Take it. To hell with you. I'm going."

He shrugs and lifts the jacket and I dive beneath the oil.

I go ten good strokes beneath that crud and something glows beside me, swims with me. It pulses with my stokes, rides along. It's a gentle blue-green. A jellyfish. Too beautiful for here. An azure fairy-tale myth. And it races beside me, its pace like heartbeats. It does not care for my story. It is seeking only food. Does not see me. Knows nothing of ships and wars. It's only avoiding the oil, evading the oil that came from nowhere. The same as me.

I pull up to the air and the raft is almost on my head and the passengers "whoa" me like a horse and pull me in.

I look behind. The boy on the gunpowder can has gone. Might never have been.

It's a good raft, only one side broken but the floor is intact. This is a wooden latticed floor that hangs from the top by lines. On the ship they are against the walls, that's why the floor of the raft hangs on lines; so as it can be stored flat against the bulkheads and not get in the way. You don't even see 'em and you walk past 'em every hour; they're gray like the steel. But adrift, floating like a lure, your legs and body are still in the water. It's only meant to be temporary. Each one is supposed to have a survival kit, paddles, Very guns and flares, wooden kegs of water. But all that was a crock of shit. That job didn't get done when we kicked off from Hunter's Point.

We were in a rush, see? We had to make an urgent delivery for a president with an itchy trigger-finger. We had thirty-five rafts on the Indy. Twelve made it off. Nine hundred men and twelve rafts. Through some mistake we had double the order for kapoks. I remember some corpsman orderly in the hospital in Guam saying that it was lucky we had all them jackets. I punched him in the face. His nose didn't fall off.

We had whaleboats too, motorboats capable of carrying twenty or more. The Indy took 'em down with her. Lucky. Lucky we had all them vests.

There was seventeen fellas in and around the raft, around and holding onto the cords that once tied it to the bulkheads. There were no officers here that I could see but that was hard to tell. Most of these boys were in shorts and vests, a couple naked, one guy in cotton pajamas like he'd fallen out of his bed at home in a dream and woke up in a nightmare with us.

"You can rest here a bit." One of the guys who pulled me in said this. "But you gotta swap with the other guys outside. This is our raft. You guys take turns."

I nodded. They all had masks, black masks. We were all strangers. It was about one in the morning I guessed. I fell asleep against the hard ridge of the raft. I actually fell asleep. I have dreams that matched. Matched my new life.

There is more diesel on the air than sea; the engine covering the maelstrom at the stern. And then I feel an objection through my feet and through my fist on the throttle. The needle is at twenty-seven revs under my flashlight. Too high, and she's barely moving.

I go grim, concentrating past the whiskey. The boat is rumbling below. Something wrong. Night and something wrong. I pull into neutral and she dies.

And then the lights go out.

A diesel engine will go on without electrics so the alternator's gone as well, or the battery. I will have to find which. And find that in the dark.

I push the throttle forward and nothing happens. I shut off

the engine, yank the lever back into reverse and start her again. That should throw the screw backward, clear any obstruction, and then I throttle her forwards and back again to shock her into response.

There is a bold attempt, a shudder from her heart, and then nothing. The searchlight gone. Only the flashlight at the end of my arm. The limit of the world. As always. The end of my arm's the limit. All a man has. All he ever has. And I know the limit.

Three minutes, three days, three weeks.

Not my limits.

I've exceeded.

I get back to the stern. Under the flashlight, under their black eyes coming back green at me, their white mouths laughing at me as they rip. Dozens of 'em. The whale hard against the transom. And I know it now. The fat corpse has entwined. Wrapped itself with the boat's screw. The dead still capable.

I'm quiet, quiet with the boat. No one to talk to anyhow. The engine has shut down, shut to protect itself when the shaft stopped turning, and maybe too much salt water has come into her. That will be an hour in the dark, under the deck. Done that before. That's not the problem.

I shine the flashlight down over the transom. The light reflects through the green, shines back at me and I can only see the whale flesh all along.

She has become part of the boat. Melded by the urgency of the white teeth. As if they had intended it so. But just fish. Only fish. Dumb fish. They didn't plan to kill my engine.

The dead have cut my passage. I'm a plague wagon. Too heavily laden for the cart to roll.

A revenge against. Against the fisherman.

I take a gaff and plunge it again and again at the meat wrapped around my stern. But for nothing. She's bound fast, the gaff-ropes

167

from the whale slack, and my play has excited the teeth still eating, hungrier now she has stopped moving. Dead again.

I still haven't spoken. Not to myself or the night. So get on with it.

Can't free myself from above. Screw caught too deep. And as long as she is held there is nothing I can do for the engine. I can get the engine going but as long as she drills into the whale she'll only stall again.

I drink long. The teeth go on. The thrash of tails. Dozens of tails. I salute the bottle to 'em. They have me here. One flashlight. The only sign of my evolution against 'em. Except my gun. That I got. That against. I'm the predator.

I'll clear the way if I can. They're only fish. Just fish. That's all they are, and I'll tell myself that they don't want me. We'd have all been dead by the end of Monday if that was so. I've been clear on that.

I'll clear the way. A little. Gonna have to.

I gotta get in the water and clear the screw.

Either that or take the VHF and call for help. Ben Gardner and his elves laughing at me from now till kingdom come. I ain't gonna do that. Don't start nothing you can't finish yourself. Told you before. And they're only fish.

I slide back the bolt. I'll clear some space against ten thousand teeth. That might make it easier. Might make me feel better. Bring a gun to the temple and the ignorant will listen.

Not a time for serenading.

"Do you know what I'll do?" said Pinocchio. "For certain reasons of mine, I, too, want to see that Shark; but I'll go after school. I can see him then as well as now."

"Poor simpleton!" cried one of the boys. "Do you think that a fish of that size will stand there waiting for you? He turns and off he goes, and no one will ever be the wiser."

19

I said that I hoped dawn would bring boats or planes. We all thought it. We couldn't be more than a couple hours from someone able to reach us. But this was still the night. Then something gray appeared. Appeared on the horizon that is.

It was a ship. Couldn't be a sub. Too big. Yet surely it was a sub that must have done for us?

Some guy had a pistol and goddamn if it didn't still work and he shot at the thing.

Someone slapped him down.

"Are you crazy! That's probably the sonofabitch that done us!"

"It's help ain't it!" He waved his gun for us to back off and fired again.

A sub would have heard us washing up our supper plates. It would take 'em seconds to home their deck-guns on a Colt going off.

He got a good punch to his jaw.

"I was trying to help!" he pleaded.

"Helping to get us killed, you sonofabitch!"

"Ain't we dead? I'd rather be prisoner than drowned like shit!"

A hand went over his arm, his gun on the water. A calm voice. I couldn't tell with all the oil but I'm sure it was the marine guard that got me outta the brig.

"I'm telling you. They'll come. Not long now. They have to. We just gotta wait."

And we waited, and the gray shape went on, went away, and then the dawn came, and something else came.

And it weren't a rescue.

The first thing that happened was that we came out of the slick just after dawn and the swells died down. Then we could see the others. Hundreds of us spread out across the sea like small islands but something in that gave us hope, and the water becoming a clear glass lifted our spirits. For a while.

We got warm with the sun; near the equator as we were she came up right fast. We even made jokes, brushed away the little fish nibbling at us with childish giggles at their tickling. And then I looked down to my legs paddling. And others looked down. And the cursing started, and the prayers from those that had 'em.

You could see maybe thirty feet through the water, and you didn't want to.

There had been the explosion, a tremor that meant death, and there had been the vomit and the shit and urine and the garbage of the ship.

And the blood.

And they had come.

Risen by the scent and the excrement and the excitement that they can feel all along their flesh. They can taste the small electricity that your body trembles with. They home in on fear. Bred for it. Born killing.

Sharks birth live young. She has eggs like a fish, sure, but they hatch inside her and they eat the weaker ones so thems that come

171

out are the strongest. They come out killers. Killers of their siblings to start their life. Earn their place. The prehistoric all dead behind 'em. The prehistoric too kind to live.

The average of us was nineteen. A ten-foot whitetip might be nineteen. And he's been killing since day one. Not a match against an Ohio farm-boy who ain't killed a German or a Jap yet.

They were coming up like they were on a spiral staircase. Hundreds of 'em beneath my boots. Winding up, sashaying their way up like Hooker Street whores when the ships come in.

Coming up to us. And with all the time in the world.

They weren't waiting on and expecting planes and boats. Maybe they knew better. The water so clear it looked like we were falling on 'em through air. I stopped looking and so did everyone else and we just stared between us in silence across the raft.

I grinned at boys. "That's a lot of sharks."

The first dawn.

Five more to come.

Now and again, he looked back and, seeing his followers hot and tired, and with tongues hanging out, he laughed out heartily. Unhappy boy! If he had only known then the dreadful things that were to happen to him on account of his disobedience.

20

I roll up my shirtsleeves and sit on the stern as I loop the rope around my belt again. Tied to my boat. And a rifle in my hands.

I lean over the transom. I'm gonna put a .303 right into their heads, right close, two arm lengths away from the nearest of 'em. The round will blow out the other side. They'll feel that.

Too close for a regular guy to be near these fish, unless they've hooked, gaffed and tail roped him. Me, I've seen 'em a lot closer, and a lot more of 'em at that. My trepidation is all spent. Mind I would have killed you for a rifle back then.

An eight-ball of an eye stares. He's tearing through the meat like a chainsaw. I pull the trigger and his eye is gone and becomes a quart of blood and milk. He makes no sound as he rolls away. Nothing ever comes from their throats. Mouths as big as a lion's, bigger, and nothing ever comes out. No roar, no howls of pain. Nothing. Too dumb to speak, too dumb to complain. Even Karloff's monster knew when he was on fire.

I don't even have to aim, they're rolling over each other like fat maggots in a bait-box. Just gotta clear a space. Empty a clip and then get in the water to clear the screw. Just get in the water. That's all.

I steady over the stock of the Enfield as they wait to catch the bullets and I lean closer, too close, like a kid on his elbows and chowing on dry cereal inches in front of the *Lone Ranger*. Fun and games. And then something leaps. A shot from Butch Cavendish to the masked man. The bad guy who had killed all his ranger buddies.

I'd forgotten they like to jump. They use their weight to drag and pull because their bite ain't all that bad. Grind and tear mostly. It's their weight that kills. The tear and rip of eight hundred pounds. And they love metal. You sometimes get 'em gnawing on the prop or chains. Dumb fish.

A world of teeth clamps on the rifle and my hands clear just in time but I've wrapped the sling around my arm like I'm supposed to and he goes down with my rifle.

The transom rams into my groin.

And he drags me over.

I'm in the water, second time tonight, tied to a tiger by my rifle in his mouth. I didn't scream this time so I got to hold a breath. And the world went black and cold.

It has a habit of that when things go bad.

You get used to it.

We were spread out over maybe three miles and on calm water. Morning on the first day. We could see each other and that didn't feel too bad. As well as the rafts there were a lot of guys in floater nets, held up by cork, not much more than a fishing net. They would be in a bad way. Floating on the water. Look just like a seal or a cod-net to a shark. And those with bare legs would have a problem. Sharks attract to pale things.

There was an officer who decided that one of the rafts should be commandeered for the sick. Sick was a soft word. We had guys with broken backs and limbs, nothing working.

I'd like to say that we all nodded and swam and got the wounded and put 'em in the rafts. But that didn't happen.

There were a lot of "fuck-yous" and silences. But some of us tried. And some of us stole life jackets off guys who couldn't fight back, guys who went under the water and couldn't complain. I think the sharks got us feeling primitive. We'd become the school-yard again. Marking the weak for recess. Making groups of the jocks and the jerks. The strong and the weak. The oil masks helped. We didn't know each other. Didn't care. Sharks were circling.

Most of those boys didn't know sharks. They'd been locked in by land their whole life, the sea a stranger, so they weren't really afraid. And there were some that were fishermen like me. We knew sharks. Just fish, big fish. Dumber than dogs. And they don't bother lest you bother 'em.

I see a dorsal, white on it like a paint splash. That was bad. Whitetips were real bastards. They didn't know from man or meat. They'd go for everything floating and at thirty miles per hour. I counted a dozen twisting around us before some asshole started pounding the water.

"Hey!" I yelled. "Don't do that! You'll bring 'em!"

They'd been told to do this in basic training by some guy who fished tarpon at weekends. I corrected.

"Punch 'em in the eye if they get close! Kick the shit out of 'em. You can't scare 'em away by beating the water."

"What the fuck do you know?"

"I know those are whitetips. And you can't see 'em yet but those black ones coming will be makos. Blues and tigers around 'em. And that shit coming through your net is grounders and barracuda. You keep beating that water, asshole, you'll have 'em all on us. Now pipe down, you sonofabitch!" That was me letting 'em know I was a fisherman.

Like I said about my charters: all men are boys on the water. You gotta show 'em you know your business. "I do this for a living," I said. "They're only fish. Just big fish. They don't give a shit about you while you're alive. So stay alive. Like your mothers want you to."

That shut 'em up. Until around about noon, guessing by the sun and the glare, and it started to get real hot. Lot of the boys had ripped their shirts and tied 'em around their eyes, so that was good. They didn't get to see.

Missed the ripped torsos floating by.

A five-dollar iron cleat and an eight-dollar gaff-rope saved me. She held me faithfully and my pants almost damn near came off, but I'd freed myself from the sling and that sonofabitch went off, thrashing my rifle between his jaws and then vanished into the black. I kicked up, my head breaking the water, the taste of whale and blood in my mouth.

I hadn't done well that's for sure. Bad place to come up.

My flashlight was rolling in the stern, gave like a candlelight under the brume, showing me where I was.

I had come up between two heads at their meal, whale flesh at my face, jaws of giants either side of me, my head like a doll's between 'em. Their eyes rolled white as they bit, ignorant of me. And they pulled back with their prize, brushed my shoulders, and the black eyes come down again and they swallow what they have. They eat like they're puking. And then they come back. And I'm in their way.

I go under as they leap.

A beast will roar, let you know what is coming. Maybe this is why their throats are silent when they come. That's how they outlived the dinosaurs: They don't give no warning.

But I'm under 'em and I crawl to the transom, their great bellies on my back and the water pulsing around me with the weight of 'em. I got my rope still on my belt and the glory of the whale consumes 'em and I don't exist no more.

I guess the night must have been pretty gruesome below us. Hundreds of us got in the water, got that far at least, but that don't mean they made it through.

A lot too badly burned to live, lot of broken limbs and backs that couldn't find a jacket or a buddy. Some probably couldn't swim or drowned anyway. And you gotta think there must have been a lot dead or dying before they got in the water. So there would have been some lucky sharks that first night. All beneath us then.

That's what we were seeing now. The headless torsos. Remnants of the shark's midnight feast bobbing up and down or surfing the waves. Guys started puking again, from the sight and from the oil and water.

Sharks follow ships, see? Told you that before. Since the old days, since the wooden world. They say it's for the garbage or the electricity from the ship or the sound drawing 'em. I say it's because they remember.

"It's a PT boat!" someone yells. "I can see the wake! See it? That big thing over the swell! Wait . . . wait . . . there! See it? It's a PT!"

Those who can are straining up to see and they're all picking up the shout.

I don't need to look.

"That wake ain't a boat," I say to those closest. "That's a tiger shark. Twelve footer. The water's magnifying him. Keep an eye."

After the feast the smell would have ushered the good news for hundreds of miles. That's why they appeared at dawn. They

178

would have been swimming all night, circling up all night. Tiring themselves out. And they needed refueling after that.

We weren't in a bind yet. Not from the sharks that is. They'd be busy clearing up the dead from just below or on the surface. They wouldn't come to the groups. They'd take easy pickings first. The strangest thing was to see 'em inside the waves. A fat swell would come up and you'd see the long black form lying perfectly inside it, frozen in space and then it would be gone as the wave fell and you couldn't help but look for it.

"There's hundreds of 'em!" a guy yelled and I shoved him to be quiet. They were letting me stay in the raft all the time now. I knew things.

"They won't come during the day. They won't mind us if we stick together. They feed at night. Someone'll be by before then." I shut myself up when a lone gunpowder can drifted by.

They all agreed on a rescue coming, but I knew we'd been rolling all night and all day. We could be twenty or thirty miles from the Indy by now. And then the night came and no boats showed up.

And everybody remembered what I had said about the night.

I'm here now. Maybe a bit earlier then I'd intended, and I'm a gun down, lost to the Landlord like I'd lost the M1 to a just as fat Landlord cop, but I'm in the water all the same. By the dorsal and tail thrashing I think I'm down to twelve dinner guests at the party. But I'm not in their interest, not yet. I go under.

Too dark to see so I gotta feel my way. The water is vibrating all around, and God knows what shit I'm drowning in, but I get hold of the shaft and feel a meaty round lump like a cow's leg where the prop should be. I pull and tear and whale slime is over my arms but I'll get there. Everything about boats is dirty work. Ain't work for the faint.

That cow's leg jumps to kick me, and my own legs fly up to the surface as I hold onto the shaft. A thresher has plowed through the meat and bumped me. Bump and bite we call it. The shark's way of testing you for food. For a moment I'm riding him as he goes beneath me, my grip on the shaft keeping me in place, and then he whips and his tail swipes across my right calf like a blade. I can't help but yell into the water and lose my air. That's enough.

I pull to the surface, to the transom, just as the thresher snaps at my heels. I kick his snout, the same soles I kicked Chule and Po with, and like them sharks he bucks and dives.

Ain't nothing I won't screw with.

I'm back on the boat, my hand to my leg. I'm bleeding; lot of me drained into the water, revenge against my bullets. My companions madder now, can taste me now. Fresh fish. Dungeness crab boiling on the dock. No gun. No engine. I smell of man and whale blood. No more clothes to change.

I've had worse.

The sharks came in on Tuesday morning.

During the night, in the dark, you'd hear a sucking sound now and then, like a plug being pulled from a bath, and you'd wake up from your half-sleep and look around. Nothing there. Look at nothing. Guys would yell out that something hit their leg or bark at each other to quit barging 'em. In the morning we found empty jackets floating around, like the rapture had come in the night. Sure, there were a lot of empty jackets floating around before, but these ones were full last night. We'd tied 'em together with the jacket's cords so we were all strung like a necklace. Pearls had been snatched from our necklace.

The first one, in the day, in the light, was like a rodeo show. I don't want to belittle him like that but that's how I saw it.

He was one of the floaters with those worthless inflatable

preservers. Without any sign, without significance, without a wake, he popped up in the air like a rocket and was running like a fish, plowing through the water. He didn't even flail or scream; might have been asleep and bless him for that. There was a slick then, a fourteen-foot wake to match the fourteen-foot tiger that took him for a thirty-mile-per-hour boat ride right through the heart of our group. Bold for a tiger. We watched him leave like we were watching an express train rattle through a station. And then he was gone. Taken home below. We closed the group up again.

We didn't say anything for a while after that.

"*Eugene! My poor Eugene! Open your eyes and look at me! Why don't you answer? I was not the one who hit you, you know. Believe me, I didn't do it. Open your eyes, Eugene? If you keep them shut, I'll die, too. Oh, dear me, how shall I ever go home now? How shall I ever look at my little mother again? What will happen to me? Where shall I go? Where shall I hide?*"

21

I pour whiskey on my leg, like your Irish father might do, and rub iodine on it like your Boston mother might. I have a kit with good bandages and I gauze and tape my leg. I can hear the throes from the stern all the while. I tip some whiskey in my ears; God knows what I might have picked up in the water with that carcass, can't be good; he might have been dead for weeks. All life living in him. All the life in the sea seeks the dead and discarded.

Their thrashing is taunting me. But that's my sentiment not theirs. They ain't got none. I drink, snap some crackers. It's two of the morning. I'm losing time. The flashlight dimming. My last light. The last step of my evolution above the teeth behind. But I got kerosene lamps too. Ain't done yet. A man still above the creatures of the earth.

I look at the life jackets that the law says I have to keep for my charters. Just look. I light two lamps. They should prefer that light to the batteries. It's formed of their ancestors.

I try the wheelhouse controls, an idiot sense that they might work better here than on the flybridge; closer to the heart. I must have cleared something from the screw. That might do. You lose one, you rig one. I got the whale gaffed and that might do.

I push the red rubber starter. Valiantly she tries, like a drunk old girl trying to get off a barstool and then gives up and slumps back down. It might be lots of things. There's a power cut-off— same red rubber-covered button—on the engine. That could be it. Just have to turn that back on. Too much salt water in her head or reservoir; that could be it just as well. Gotta get down into the engine, under the deck. I got the blue leather-bound Superior manual down there; could strip the thing if I had to. Made in Springfield, Ohio, like the M1 I wish I had now. I wipe my hands and take the flashlight, ignore my guests.

I pull the panel by the transom, check the shaft 'cause everything else be a waste of time if that's gone. She's fine. A little water under there but not a worry. So it's up with the other panels behind the wheelhouse, where always at night your fingers are too big and too fat to pull 'em up by their stiff little rings. The deck rolls as my guests munch on. And new guys are bumping the boat, muscling for position, for game, like a fat offense team. Have to take a look at them when I'm done.

I go below, lay on my side to check under the engine for any leaks or water. She's good, or as good as I can tell. I sit on the ledge provided for me to oil and maintenance.

The water reservoir is too high, so that's it. Engine flooded with salt water. Not too bad a problem for a diesel, and the Superior only ever wants to go on, so that's just ten minutes work. That would have stopped the alternator but the engine will go on without electrics. Can't fix the alternator here but the Rolls battery will hold enough charge for the starter forever; tell that by her willingness to start. She wants to go. No spark-plug worry on a diesel; long as she's got fuel she'll run. I rub myself free of the water and grease from the whale. Always wet on a boat. Some folks hate that. Me, I'm wet to my bones always. Part fish. Earned that.

I run my hands down my face and smell the whale ingrained. Two of the morning. If I wasn't wet I'd think I was asleep. Been that way before.

Empty the reservoir on the engine. That might be all I have to do. Let the head drain a few minutes and crank her again. Just a few minutes.

I get to it, with the flashlight balanced on the deck watching over my wrenches and it jiggles as the bodies bump my side. My boat's black now in the water so the Monsters are wondering what I am. They're testing and nudging the hull like trying to tilt a pinball machine. My hands are cold and weak. Every twist of a wrench a small teeth-gritting pain. That's what water does. Always cold, always numbing. Expect it. Angry thumps all along my hull as I work.

By Tuesday afternoon we started to get the measure of it. We'd seen dozens of planes and the boys hollered and splashed at each one. The good rafts, not ours, had signal mirrors and yellow bunting that you waved in the air like cheerleader ribbons but no matter for all that. A pilot don't look down at the water unless he's looking for something. We didn't know no one was out for us so we thought the planes were scouring the sea for survivors. They weren't and we cursed every one when he didn't turn, just went on without us. No one was coming. No one knew we were here. We'd delivered the bomb to end all, to change the world. The first atomic bomb to drop on civilians. And you had to keep that secret, keep that quiet. Not even tell the mailman delivering. I bet there wasn't one voice in that war office or wherever they decided such shit that piped up for us.

"But what if the ship gets torpedoed? On their way out there.

That could be disastrous. All that uranium. What if they get hit after? No one knows they're there. That's twelve hundred men on their own."

"Oh they won't be on their own," some brass would say. "Them's shark waters. No one will ever know they were there. Our secret in their graves. And they won't even have those."

And maybe that was it after all. Maybe we weren't supposed to come back. Maybe it wasn't a Jap after all. You get to think like that after the first thirty-six hours. And then it don't matter.

You start to go plain insane after that.

I've done what I can. I got the reservoir empty and wire-brushed the terminals of the Rolls battery and reconnected. That battery could run a plant; I know it's got charge. You could leave a red Rolls battery to your grandchildren. And just like the lamps on my Dodge the flashlight fades when he's spent for me. I slap him a few times but he's done. He's tired. He stayed when I needed. He goes to sleep, gives me the dark, winks out as if to say he'll wait for me. Only the two kerosene lamps now, not much more than candles, and if it comes down to it I got candles as well. Long as I have light I'm better than them. Light to keep the wolves at bay. A caveman bold in the dark, the beasts just past my fire-light. Better than them.

I carry a lamp to the stern, hold it over the water like I'm calling lost ships, calling up the dead. The boat rocks against the light, only it ain't the boat. It's been hours. It always takes 'em a time to come. Always the last to the party, always the last to leave. The Landlord shutting the party down. Closing the door.

Four of 'em, like in that painting in Frank Silva's office, the painting with the Black guy in the boat. Mouth, dorsal, tail, all in that painting. All above the water, circling his broken boat. You can't tell if the Black guy's hoping or expecting or given up.

That's what makes a good painting. It ain't the scene. It's what came before it, it's what came after. That's what makes you not want to turn away.

Fifteen-footers, maybe a little less. Fat porkers beating away the others. Their whale now. The others retreat away. Respectfully away. Their Landlord's here.

They are gliding along my sides, right where I might put a gaff in 'em.

Two of 'em, nose to tail, churning the water into cream and, together they're almost the length of my boat. Their hide shines under the moon like polished stone, like a kid's rock collection, and even in the black of the water and the night it glistens gray.

I watch 'em go around my bow, silently, while their brothers ascend on the meat and wait for the report to come back on the long black thing attached to the whale.

I go to starboard, hang the light over their study as they come round back into view. An indolent roll and a black eye looks through me, disregards me, my lamp glowing back at me from its hollow stare. He shrugs and goes past for the flesh that brought him. The other follows, slow as if asleep and drifting, a contemptuous slap of his tail against my wood and I have to step to keep my place.

I put my toothpick back in my mouth, roll it back and forth.

And I grin.

Exposure is a progressive thing. The water's warm, gets hot even, and we steam, but still below body temperature. Good for a swim, for an afternoon, not for days on end and most certainly not for nights when it loses another ten degrees. I said that some of them boys were naked and some just in shorts. They went mad first.

You can feel your legs getting thinner, tight like they're being tied like twine around a pot-roast. You can't feel the little fish nibbling no more, and the worst was the rise and fall of the mercury. At day the sun baked you, at night the moon blew you cold. By late Tuesday we knew we were dying.

I guess all the weak and wounded had already gone. Gone to the water or gone to the sharks. Now it was the turn of the healthy.

We'd got down to just four in the raft and a few floaters outside. The boys who had been sipping salt water went first. Forty hours without food or water. There were carrots and potatoes floating around, each one poison, but a lot succumbed. The whites of their eyes would get wide and they'd get real angry. You kept away from 'em. The night was the worst.

During the day every floater would tie up together. Some of the stronger guys would lay back and cradle a weaker one between his legs. But at night the deliriums, the terror, came hard and fast with the dark, like children afraid of monsters. Only here there was no mother to leave the door open a crack. And real monsters were amid. Real fangs.

Your parents tell you that there ain't any monsters, that there ain't ghosts. And there ain't. Not in our world. They have their own world. You have to step sideways, off the path, to find theirs. All fairy tales tell that. And we make our own ghosts.

We'd untie the floaters, 'cause they were going crazy, let 'em float away.

In the morning a lot of 'em would be gone. If they drifted out of the cluster you'd guess the sharks got 'em. Someone would spend a while collecting kapoks. They'd always remark how many were still knotted up, like the floater had just been sucked out of it. Wednesday a bad day.

The kapok stuffing in the jackets had become water-logged. If you were a floater the water would be about your ears and in your mouth with every wave. But if you got rid of your jacket you drowned. Damned. If you do. If you don't. The floaters started calling for help then and each time they did they took in more water.

"Don't go," was the opinion. "Don't help 'em. They'll drown us in the night. Too much weight."

The raft was in a bad state anyways. The balsa bottom had started to fall away and we'd lost one end. And a whitetip advantaged on that.

He burst through the frayed netting and we hadn't seen him coming. He wasn't there, and then he was always there. Like they always do. The water punched open by a scarred bloodied maw reaching for us.

We clawed to the back of the raft, elbows and heads slamming. One of the boys was screaming and kicking at the snout like starting a motorcycle. He had no boots; lot of us left the ship with none or took 'em off 'cause they got heavy. His foot scraped the side of the head and the rasped hide took some flesh with it. Even their damn skin's like a razor. I leaned in, punched the bastard's black eye and he thrashed like I'd hooked him and he backed out, forgot we were there.

I looked down past my feet as the other guys were swearing to Jesus. I saw him below, thirty feet straight down, spinning round and shaking his head. And then he forgot about that too and glided off. We were pissing our pants. He was just having another day in the water.

Before we'd settled with that, one of the floater nets got a visit. Those poor bastards, dozens of 'em, had been lolling together for days, bruising each other as the waves smashed 'em together, hour after hour. The naked of 'em beyond us now, their backs just ulcers, flesh rotting off 'em. When they had a dead guy the only thing they could do was roll him over 'em all until he got to the edge and down he went. The sharks got used to this, expected it, and then it was like they were feeding 'em. The whitetips corralling 'em in all day long, waiting. Waiting for the splash.

So this net erupted in a volcano of blood and bodies. A whitetip had reared up, like one of those rockets off the Cape, right in the heart of 'em. I know they can bullet it at sixty miles per hour and all that white flesh must have looked like a nice lot of seal. That's what they like to do, see. Charge and flip their prey in the air, out of their home, out of their senses, and then use their weight to take it down. Like it was never there. Lucky most of those boys were already out of their senses. Lucky. Lucky we had all them life jackets.

None of 'em fought or hollered. He ripped the net to shreds as he took legs with him. Boys flung out of the net like ragdolls, and he came down, his face all red but you could still see the white teeth glaring through the meat in his jaws.

He took the net and took some of the boys who'd got snarled with him.

He'd caught 'em in a net.

I think about that a lot.

The floaters weren't floating no more, they were paddling if they could. Then the fins stopped corralling. Stopped waiting. Went below.

The water went white, boiled with the thrashing, and then it was a pink spray and foam spreading out, coming to us and to the floaters in their water-logged jackets, with their heads, with their mouths right on the water.

The pink slick was rolling to our raft, the spray from the thrashing hitting us, and we began to mad paddle with our arms out of there, sure that we couldn't hear the cries for help over our plying through the water away from that slick, worse than the oil one before.

"I thought you said they come at night!" Me getting blamed for this.

"They ain't afraid no more," I said. "We're the landscape. They're getting drunk on us."

"How much I do thank you!" said the Marionette.

"It is not necessary," answered the Dog. "You saved me once, and what is given is always returned. We are in this world to help one another."

22

I take a drink, and I'll say it again: don't ever think that a bottle can't help. Your life is too subdued, too easy, if you think and preach like that. It always helps. Sometimes the only thing dying towns have left is the drunks. The last to be buried. The bottle only hinders if you are already beyond help, beyond meaningless.

I'm in the wheelhouse, my thumb over the starter. I pray. Only to the boat.

"Good girl."

She splutters and grinds but I know that sound. An engine just off. Lulling me to sleep. Like water lapping at my ears on the ridge of a raft.

The prop kicks off the last of the flesh, screws the water. Screw the water.

My boat. Part timber-flesh, part engine. Part natural. Part me. And I'm moving again.

Slow, but faster than they can bite and they get mad as the glorious whale slips away.

"Come get it, you sonsofbitches! I'm still here, you bastards!"

They thrash and fume, then put their heads down.

"Come on! Come get it!"

Three knots. My eye passes over all my needles. All treading halfway so all good. No speed from them following. A walk in the park. Dorsal and tail chugging behind the whale. Measuring the black thing pulling it away. Working it out, working on it. But it is food, and they have come a long way for it. They will travel hundreds of miles for a taste of it. We get stores to deliver in paper bags. You can't match that passion, that desire. You have to understand that first. And that thirst. Wolves and sharks will go hundreds of miles just for a scent. You can't compete with that. That's why they go crazy when they get there. Can't blame 'em. Come a long way for it. I push the throttle harder.

I can still make it in for dawn. Drop the whale in my quarter. Not too shabby. I'm done with getting wet. Whites on my tail. A full stern for Sunday when I take 'em to the whale. My name etched on Amity forever.

Quint. Amity. Akron. Shark.

Five letter words. Better than stars for divining. Fate's a four-letter word.

"Come on, you sonsofbitches! Come and get it!" I push harder, sing louder. And they follow. My four brothers.

"And here's to the ladies and here's to their sisters! I'd rather one miss than a shipload of misters!"

Wednesday night. The sun drops fast here. It is a long night of screams. I think now we're on the outside of a group. During the day, over the waves, we've seen hundreds of us stretched out over miles. All of us having our own little stories. No, not little stories. Our own little pieces of shame.

With the moon comes madness.

Guys would shout out, "Hey! There's a Jap here!" And he'd start beating on the guy next to him, and then others could see the Jap and join him in beating this poor sap. That went on all night. Some died at that.

Most got kicked away from the group when they started yelling. Some right imaginative.

"There's a Jap sub under me! They're pulling me down! I can feel their arms! They got me! Help me!"

You swam away from 'em then.

"They cut me! They cut me! I'm bleeding!"

Swam right away from 'em then, made a new group.

Probably better if they thought it was Japs. A comfort in madness.

The day brought the first of the hallucinations. The guys who thought they could swim down to the ship and the guys who thought there was an island "just over there". Everything was always, "just over there". A big bunch thought that if they all tied themselves together in a row, in tandem, they could swim through the tide, it would take less effort, and off they went like a big conga line over the swells for the island. They were happy, confident. That's where the officers were they said.

Never saw 'em again, which made it worse 'cause then other kids would try the same, thinking they must have made it. You couldn't reason with anybody no more. Didn't bother. This was our life now, this was how it had always been, would always be, until the day when we weren't here. That's what death had become. No hospital, no crying bedside, no funeral. You just weren't here anymore.

I still had that potato crate bobbing around, following me like a mutt. I thought about the guy who'd branded the word on the box, sure that it would have been prison work. I wondered what he'd done, what he maybe didn't do that got him caught, wondered where he was now. An afternoon in Folsom. Lying on his bunk looking at the ceiling waiting to be called to make more potato crates for those lucky Joes sunning themselves overseas. I'd read the word "potatoes" a thousand times. He'd printed it a thousand times. I knew every defect in the black writing. Did he get punished for that? Would he swap with me now? I would with him. I'd take all his life sentence to be out of this water for just one hour. Would he take me up on that?

But there was always the fear that maybe you couldn't come out of the water. What if you were rescued and you died anyways? What if there was too much salt in your body already, that your kidneys were too far gone, that you were infected, that the fish biting and the life of the sea had given you some disease. Wouldn't that be worse? To be saved only to die a week later. The water to get you in arrears. To be out only to never be out. What shitty story would that be? What point, what meaning to stay alive?

The guys with wives and families endured the best. They just tried to sleep. To live or go and pass quietly. To not give up and to not aspire to survive. They didn't think that anyone was coming, and I guess none of us thought that anymore. The Japs had won, America was invaded. There were no search missions for the defeated.

The young single guys just either went crazy or drank cool seawater like beer, laughing at you to join 'em because it was great and we were the nuts for holding out for so long. They laughed and kept drinking even when their lips went blue, when syrupy blood started to hang from their nose.

Some got angry and swam off. They'd sidle up to you and whisper, "To hell with this. I've had enough," or something like that, and then they'd give you their ruined dollars in their wallets and sing, "So long!"

They weren't giving up, it wasn't like that. They just didn't want to do it no more. Done with it. Not with life. Just this miserable part of it that no one told 'em about.

They took off their jacket and went swimming, like it was any summer Sunday on Coney Island. Sometimes they'd wave goodbye when they were too far to shout. They'd smile and wave and then just lie face down or dive. You didn't try and stop 'em. You understood. You tomorrow.

Sometimes they came back.

And that was the worst.

Sometimes the deep current returned 'em, if the sharks didn't get 'em. You'd look down through the window of the water and there'd be a body lying twenty feet below, lying flat out like he was sleeping, but he'd be looking straight up to your gaze, the oil washed from him and he was the fresh boy again. Then another current would get him and he'd go shooting off sideways like an octopus might, like a rocket, and he'd be gone. That was worse than looking down and seeing a shark beneath your feet. Got used to the sharks. I feared those dead hands wandering over my feet, a face with eyes eaten out coming up between my knees. Then we saw a plane. Flying low. For once a plane under the sun. The first time this had happened.

His wings turned.

The boat jerks and the wheel hits my gut right above where the transom caught me when I went over the side. Been punched twice in the gut by my own boat.

The bastards are ramming the boat, ramming the stern. Probably trying to get deeper into the meat but their pounding will count. I can't push faster without risking the engine going out again. But they're driving the meat back into my prop. Four fat porkers ruining all that I have. If I was afraid of 'em they would win. I'd panic and they would win. Win again. They'd go through the meat and then they would start on the boat. Like that Black boy in the painting with the broken mast and boat.

197

They would circle and grind you down until all you knew was the dorsal and tail and the long wait. But I already know all that they have. They'd caught a tartar. That's a saying from the old world. From the old sea. It means you came up against an enemy that won't quit, an enemy too strong, one that knows all your play, that ain't afraid. I throttle back.

Captain McVay had Very rockets in his group—flares that is. He had spam and biscuits and malted milk tablets. Lucky sonofabitch. We never saw that group. We had shit. Best we could do was huddle round a guy when he took a piss to get some warmth or try and grab the pilot fish from around the sharks without losing our hands. We never did. Those pilot fish don't make for good eating anyhow. They have a partnership with the shark, same as most predators have something small and weak that cleans their teeth or eats their mites. They consider them sharks "their" shark. Heard of a ship that left France and caught a whitetip for sport. That shark's pilot fish followed the ship all the way to New York. The sea is the strangest place. There ain't no reason to it.

I got Very rockets of my own now. I go below and get the wooden box. I check and break the brass gun. Load.

I go to 'em.

I'm at the stern. I balance myself, level my eye against their dead eyes.

"Come and get it." I pick the largest of 'em. Aim right in the eye, from my eye. "Get the fuck from me."

The magnesium fizzles, the shot slow as it leaves the muzzle but it picks up real fast and I see it fire red into his head and explode like a grenade.

His flesh burns, his fat bubbles, good like it should. His eye gone but he don't say nothing, don't roar nothing. He rolls off the whale to cool his head in the water and I can see the red-flare burning, lighting the water as he goes deep. I'm done with him, break the gun again and slip in another. I got flares for all of 'em.

I take aim again. They don't notice their buddy has gone, don't care, no fear in 'em of the gun.

But this shouldn't be the way. I lower my arm. This ain't what I do. What tale to tell? This ain't it.

Boys in my arms, strong in my arms. Lived nine years now more than they ever did. They were angry. "*To hell with this,*" they said and swam away. They didn't give up. They weren't mad. They'd just had enough.

"*To hell with this.*"

I don't owe 'em nothing, or myself, and the shark just does what he was born to do. It ain't revenge. I don't deserve killing 'em with flares. And neither do they. I'm not like the archers and the shooters. I'm better than them, and I'm better than these sonsofbitches at my stern. I just have to show 'em. Carry 'em in on my gin pole. All them fat ladies and sticky kids squealing.

I keep the chair in the quarters fore, where my charters sleep on straw-packed vinyl mattresses when we go out for the weekend. I put the gun down. Not to the box. Might need it quick.

The plane dipped his wings either side as he went round. That meant, "I see you."

Holy shit! He's seen us! Three nights, near four days in the water, hundreds of planes, and one sonofabitch had seen us!

Not by design. He'd gone low to fix his antenna after nearly losing it and his second wind-sock that morning and was mad as hell. I now know that's how the Lord works.

His PV1 was set to look for and bomb subs. His faulty antenna was whipping the shit out of his fuselage and he'd gone low and opened the bomb doors to try and grab it, or something, he wasn't sure what, and then he saw an oil slick.

199

He figured it was an injured Jap sub and followed the slick. We didn't know it but we were about a hundred miles from the sinking. He ran up the slick and then he started to see bodies. And some of 'em waved.

They were black bodies, covered in oil. He thought they must be Japs. He'd have heard if there was an American crew missing.

He'd have heard.

He had Tarpok depth charges, two .50 caliber forward guns for strafing and six .30s for picking flies. There were Japs in the water. Hundreds of 'em. His plane's call sign was *Gambler*. He went lower. To take a gamble.

He was better than his president. He didn't pull the trigger on unknown faces.

I see you. Wings dipped up and down again. *I see you.*

That was Thursday morning. And one plane don't make a rescue for three hundred boys. Some of 'em got so excited that they splashed and yelled and the last of their engine puttered out. They drowned with only ever seeing a dip of wings. *I see you. I see you.* And maybe they did get rescued at that.

The next twenty-four hours were the worst.

It only takes ten minutes to bolt the chair. Wet hands and wrench, good enough pain. A fighting chair is much like a good barber's chair. Leather cushions, foot rest. Only the stirrups and braces tell it for what it is. And the bucket for the rod's hilt; a scabbard for a sword. We wear a harness for the monsters, like those braces they give to cripples, to polio boys. It holds against the shoulders and the lower back. Takes the strain. In practice it just shows you where the strength needs to come, where your arms ain't working and makes you pull harder. You're tied to the chair, chair bolted to the deck. Not a place to be weak.

I got a leader of piano wire but no mate to pull it so I'll fight

200

where it hangs. Bamboo rod, Penn 60 and 100 lb test for the chair. I don't have to bait. I just lay my hook over the whale. Wait for 'em to bite. And they bite all the time, up and down like a steam-engine.

No drift-anchor, no engine. Kerosene lamp and whiskey and crackers. Three whites, the one I shot in the eye gone. Twelve foot the smallest, all of 'em at least half again in girth. As old as me. They lived through a war also, traveled the same oceans, been around the world dozens of times. And a skinny Boston-Irish is gonna send 'em home.

"I'm still here, you bastards!"

I switch the marine-cap for my Indy one folded in my field jacket.

The marine one too tight sometimes.

"*Tomorrow your wish will come true.*"

"*And what is it?*"

"*Tomorrow you will cease to be a Marionette and will become a real boy.*"

Unluckily, in a Marionette's life there is always a BUT which is apt to spoil everything.

23

I could hear footsteps. I was asleep but I could hear someone walking slowly all around me, right by my head. I felt real peaceful about that. Then someone grabbed my neck and pulled me up out of the water and pushed me back against the ridge of the raft. I had been sleeping under the water. The footsteps were my heartbeat. I didn't say thanks. We didn't do that anymore. Hard to speak anyways. Lips just bloodied scars in our faces. Our necks were like we'd been hanged. Bleeding raw from the jackets round 'em. They weren't built for comfort.

It was Thursday afternoon. The PV1 had gone but he must have been doing something. I can't say that our spirits lifted. We were pretty empty. Rescue didn't seem possible. Just arithmetic that's all. Pencil and paper. "Sit down, class." An arithmetic problem to solve. "Johnny has three hundred men in the water. Mary has X number of planes Y distance away. How many men must Mary let die?"

It would take dozens of boats and planes to get us out, take maybe a couple of days. We didn't have days. All I could think about was if they just dropped us some water we could stay here for a little bit longer. We could live here now. That would do. Just keep dropping us water.

Some thought we'd be picked up in hours so they started drinking the seawater, thinking it didn't matter now, that there would be some miracle cure that would take care of it back in Guam. No one fought the sharks anymore. They were still taking the dead mostly but they'd got used to the plentiful of us and we'd got used to them in the reaping of us. We couldn't see very well by then anyhow. The lack of anything inside us, the sun's relentless burning and the oil had got to our eyes so all we saw was a dark blur powering through a pale blur, and it had become ordinary, like swatting flies, just one infinitesimal act against another. A rush of noise, a blur, and done.

More planes, and now they dropped life jackets and orange dye to mark where we were. Some managed to swim to the jackets, to swap 'em for their own, knowing that the jackets would have pockets with water beakers in 'em. That turned out to be a bust 'cause the beakers were made of wood. They exploded on impact. I had a mind to kill the man that made them beakers and the cheap sonofabitch that signed off for 'em 'cause metal ones were too much to pay for.

"What's the point of giving good canteens to dying men? What's the point of giving 'em a life jacket that lasts a week? They'll be dead. Why give every raft a survival kit? For maybes? We need bullets not bandages." And then he goes home to his wife and kids that we were fighting for. He ain't killed anyone. He just didn't save anyone. Got a bonus for saving nickels. Bought his kid a toy battleship and wooden toy sailors for Christmas.

Because Daddy's in the navy.

They picked up the floaters first and we were spread over maybe twenty or thirty miles so we went into Thursday night still in the water with our busted raft.

We'd lost sight of the Father days ago and I could imagine him ordering his boys to hold on, that help was coming now, only a few more hours. We had no one like that with us. Our only god now was the one that the Japs, Africans, and Hawaiians revered. The one constant in all our days. He would choose who lived or died. He would spare none of us. Not from his memory leastways. That we would take with us. Like gods want. He just wouldn't kill all of us. He'd just take some sleep away from us forever.

Nine hundred men went into the water. We were down to just over three hundred. That's about one hundred and fifty men a day.

A day.

One hundred and fifty men gone per day.

Think about that when you come home from work. Look at the cars in front of you, rolling past in the other lane, the guy in your mirror. Look up your railroad car, through the doors, and think about that. Count all the cars. Count all the bodies in your railroad car, the next passenger car. Think on their faces, not numbers on paper. That New York special carrying them desk jockeys. They couldn't fish that hard if a saint gave 'em grace to do so. One hundred and fifty men a day. And if each one had just one person, just one person who had a picture of 'em on a nightstand, that's three hundred people. Gone forever. Not just the dead. The living, the living that remain, gone as well.

Some of us never even saw a shark, never saw anyone taken. The PBYs, the Catalina sea-planes that landed to pick us up, saw boys taken before their eyes; even when they were scooping us up. In some way that justified. I hated to hear those guys say they never even saw one. They were usually the groups that had paddles and tins of spam and biscuits and Very's. They must have been on a different damn sea from a different damn ship.

Maybe there *was* an island where they all hung out. Maybe we were put down exactly where they wanted, where we couldn't tell no one ever of what we'd done and there was an island for them that knew about it.

Maybe a doctor had told the brass that nobody could survive. Could not survive the exposure of the sun and the water for five days, no water for five days, and a natural tempting poison all around, and the greatest predator to defend against.

"We didn't do it," they would say. "It was nature. We would have no blame. Just wait five days and go and pick up the pieces. We'll give 'em a nice bit of marble as a memorial for folks to look at."

Wednesday we'd done a call-off. We had sixty-three guys in our group, our spread-out group. Thursday we were down to twenty. Thursday night my last. They would come to pick up only the pieces. Like they planned all along. The which, the why, the wherefore.

I don't know if I had the same guy next to me all the time. We'd come and gone, and names didn't mean much, all our faces black anyhow. Masks separating us. We had to squeeze our eyes open just to see the smeared world, and when we did it burned, and when we closed 'em it burned. I'd set to be blind, accepted it. But this was the guy who had lifted me up when I'd fallen asleep and he was by me Thursday night. We linked arms. Alone now, lost our last one from the raft that morning. I knew him. The guy who had cajoled me about the Saint. Herbie Robinson. Bosun's mate. Year younger than me. Twenty.

Our teeth chattered together and we listened to the thrashing and the sucking sounds all night. No one screamed anymore. Just flowers being plucked. Planes and boats were coming, but not for us.

In truth I was afraid of being saved. I still dwell on that. As I said before I dreaded the hospital and the white coat that would write me off. I was blue-white, flesh swollen, eyes hot and fading, my own throat throttling me. I had pains deep in my back that I didn't want to think about. And what if they pulled me out and I just stretched like putty, my spine withered to nothing, or worse and my legs were only held on by strings of meat where the sharks had been and I just couldn't feel it; alive in ignorance.

More afraid of living than dying. And that's the worst a man can be. Meaningless. That's how young healthy men die, that's why they take their own lives. Their continual living is meaningless. It wouldn't be suicide in the water. No one would judge you. You might be honored. If you lived you might just warrant a space on a porch in some afternoon sun at a veteran's home where you had to change your own diapers. The sea taking you in arrears. The Landlord taking his due from your five days in his debt. You never got shot, you never hand-fought no Jap or liberated no town. You just got damn wet for five days.

"Do you believe in angels?" His voice was rasping. We'd stopped talking days ago.

"No," I said.

"I think those planes were angels. They didn't look like planes. I don't believe anyone's coming."

"They were planes," I coughed and some rotten shit came up in my mouth. "Your eyes don't work. They're just taking their time. Hold on."

He waited before speaking.

"I think they want us to come to them. I think the world's ended. We lost the war. The world's dead. We're the last alive. They're coming to bring us to glory. I can hear them."

The last corner of the raft broke away; the only thing holding it together was us. The others had gone. Drowned or eaten. We'd dozed and missed it.

"The angels are coming!" He'd gone blissful.

207

Then *he* came.

He did it like they always do. Not there. Then always there.

White and gray. Blood, and teeth hanging with meat and cloth. They energize in the sun. Use the night to expend. Run over you, pour over you like a wave. I see my right arm in his open throat, half in the water, half in him. I wasn't afraid. Waiting was the only fear. This was release.

I was pulled away.

That guy threw me back, back behind him, and the maw came on.

I can't say that he meant it, he just reacted, but I was thrown to the other side of the broken raft and the shark tipped him and bit through his belly and he burst like a water balloon.

He didn't make a sound. The shark choked, extended his gape in a gulp and took a deeper bite that went right across the boy so that now there was a top half of head and torso and then a gray thing like the hood of a car and then legs hanging out the other side. One boot off.

I remember that it was quiet, like a silent movie, and for a moment the sight froze while they changed the reel.

Changed the reel.

Click-click-click-click.

I watched both their eyes. One machine killing another. As calm as shaking hands. Neither of 'em concerned. Just natural. I wasn't even there.

The water boiled, and the shark pulled back, shook the ragged body like a hound with a squirrel. And then he was gone. They were gone.

The sea calmed straight away. A burglar closing the window behind him. Like he was never there, like they both were never there and I'd only dreamed it, as the world had become a dream, waking and sleeping all the same.

The water was milky white and then black but not because it was night. A different black. Thick. Things in it. And I kept my mouth closed.

I was picked up Friday afternoon.

They came to the rafts last. They figured we were not the worst of us. I was picked up by a Higgins boat. I had to climb up a Jacob's ladder. The boys had got in the water to get me and then scrambled back in when they saw just a few of the sharks that I'd lived with. They threw me a monkey-fist and dragged me to the ladder, assumed I was strong enough to hold on. They remarked and reminded me how lucky I was that I had been in a raft.

"Screw you," I said. I didn't know my own voice. "You got water? Put me back if you ain't." And I meant it.

They dropped the bomb on the Monday.

They'd built it while we were in the water. Guess they were too busy to think about us, the ones that brought it. We'd changed the world. All men that change the world get punished.

Look it up.

Pinocchio's heart beat fast, and then faster and faster.

He redoubled his efforts and swam as hard as he could toward the white rock.

He was almost halfway over, when suddenly a horrible sea monster stuck its head out of the water, an enormous head with a huge mouth, wide open, showing three rows of gleaming teeth, the mere sight of which would have filled you with fear.

Do you know what it was?

24

I get one straightaway, close as they were. He don't run. He's taken a craw-full and my hook has taken its bite of him, down his throat while he's still swallowing the flesh. I reel back, line taut so he might notice. He's only feet from the transom so this won't be no fight. I lock the reel and unclip the harness from it. Put on my gloves. I've only got to pick up the leader, my piano wire leader, and use the chair as a mate, the rod in one of the chair's holder sleeves, and then hook him with a tail rope. Two-man job. But like I said: don't start anything you can't finish yourself.

If I can haul him up by the leader, haul his snout up, he'll show me his tail. Roping that will be the only struggle. Could break my arm on the side of the boat if he thrashes well enough, could slice an eye if I get it wrong. But get him by the tail, winch him up from the gin pole, and he'll hang helpless. They give up then. Every animal does if you get 'em upside down. Rule of nature. Man started fishing and hunting when we found that out. Before we could talk we found that out. And if you observe hunters and fishermen we're still the same. The moments when the trigger's pulled or the leader is hauled up. We don't say nothing. Talk shit all day until something has to be exploded or gaffed. Them's the moments we become our ancestors.

I got a gaff tied to another cleat and that will hold him when I run it into him.

Hook, gaff, tail rope. The Holy Trinity. All you need.

Pull up the leader with my left, gaff him in the head with my right and let the reel and line and the gaff hold him while I bring up the leader and hook the rope round his tail. That's all I gotta do.

On a twelve-foot Great White.

In the dark. Alone.

Never said I didn't work for a living.

I must have been in better shape than I thought 'cause once they got me to a ship I didn't go straight to no medical. They sat me in a shower on a stool and left me there. I just let the water roll over me and even managed to stand so I could lap at the water like a dog. Drank straight out of the shower-head. I did that for half an hour at least, hanging off the chrome. It was odd to see metal again, to see turning taps, to see anything man-made. I got out and there was a towel but I didn't use it 'cause I thought my skin would come right off if I did.

I got into the shorts and shirt they gave me while still dripping wet and no one said anything. I was escorted to the doc and had to wait in line. There were about fifty of us. We stood in line, leaned against the steel walls without a word of complaint. Expected nothing else. Ain't no space for chairs in a ship's corridor.

At Base 18's Guam hospital we were washed with diesel to get the oil off and had our heads shaved for the same. The oil had saved our skin, saved our eyes. Funny how that shit works out.

We thought it was killing us. About a week out of the water, bandages off my eyes, and I was on crutches while other guys were all still in beds. Maybe my fishing days had done me some good. I was accustomed to the water. *Paddy's bones float.*

I hopped around the ward and ate the fruit bowls dry and pocketed anything I could in my dressing gown and pajama pockets. I kept a jug of water within feet of me all the time. Whenever I went to the kitchen or hovered over the head—I couldn't sit down for my sores—I kept the door open just so I could keep an eye on that steel water jug. I prized filling that jug. Never let it empty. I didn't sleep much at night so I used to reach to that jug just to touch it before falling back into my half-slumber.

They kept us under marine guard, keeping us a secret, keeping the press and everyone away, probably wondering what to do with us. We were even ordered not to talk to the corpsmen nurses about anything 'cept our ulcers.

Admiral Spruance visited us and shook our hands in our beds. He pinned Purple Hearts to our pajamas. The Indy was his flagship. Not one of us asked him why we hadn't had an escort for our mission. An escort was standard practice. That would have saved us all. We still didn't know we had the bomb then. It had been dropped and we were a few days away from the next one, a few days from the end of the war. We'd carried the parts for both. Still didn't know it. The pilots that dropped the bombs wrote their thanks to us on the casings.

Captain McVay came into our hospital barracks the day before Truman announced the Japanese surrender. The captain visited us all the time, and he looked good. We were rags of men and he looked fit and found as always. I guess officer material is in the blood. He stood in the door in newly pressed khakis and dabbed a handkerchief across his forehead.

"I have to have a driver," he said and looked around the room. "I need someone to accompany me to CINCPAC." That was the Commander-in-Chief Pacific headquarters up in the mountains. "I'm guessing I'm to you boys and saying I don't trust any of the drivers here to it." He looked around the beds expectantly at first. At first.

I was standing on my crutches by the fruit bowl, waiting for it to be filled up. I was the only one not in a chair or a bed and I watched McVay's eyes lower.

I walked off my crutches, let 'em drop and he and everyone else looked up at the clatter.

"You got me, Cap'n," I stepped toward.

He nodded. "Can you walk OK, son?"

"Walking I can do," I grinned. "Reckon I can't swim though."

Didn't mind me not saying "captain".

"Check out some khakis, son. Go get me a car. My Quonset is the last on the block. I'll be outside."

I didn't get no trouble getting a jeep. I went to a corpsman and had him patch up my behind like a baby so my ulcers wouldn't bleed through. I got pants and a shirt from the orderly and walked straight to the car-pool with my shaved patchy hair and skeletal face and no paperwork and they let me have a car just like that. The service can be queer in that way. Sometimes you can't get a new pair of boots but they'll let you drive away in a jeep. I brought two cans of water to roll around under my seat. Took me a time to fill 'em up because I kept drinking 'em when they were halfway full.

Me and Captain McVay drove up the mountain to Admiral Spruance's place. We were quiet because you can't really talk in a jeep, no more than you can atop a threshing machine, and I could feel my ulcers popping with the bouncing on the road because a rocking chair's got more suspension. When we stopped

I waited 'til the captain got out and then I followed with a can of water. I asked him to hold up.

He turned and waited for me to speak.

"Cap'n," I said and turned my behind to him. "Am I bleeding, Cap'n? I don't want to have to salute anyone with blood on my ass."

"No, son," he said. "You look fine, sailor. Fine. Come on in with me. Best leave your can there."

I looked at the water in my hand.

"No, Cap'n." My tone wasn't speaking to a superior officer then. "Can't do that."

He pretended not to hear.

We waited in the corridor for a good while. I didn't want to sit because I could feel the pressure building up in my sores but had to because Captain McVay was pacing up and down and I couldn't stand while he was doing that because he was my officer and all. He broke his walking to talk to me. A captain talking to a seaman. A man talking to a man.

"I think they're going to hang this on me." A survivor talking to a survivor. "Nail it on me."

I didn't know what to say. I'd always avoid a captain's attention but he was going gray in the face so I stopped concentrating on the pain in my rear.

"You couldn't do nothing. We went down quicker than frying a steak."

He took up pacing again. "They should have been looking for us Tuesday. When we were overdue."

"So why didn't they come?"

He stopped again and looked me right in the eye, in my scarred face.

"I don't know, son. I really don't. But they gotta blame someone."

I then braved something that had bothered me all the hundred and more hours I was in the water.

"Cap'n," I shifted on my sores and he could see it, saw me wince. "You had food didn't you? Guys said you had a full kit. And you didn't see sharks. And there weren't no island that you all went to? Was there?"

He was puzzled by this and showed it all over his face.

"No. There was no island, son. We were maybe thirty miles away from you boys. We had a kit, but we were hungry too, sailor. Water was a crock. I'll make sure there ain't anymore of them wooden beakers. We had some sharks. Named 'em. We had some boys in another group that were bit, further down from us. I think they did all right. I've seen 'em since."

"I was in the brig, Cap'n," I smiled cold, kept his eye. "Sunday night I had two slices of bread and a mug of water. That's all I ever had. For five days. We had sharks every day and every night. Every morning we'd push the guys next to us awake if we were first up. Thursday morning, Cap'n, I had Herbie Robinson next to me. I knocked his arm to wake him and he slid up and turned over. His jacket was bit right through. His face asleep. He floated off with nothing below his waist. His insides were white. Hollowed out. He had fish inside. Living in him. Eating him. That was Thursday. The day they found us. I still had one more day than him. We had that all the time. Every hour."

The door opened and a clerk called him in. He took off his hat, still looking at me.

"I'm sorry, son," he said and went to the door.

I raised my voice so someone in the room might hear.

"You tell 'em that, Cap'n. It weren't no one's fault. Except thems that didn't come."

He nodded. No salute or any of that shit.

"I will, sailor." Then he closed the door and I sat and waited.

I had a slice of apple in my pocket and slipped it in my mouth when I was sure no one was watching. I had the can by my foot, touching my foot. Making sure it was there.

He came out whiter than when he went in. He didn't speak to me no more on the way back.

That sea monster was no other than the enormous Shark, which has often been mentioned in this story and which, on account of its cruelty, had been nicknamed "The Attila of the Sea" by both fish and fishermen.

Poor Pinocchio! The sight of that monster frightened him almost to death!

He tried to swim away from him, to change his path, to escape, but that immense mouth kept coming nearer and nearer.

25

Watery blood spurts pink from the gaff I ram into his head. Not a good blow 'cause I had one hand on the leader wire, but the strike was good enough. You learn to tell.

He looks into me, so I know he felt it. He falls back in his defense, his weight his defense, and then he realizes I got a hook deep down his throat and a spike in his head.

I roar at him.

"What you gonna do now?"

The rod and chair holds him. I yank him away from his whale, make one loop of the wire around my glove, biting through the leather and canvas, and up comes his gaping mouth and his thrashing tail. Eight hundred pounds of him at least and I grit my teeth. I let the rod and gaff hold him and I hook the rope over his tail easy as roping a lamb. I got the tail rope rigged to the gin pole so I gotta leave him to wind up the winch.

I'm breathless. *Click-click-click-click.* The winch, and he's up out of the water, hanging beside my boat.

My boat, my deck, a black horizon. And me and a fifteen-footer the only life on it.

I got him.

But he ain't dead.

His jaws are still chomping on meat that ain't there. He's thrashing but he don't know the why-fore he ain't moving anyplace. I put my hand on his hide, can feel the rasp of it even through a quarter-inch of glove.

You get some orcas that only eat sharks. You can spot 'em 'cause their teeth get worn down from that saw-tooth hide.

I can feel he weighs four times my size, like pushing a car. His gills flap as his heart panics, his eyes roll up and down in his head. Black and white, black and white, as he tries to figure why the whale has gone and what is this new world he has come to.

I draw out the gaff from his head. I have to wrench it out like pulling an old nail from a joist, pushing him away with one arm so his teeth don't come too close. I've got moments before he might loose the rod from the chair, before I'd lose my mate.

I winch his tail higher with one hand so he loses the bend of his spine which would give him muscle and he is above me, and then I draw back my right with the spear of the gaff, like a Spartan, like the image on those Greek soldier's badges, and I shove it through his damn gills and out the other side.

He sees death then, curls like a snake, a reptile, like he should have been all along and not of the water.

He gulps and gulps and bleeds over my gunwale. I twist the gaff out, take as much as I can with it. It hangs with white meat, same as his rows of teeth which are still biting the air, reaching for the whale, seeking me.

I got both my arms for work now. The winch and tail rope have him, the rod and leader holds his throat. It could take him half an hour to die. I ain't got that time. I got two more of his brothers to bring.

I run the gaff through his eye with all my weight and feel it grind his cartilage skull. I leave it stuck, step back to watch. I've my heart pumping in my head. That Chinaman in San Fran not half his size. I've beat him now. Gaffed me a Chinaman.

I let him keep the spiked gaff; I got four more. Four more left. Two in the whale, one in him. Always take twice as many gaffs as you think you need. Might get lucky.

The kerosene lamps dance against his swinging flesh. I gotta take a breath, and a drink, watch him swing. I hear his brothers still going at the meat. They don't miss him. He just weren't there no more.

I give him four more clicks of the winch, feel hundreds of pounds of him straining against me. We've both done this before. Maybe him not this far.

But he just met me.

I wrap another tail rope attached to a side cleat so I can remove the first that I'll use for his brothers. He'll drag by my side now, dead now, part of the boat, his day done. Two more to go.

I heave out the gaff and cut the line, release the leader. Can't take the hook out of him in the dark. Gotta rig one more of both, hold 'em in my teeth and walk back to the reel to start again. He falls to the water and I'm done with him. I gotta move fast. They're still pushing the meat into the prop. I don't plan on going in the water again.

I'm long done with that.

When I got back to base I had a clerk tell me that they didn't have no record of family to send a telegram to.

"What telegram?" I asked.

"We're sending out your MIA. To your family. Your wife maybe? Your parents."

"I ain't missing."

He sighs. "Your folks get an MIA. The world don't know about you yet. That's the procedure. Once you're officially found they'll get another. Don't worry about it. But I ain't got no record of your family."

"You got my address?"

He checks his paper and confirms my Boston one-room.

"Then send it to me." And I went to fill my water again.

We came back in late September, shipped to San Diego. There was a welcome given by the Salvation Army. They gave us a kindergarten bottle of milk as we stepped off the gangway.

We'd missed the parades and the big parties for VJ Day. We came back to San Diego not San Fran. Hiding us still. No parade. No party. And the Salvation Army gave us some milk. I don't think we wanted a parade anyhow. Wouldn't fit. We wanted to be shadows.

In December they court-martialed Captain McVay.

They determined that if the captain had "zig-zagged" (that's what they called it) he could have avoided the incident. They failed to cite that he was crossing the Pacific as fast as he could for them. And no one questioned why we didn't have an escort. Why there was no little ship that could have sent word, could have gotten help. Hell, you got an escort if you were just carrying beef.

They went as far as bringing over the Jap captain that sunk us. But he didn't say what they wanted him to. He told them admirals that it wouldn't have made no difference, zig-zagging or not. He'd heard us on the water and that was it. He was sweating, and small in a suit too big for him, but he stood up for the man he tried to kill. Gotta admire that. He was in the land of his enemy but he stood up for kinship, captain to captain. He must have had all sorts of pressure to do otherwise. But he was talking of the sea. He knew what that meant.

They also charged the captain with failing to abandon ship in a "timely manner". We had twelve minutes with more than half the ship asleep. I wondered how they defined "timely".

The captain didn't mind. His punishment was to survive. His men dead. No man could convict him further. The title of captain is a sailor's greatest honor. And it's his curse. There was nothing more a court could do to him that hadn't already eaten him away. We knew that. Every day after we questioned why we were alive. The why of us. I sat in that courtroom and could see it in his eyes. If they hanged him he would thank 'em.

He was the first captain in US history to be court-martialed for his ship being sunk by enemy action. It don't make sense anyway you read it. We had a lot of firsts, lot of lasts.

We were the last US battleship of the war to be sunk. The captain of the sub said we were the first enemy action he'd seen. We'd carried the first atomic bombs, and as a consequence, as punishment from a Japanese demon, revered and feared, we suffered the largest naval disaster in our history.

I'll tell you one thing, and you can go to sleep on it.

When we built the first naval station at Pearl Harbor, at the start of the century, we uncovered a Hawaiian arena. An arena of gladiatorial proportions. We dug it up while trying to make way for the foundations for the dock. The locals told us that it was an ancient place where warriors would prove themselves armed only with a shark's tooth roped to a spear. A gaff of the ancient.

It was an underwater arena. And the warriors had to prove themselves against sharks. I bet even the Romans couldn't think up that shit.

The sharks were fed on live sacrifices so when the warrior got in the water the sharks knew what he was and went right at it. Being Americans we nodded and acknowledged and then built

223

the dry-dock right over it anyway. Weren't our history. An under-water quake thirteen years later destroyed it. It waited 'til it was finished and done and with plenty of men on it. Plenty of new warriors. We built it again. And you know the rest about Pearl, and what happened to me and nine hundred other boys.

Some gods you don't screw with.

Not if they still roam.

Two down. One shot with flare, one hooked. Two brothers left and only two reasons for all of this. One: clear 'em away from my prop to drag the whale, and two: bring 'em into town. Show I mean business. Photograph in the paper and hang 'em from the dock like the pirates they are. No other reason. Just business.

Just business.

The line clicks, the rod bends. Another taking the hook laid along the meat. I let the chair take it and I go for the gaff and the leader, the gaff that's still got the gore of his brethren hanging off it, laying on my shoulder as I hold it high. I know how Ahab felt. And hundreds of boys stand behind me.

"Come get it."

He shows no surprise, no meaning of any of it. He takes the flesh and the leader, the hook. And he's mine. The gaff held by the cleat. Got him right through his snout. His nose bleeds like a child's, like a boy's after he drinks salt water for days.

His brother retreats below, under the water with his pound of flesh. His turn next. Last.

I have done this a hundred times. They will do it only once.

Pull up the leader, tail rope on. My arms do this with memory in 'em. He fights. We fight. I'm doing the work of two. Of hundreds. Of the hundreds expecting of me.

He's up but I gotta drop him to reach for the winch, same as before. Faith in the gaff and the rod. I wind him up, heavier than the last or I'm weaker, growing tired. But I can't be that tonight. So I get on.

He's mine, and I pull the gaff and him to the boat, my arms over the gunwale, over the water. And then the water explodes beneath us both.

His brother leaps, like they all leap, like a train derailing, and I let go and fall back as he takes his brother into his terrible jaws. A head takes a head.

For a gasp, mine and theirs, they hang together, the gin pole groaning with the weight. I'm reminded of some Chinese symbol again, like that blue eating his own innards again and again and the water crashes and I'm left with just the tail and body swinging, the gills ripped and hanging where the head once was. Leader gone, piano wire snapped, gaff gone. Other men might mind. Not me. I brush myself down.

Lose one, rig one.

If I was not the fisherman I might think he was trying to break my gin pole with both their bodies, take away my terrible wire leader. Or reach to me. Over his brother. To me. But I'm the fisherman.

And they are only fish.

Alas!
It was too late.
The monster overtook him
and the Marionette found himself in between the rows of gleaming white teeth.

26

We got leave. Most of us a good couple of months which meant whiskey and no sleep. That's if we could walk or had the right number of limbs. We got back to the regular world with the same problems as any veteran, and sometimes that meant we didn't take any shit from those who before the war we might have placed above us. It was common for us to go work for ourselves. Carpenters, body-shops, fishermen. War and prison teaches some to be on their own, to think for themselves. Some think that holding prison bars in your fists is the lowest you can go, your world over. You know how many guys come out of prison and become millionaires when they can't even spell millionaire? I've had enough of 'em on my boat. Prison bars are the bottom rungs on a ladder for the right mind, and service the same. Done with orders and following the guy in front. Let someone look at your back for a while.

I took my pension, done with the navy. It weren't my career. I was drafted so now I was drafted out. They'd dropped me in San Diego and that meant nothing to me. I thought of going up to San Fran, get some crab or lobster work, but this weren't my coast. I knew where I had to be.

I went to the bus station. The saddest places anywhere. They're like hospital emergency rooms. Full of the dissolute and the poor, the lost and the hopeful soon to be lost.

I had my bag over my shoulder and my field jacket and asked a fat lady behind glass where forty dollars would get me.

"Where you want to go?" she asked.

"East," I said. "Boston maybe."

She shook her head. "We got a special that will get you to Florida for thirty dollars? Only takes three transfers."

I looked over the drunks and the pregnant lonely women waiting for their transfers. A few Japanese trying to be invisible in corner seats.

"They got the sea there?" I asked. I didn't know nothing about the shape of my country.

"Honey," she said through cracked lipstick, "that's all they got."

I paid my thirty dollars and I was done with the war. I was twenty-one. The only thing that remained of the *Indianapolis* to me was a tattoo on my arm and the shadows of people burned into the ground that the papers liked to print for our glory.

I would find me a boat.

I climb back to the flybridge, hand on the starter. I got one shark dragging along the side and a half of one on my gin pole. I need to see if they've done for the prop again. My thumb pushes the red rubber down, wait for the feel of power under it.

She grinds, turns over and over and finally hears me calling her, knows I'm still there, and up her pistons come. I push her out of neutral and even from the flybridge I feel the prop drilling through the meat. She's clear. We're clear. The whale still mine.

I turn her to make the journey back, to dump the carcass in my quarter. Done enough now. Got wet, got hurt. That's just fishing, no harm done. A burning in my arm where a Chinaman pulled me over and a bandage on my leg where a thresher cut. No harm done. I'm coming in, Amity. Tomorrow I'll make shark-fishing your reason for being. Rich by Monday. Rich enough to buy real bait at least. The whale might last a week yet, another weekend where only I know where she'll be. All my sharks.

Something bumps the boat. Bumps it hard. I throttle back, back to neutral, down the ladder to the deck with a curse. I pick up a fresh gaff. One more to spare after this.

"Ain't you done yet? Ain't I wet enough, you bastards!"

The one who ate his brother's head has come back, and in the searchlight's glare so has the one whose eye I burned out.

"Don't you know when you're done, you sonsofbitches!"

They've lost interest in the meat. Their gray heads, big as refrigerators, are pushing at the prop, gnawing at it. They go for metal. Something wired in their brains to go for metal. Always talk about monsters going for the prop. Maybe it ain't the metal. Maybe they know what drives the boat, maybe they know what they have to do to break you. Because then you're only wood, and wood they can go through. Like worms through a coffin. They have seen and counted me for just one man. One man alone in the dark. They took my gun, took my leader wire. Only wood between us. And a lot of lone fishermen don't come home. Towns like to keep that quiet when fishing is their life's blood.

I lean over the transom, thrash at 'em with the gaff, into their heads again and again. They thrash back, heads side to side, trying to dodge my steeled barb. I'm cursing and their teeth are moving up and down as if they're trying to curse back, that after millions of years they've finally learned to speak and they save it for moments like this when blood is running in their eyes.

They slink back, just under, under their cloak, the prop clear and I stand and take a breath, rest the gaff on the transom, and the water explodes with teeth again.

229

He-Who-Took-His-Brother's-Head leaps at me once more, across the transom and grabs the gaff and I let go as he takes it down and soaks me, mocks me with his fall back to darkness.

I shake the water off. One gaff left. I think about the Very rockets again. But that wouldn't be winning, not a contest. That would be only surviving. And I'm done with that. For all time. I don't play that no more.

Two whites. Maybe twenty-five foot of 'em put together. High on whale meat and angered by my slaughter. No. They don't think like that. That's me. That won't work. To give them human reason won't work. They're just fish. They didn't take my gun. They didn't drag me into the water nor take my gaffs and leader or the head of my prize nor try to break my prop. No fate here. No God. No Devil. Me and them and the dark. If it was day I'd be laughing. If I had one more man I'd be laughing. It's the night that brings doubt. It's the caveman in us. Gotta get home before dark despite our electric lights. Make a fire, light a lamp, draw in against the night. That's when the animals come to hunt, and we keep that. Keep it inside us, locked in our historical brains. The neon, the cars, the TV, but still born with that piece of slime in the brain that makes you huddle away from the long cold nights. From the dark.

There are still monsters in the night.

And that's when they feed.

All our old enemies still alive. Evolution hasn't done for 'em. Every animal enemy man ever had is still alive, still shares the earth with us. Think on that. What did we win if evolution ain't a contest? They're still there. Waiting for their chance, their time. And they'll be back when the lights go out. Wolves waiting for the light to fade. And we shouldn't be in the water. These water-wolves don't even care about your light. They'll eat it. And eat you. Don't have to finish you off. Those scientists and nature lovers will only tell you about the lack of deaths by sharks compared to tornadoes or some such shit. Let me tell you this: it ain't about the deaths. Every hospital near the sea right now, the world round, has at least one diver or swimmer bandaged up to the knee or elbow. Weren't no bee that done that. Ain't about the deaths. And the more we get to the water, the worse it will be. Mark me. I've seen it. Ain't about the deaths. Count the injured.

Don't get in the deep. That's my best word on it. We don't belong there.

Every time you get in your car you up the chance of a drunk driver plowing into your side. But that ain't a reason to not get in your car. Every time you get in the water you up your chance of something biting. Averages. That's all we ever have. All life is the average of the undefined, the unknown. If you don't want to get shot don't own a gun. No man ever got killed by another by not stepping out his door.

But he never lived either.

So take the whale and let 'em follow. Let 'em to their worst. I'm gonna start her up again and make my dawn. I climb the ladder to the flybridge. I'm at the last few rungs when they ram the hull hard and I fall, hit the deck, jar my back like a strike from a baseball bat, the stern yaws.

Bastards.

I get up, yell over the transom at 'em.

"You think that's funny, you sonsofbitches!"

They don't think it's funny. They don't give a shit. They didn't wait 'til I was half up the ladder. Didn't even know I was climbing. They don't care if I'm still alive. Don't care for nothing.

"I'm gonna make douches out of your lungs, you bastards!"

Leader wire. Hook. Line. Rod. Chair. Five furious minutes and I sit down. Gonna reel 'em in, hook 'em and reel 'em. I owe 'em that much.

"Come get it!"

I'm idle on the water, neutral ticking over, diesel fumes up their snouts and they circle the boat. I can't see 'em but I can feel 'em. They're checking that the whale ain't moving no more, maybe checking their brother lolling upside down along the side. Biding. Biding.

I got one hook laid. Just take one and the other can go screw himself. In daylight I might use the harpoon points I got, for a fish far out, for marlin or bluefin, and for the happy assholes who just want to bag and snag something for a Polaroid for their Monday morning show-and-tell. But the Landlord's always close. Barbed gaff will do, will make do. For him. Plus it ain't the sport if you harpoon; against the rules. The deck I come in on might disparage if they see a harpoon spike. And ain't this a game? A dame of a game. You can only harpoon if you plan to eat the meat. And no one eats shark. Can't harpoon anyway without a mate. Can't tie a harpoon line to a cleat, lose it else. Need a buoy, need a harpoon mate to take care of that. As I said, one more mate and I'd be laughing, this'll all be joy. Don't ever aspire to be alone on the water. Be a right sight if I go in with three whites on my boat, even if one ain't got a head. I'll tell Ben Gardner I got hungry and made me a sandwich.

The leader bites and I wind it back. Hope it's the sonofabitch that bit his brother's head and took my gaff. I've named him now, like we did in the water. "Hey, Oscar's back!" we'd shout, or, "Scarface is coming in! Watch your back. He looks mean this morning, boys!"

"He-Who-Took-His-Brother's-Head." That's what he'll be. I'll mount his jaws on my flybridge.

I can't see 'em from the chair; it's set in the middle of the deck for looking over the water, for fighting fish hundreds of yards out. But I can hear 'em, can always hear 'em. Even in sleep.

The gear runs, the rod bends as the wire pulls. I imagine him gulping down the hook with the meat, see its two inches claw into the roof of his mouth or along his jaw, pulling it into a rictus, and then he's wondering what's holding him back and a Boston-Irish leans back in his chair to let him know.

He tries to go deep first. That don't work, so he shakes side to side, head one way, tail the other, and it gets worse. He bites and swallows, sure that will clear anything that comes against him—always has—and then, last of all, he runs.

The Landlord. Always last to run. Of all of 'em they run last. Fight first. Run last.

And then he knows.

I reel back, rod in the well, in the bucket shaped like an oversized shot-glass, feet pushing on the footrest, and the chair creaks, feeling its pain now. I won't feel anything 'til tomorrow. I reckon on charging five dollars a head to fill my deck when those happy assholes see what they could fish for.

Up he comes, bucking like a green-horse. I still can't see him. Through my arms I can feel everything, see everything he's doing. He's rolling his eye down at the whale, then at the transom, then up at the black stick waving against the background of stars, the strange stick that bends and holds him, the piano wire cutting through his teeth, something cutting through him for a change. If he ain't been here before then I got this easy.

I pull him hard for a couple of clicks and he's biting and kicking so I gotta be quick. I lock the gear, unhook the brace and slip out of the straps, heave the rod to wrestle it to the chair's sleeve, to hold the shark for me. The whole chair complains. I'm wary she can take it. Older than all of us out here.

"*I'm OK*," it creaks. "*I'll hold. Do your half.*"

I pick up the tail rope and the gaff, the last gaff. Spray is coming up over the stern, he's mad now but he'll rest a bit, he'll take some breaths when I pull up the leader.

I got a good trick to show charters when the shark's roped and gaffed. Roll 'em over on their backs, show their white bellies to the sun. The shark becomes hypnotized then, goes to sleep and you can stroke 'em like kittens. That's how the orcas kill 'em. They flip 'em over and the shark goes dead. And then he really does go dead when the blackfish bites. Never knows what happened to him. He was asleep. Bitten in half. While he was asleep.

Killer whales. Shark killer.

Ain't a whale.

It's a dolphin.

Look it up.

While talking in the darkness, Pinocchio thought he saw a faint light in the distance.

"What can that be?" *he said to the Tunny.*

"Some other poor fish, waiting as patiently as we to be digested by the Shark."

"I want to see him. He may be an old fish and may know some way of escape."

"I wish you all good luck, dear Marionette."

"Goodbye, Tunny."

"Goodbye, Marionette, and good luck."

"When shall I see you again?"

"Who knows? It is better not to think about it."

27

My gloved grip hauls the leader. I'm looking at him now. He's gulping air, drowning in it, gills pulsing like heartbeats. If that were you or me we'd look pitiful. He's just mad. He's trying to eat the air, eat the world. He doesn't get to see this much of it, and anything he don't know gets a bite taken out of it. He's biting at the stars. I can bite too.

I put the gaff through his gills and it shivers up my arm, horrible to us both. He's got both his eyes so he's not the one I half-blinded. I'll call that one "Blind Bill" when he comes. Don't see him now but I'm too busy to look.

He-Who-Took-His-Brother's-Head hangs limp and I pull him up some more and wrap on the tail rope. Easy. Easy night. I drop it and let his fall tighten the rope. He crashes home like he's dead already. I walk to the winch where the end of the rope is clipped, where it runs over the gin pole. Just wind him up and all's done. Let him drown. Drown in the air.

I crank the winch. The chink of its rattle reassures. It is a machine working. The engine's *thum-thum-thum-thum* and the winch. I'm not alone while I have these sounds. You ever watch a carpenter work? Or anyone with a machine or tool, any man that works for himself, with his hands? They're happy at it. The noise, the machine, drowns their woe with the world. They look miserable at lunch when the only sound is their chewing and even if the rest of their life is a piece of shit there's destiny in hitting a nail with a hammer. Something will come of it. You know the man that kills himself? That's the man who sits in a room in silence with nothing to do. There ain't no such thing as being unemployed. There's only guys who've decided to become meaningless. You don't have to get paid to have worth. Do you think them cavemen were unemployed? Ain't you better than them? Go pick up the garbage in your street, cut back a tree. Even in a concentration camp somebody swept the floor and he was probably a doctor before. I got no sympathy for you. It's gotta rain for grass to grow.

His tail comes up above the transom and I'm winding hundreds of pounds into the air and it takes ten turns of the winch before his head shows. I swing him out with the gin pole, five feet over the starboard, over the sea, and I watch him. He's breathing hard, he's dying. It'll take him half an hour. I was in his lair and survived for five days. Better than him. He won't last five days. I'm the Monster here. And then the boat rocks and near sends me to my back.

I scramble to the transom and in the white water there's Blind Bill on his side, gray above and white below, his big angled mouth latched onto the corner of the boat. Even through his plashing I can hear the cracking of wood. He's grinding through it like a sawmill even though the whale is right there, food right beside him. Maybe I damaged his brain in the shooting of him or maybe this is something else. No. Can't think like that. Can't give 'em emotions, can't give 'em thought even. No brain there. Just impulse and instinct. I made a point when I slit that blue to those happy idiots and he ate his own guts over and over. I was saying something. Something above the show and entertainment of it. But it's a hard thing to put down in words, onto paper. You have to feel it yourself. And I hope you don't have to.

I grin at him eating my boat. He's going at the edge of it, where he can get the most purchase, where his jaws can do the most harm. He's working. This is his work. His employment. He don't want to get paid for it. His reward is me.

He's twice my size, maybe four times my weight, his girth my height. He's sure he can eat my boat. He might do this once a year. Easy pickings. He might know that I need wood to float and if he chews at it enough, eats enough, I'll come down to his world and we'll have a different story between us.

But I grin. He don't know I've been here before. I met his father. Like in that alley behind a Chinese restaurant in San Fran. Got pushed into an alley. Came out alone. I've been in his water-alley too. So I pick up my bloodied fly gaff and watch him grind at my boat.

I have at him. Plunge the gaff into his snout again and again. That's his sweet spot. He can feel that. What he lacks in brain he makes up in nerves all along his body and in his head. And nerves hurt. The only thing about him that hurts.

He bucks and I swear I hear him growl and the eye I burned out of him stares blankly at me for the one moment I stop stabbing and take my breath. He plows back into the wood as if I've gone, ignores the blood running off him.

The side he's working starts to crack. He's going through two layers of strakes like cheesecake. I admire it when I should be killing him. No matter, let him have his play. I can just pull the blackfish now and drop him in my quarter. The night done. I pick up the whiskey and take a drink then pour a slug over the transom to Blind Bill. I get it right in his charred eye.

"Here's to swimming with bow-legged women," I salute him. Then I look down to the water running off my boots.

The deck is washing. Only puddles but she's taking water.

Sonofabitch. Bill and his prehistoric senses have found a weak spot, old wood, tired wood. I can see it beneath me. The prop getting flooded, salt water getting to the engine, the well of the boat getting deeper, lowering the keel. He might have been working at it the whole time I thought him gone. The whole time while his brothers kept me busy. The whiskey makes it bad. I see horror now because of it. The drink is my weakness but if I don't drink I don't sleep. Not since. But drink and water don't mix as well as it should and Bill with his senses can smell it. I should know that. Every guy who ever hit a reef or ever fouled had an empty bottle on board. I should know that. I feel my head flush and I run to the wheelhouse and push the gear forward. Sonofabitch has me holed to be sure.

She responds. She growls and the Superior engine plays her tune. I got three knots, make five if I push her, but I don't need that yet. All I need is a slow run to take me to my quarter and then I can cut the gaffs from the blackfish and make Amity. But Bill behind me can go fifteen knots if he wants to. If he wants. If he wants me.

I look astern, back through the wheelhouse. I know I can't see him but I want to see my wake, see if he's gone back to the whale. I got a hand pump and my scuppers so an inch or two of water ain't no real worry, not now that the electrics have gone anyhow. But I'm a man alone on the water with two kerosene lamps and a boat taking water.

And a fifteen-foot white on the stern with my whiskey in his dead eye.

The lump of the whale is there, glowing in the cream, but I don't see no dorsal on him. Screw him. Maybe the burned eye and the whiskey and the stabbing gaff have given him enough to move on.

The boat lurches forward and the wheel hits my gut and everything in the galley falls like I've run aground. I pull back to neutral.

Bastard.

He's showing me his speed, elbowing me with his might like that guy in the Charles Atlas ads in the back of the paperbacks I read. The bully on the beach muscling to the ninety-pound weakling with the pneumatic gal that shouldn't be with him in the first place. The sand in the face. The ads are always about punching folks flat. You can't be a man they're saying unless you can punch-out a guy. You gotta get big to do it. You gotta be bigger than them to be a man. You can solve everything with hitting folks and your gal will love you for it. Hit 'em hard, hit 'em strong, get strong. Drop the biggest damn bomb on all of 'em. And then the world will change.

I can feel the boat shift under my boots as he gnaws at the wood again. The Very gun is still beside the chair. I go and pick it up and curse my own dumb ass. I'd left it sloshing in the water on the deck. Useless now. He's kicked sand in my face. They have taken my rifle, my gaffs, the flares. Whittling me down to arms and legs. As they always do, always will. No. I'm still giving him too much. Giving 'em all too much. It's the dark. Just the lonely dark. In the day the sea is a place to be lonely, you welcome it as the houses melt away, the cars and prattling folk silenced. At night it's another thing. You lie in your bunk, the waterline beside you, at your head, two inches from drowning, and things pound at the bulkhead and you look up at the overhead just above you like a coffin lid and wonder why you're out there.

That's important.

It's not "out here", mind. It's "out *there*".

A sailor ain't a seaman. Seamen go "out *there*". And only seamen know the difference. And every seaman has that tale of when he near didn't come home. Before that you're still the green-horse, the sailor. I'm going for two tales to tell. Damned if I could survive a third.

And the water on the deck is playing over my boots.

"You must know that, in the storm which swamped my boat, a large ship also suffered the same fate. The sailors were all saved, but the ship went right to the bottom of the sea, and the same Terrible Shark that swallowed me, swallowed most of it."

"What! Swallowed a ship?" asked Pinocchio in astonishment.

"Today there is nothing left in the cupboard, and this candle you see here is the last one I have."

"And then?"

"And then, my dear, we'll find ourselves in darkness."

"Then, my dear Father," said Pinocchio, "there is no time to lose. We must try to escape."

28

If I had other hands, other mates—ones that weren't ghosts—I'd give one the hand pump, set one to the wheel and me to the shark. But I don't have that. It's just me and him. I check to the Montauk lighthouse on my port and steer away from it, spin the wheel back to Amity until its South Beach light is in front of me through the glass. The tide will be in soon. Enough. I can ride in on that if all else leaves me. I click the navigation-light switch up and down, the green and red mast lights, starboard and port lights. Still nothing. Going in dark. That will be bad if there's an early fishing boat that can't see me. I look to the radio. I press the beacon button, and mind that ain't asking for help, that's just helping others. That don't count for pleading. Then I realize I'm the dumb Mick who thought the radio would work without power and never got around to replacing its inside battery. That's the diesel engine for you. She's running so you think you got power. You know how many weekend sailors you see on the dock scratching their head to the harbor master? "But the engine's working?" they say. Always one. Me dumb as them now.

The boat lurches again. Bill still there. Piece by piece eating to me. I wonder if he swallows the wood, if he can digest it and its paint or if he spits it out like tobacco, like guys in cowboy movies before they roll up their sleeves and get to it in those bar fights. Blind Bill spitting it out before he gets into the whirling fray. Or is he just a hulk of a monster scything through a field of lambs, my wood just fence posts in his path.

I gotta keep an eye to the water ahead, look for boats and keep a course. Can't mind him now; only got one gaff. I could hook him maybe. Hang him with his brothers. But that would mean switching back the engine and maybe she wouldn't start again. Everything about boats is minute to minute. You can spend your whole day doing nothing and then you gotta do a hundred things in five minutes just to stay alive. Wood and water. Between wood and water. Between the Devil and the deep blue sea. Just as they say. Just right. The water's in the wheelhouse now, lapping at my heels. The Devil on my tail.

Judging by my speed, my dead reckoning, I'm in my quarter, the place where I first put myself between the lighthouses. I've got a machete that I keep in the wheelhouse. I use it to cut mackerel for chum 'cause no one wants to take them home for show. I don't pull back to neutral, can't risk it. Just pull back the throttle one notch so I'm down to tide and one knot. I drag the machete out and go back to the deck, pick up my only gaff on my walk to the transom. Steel in both hands. A man can't do much better than that. Spear in one hand, blade in the other. If I had a shield I'd be in the Bible for sure.

I'll be thirty soon. Married three times, widowed once, lived five days in the deep without food or water. And I delivered the damn bomb that changed the world. Don't tell me I can't do this. I bet at my age you were still whining to your mother and dipping in your father's pockets. Men like me had been in two Asian wars.

244

I missed one but only 'cause nobody called. And our country was now fixing on building rockets for the next. Germans gone now, Japs gone. Any other race will do. Killing all our fit young men before they can breed. And we're left with fat mother's boys driving buses and the rich who can afford not to send their young men to fight. Morons doing the work. Rich kids ruling over 'em. That might be a plan at that. Only send the fittest poor, the A1s. Leave behind the weak so they can breed weaker. Send the best of the meek to die. What a country we'll have.

I don't see Bill. I got two of his brothers in the air beside me hanging off the gin pole, the other dragging alongside. I got a ton of 'em already. That will do for Sunday morning. I raise the blade high, the light from the lamps enough to see the lines. Just cut the whale free and into home. New home. Always a new home. Never got a welcome back from the war. Went to Merritt from the bus and bummed for fishing jobs like a box-car boomer hobo. Got my own boat, got a new wife, built my own home. Sickness took my wife, Indians took my home. Got my boat. Got my arms. My boat. Ain't no fish gonna take that from me.

I bring the blade down through the cleat-lines. Two strokes and the whale is off me. My whale. I stand and look over the transom, steel in both fists, the engine ticking over, water running at my soles. I got hours yet to worry 'bout that. Tide will bring me in if she has to, on a plank if I has to. I'm waiting. Waiting for him to show. Waiting for ghosts to show.

"Come on, you sonofabitch. Come get it."

I don't wait long. Don't ever have to wait too long for sharks.

He rises a hundred yards off my stern. The whale, or the boat, has drifted. Just two dark shapes on the water. And then there is the fin cutting like a knife. A finger against the horizon that is slowly turning to blue. You can see all the planets now. Low off the horizon. All watching.

He doesn't sweep side to side. He comes like on a line. Like an arrow. That silent shard of a dorsal like a lone tombstone in a new graveyard. Solemn and distinct in the predawn. A moving living fossil.

I should get out the hand pump, leave my steel and get rid of the water creeping over me. But I wait. I've waited a long time. All that fishermen ever do.

The dorsal goes below, like a sub before its attack, and the water goes still. Normal men might fear at that. Afraid of what they can't see, afraid of the invisible. But all fishing is invisible. Only in the last moments, when the color and the teeth and the tail show, does it become the sport, the game. The fight.

He comes up, right on the stern. I see the white of his underbelly as he comes close to the curtain of the water for his reveal, as he rolls to get back to the same spot he was at before and he gets back to biting through it like he never left. Like he's never left me.

I can't reach him with the machete so I slam it into the gunwale, for later, and have at him with the gaff, half of me over the transom.

I stab through his head with both hands and the wine of him spills out. Again and again I thrust, slippery with my gloves and still he goes on. I haven't tied myself to a cleat but don't regret: I might need to move fast, to the engine, to the wheel, and above all that I won't be dragged down by my own boat. By any boat. Not again.

I'm not cussing or singing now, and him, he's always been quiet. Just the two of us fighting in dead air. Me ramming the barb into him in time with the rhythm of the engine and he with his own pace, his own machine, half of him breaking the water, his mouth full of it and my wood, and my sweat falling into his burned-out eye. The only sounds on the earth. The ripping of flesh, the tearing of wood, the thrash of water, and the calm beat of the engine under it all.

I hear the crack of strakes and he does too. He takes a breather to roll, to sneer at me, like he remembers. Wood floats over him. My boat. In pieces. I spear his white belly and he continues his roll and out the gaff comes with his white meat dripping off. I ain't got nothing else. Just the barbed hook of the gaff. And me. And he knows it. He's counted all the bits of me that have fallen to the water, to rest forever in the deep. All my evolution. And he goes calmly back to the gap he's made. One of us will write the last page. We're just fighting over the pen to ink it.

Just one more set of hands, that's all I need. It would be good fun then, bit of sport before a good breakfast at Cy's Diner. But I ain't got no help. So screw that and get to it.

He's got his gray back to me now. Can't do much harm through that so I keep driving at his head, at his snout, where he can feel it. One of us will give soon. My arm is squalling where that Chinaman pulled. That will tell, that will be it. But I can't die 'cause my arm hurts.

The boat's rolling now, chugging on like "The Little Engine That Could" but I'm about done. Not in my mind; just the hours bearing. A Mick too skinny for this. He has hundreds of pounds on me. I'm punching holes in him like pencil through paper and he don't mind. I could write my name in him with my spear and he wouldn't mind. He's still got his winter fat. It bubbles like pus out of his hide. He's as old as me, traveled the same waters and seen it all.

I move away, gaff in the crook of my arm, and pick up my bucket of butterfish chum. The boat starting to list, a camber on the deck, and the scuppers are starting to choke, vomiting the water back up. I pour the bucket over his head, try to distract him, to get him away just a bit. I'm two hours from shore, two hours from taking too much water to make it in. I gotta get back to the throttle and drive her home hard. But he's still there, still eating his way to me. The blood of the bucket does nothing. He shrugs its coat off him. Ain't butterfish he wants.

I throw the bucket to his head like a hammer, hard as I can. It ricochets off his bulk and drifts away. One more piece of me gone. I watch it float to port across me, across us. *There.* That's my tide. Coming in good. I can do this. Get back to the wheel-house. With the engine on full and five knots, the tide will give me just about eight. I'll be at Amity in two hours, before the dawn. Sausage, eggs, beans and black coffee at Cy's Diner. Sunday-morning breakfast.

More cracking. More wood setting to drift with the bucket. What will beachcombers make of that come morning? Folks walking their dogs on the beach. A bucket. Chewed driftwood. Pick it up for the stove. Cross themselves and walk away from the beach slower than when they walked to it.

I'm gonna need charters tomorrow. Five dollars each. Maybe a dozen of 'em. I'll have to get credit to buy new gaffs. Don't like starting in a new place with debt but little choice with all my steel gone. Crazy thinking. Thinking of spending money to come. Water around my feet and I'm thinking on bargaining for gaffs tomorrow. Seeing my stern full tomorrow. But what stern? I'll be lucky to get her in. I won't be taking anyone out tomorrow. But I'll be in the paper for something.

I'm done now. Can't beat him unless I get in the water with him and he'd be right keen on that. Ain't that what he's going for? No. Just throttle up and get back to shore. No hurry to bring him in. He won't go nowhere while there's still the whale. And ain't I marked him? Another day. One more day. Come back with my teeth instead of hobbling on crutches, like back in Guam when his brothers done for me before.

There's a complaining from the deck, from the wood under me, whines like a dog in pain, I balance and check for boats along the growing white line circling the earth. Not looking for help mind; just don't want to run into nobody and scupper for good.

I see the island now. Amity near to waking. Her white street lights like a landing strip. Her lighthouse waving me in like a long friendly arm as she sweeps fore.

And then something else.

Something else comes out of the water in front of the island.

Black. Moving between me and the promise of land. Not there, then always there. Gliding along the dawn horizon, slicing the night. Not dawn yet, still their night. He's late. Last knockings. Rent due.

Gliding, pushing the water away softly like casting a roll of silk over a table. The fin goes narrow. Narrow as it turns. As it comes toward.

Its wake spreading like a grin.

"Dreams, my boy!" answered Geppetto, shaking his head and smiling sadly. "Do you think it possible for a Marionette, a yard high, to have the strength to carry me on his shoulders and swim?"

"Try it and see! And in any case, if it is written that we must die, we shall at least die together."

Not adding another word, Pinocchio took the candle in his hand and going ahead to light the way, he said to his father:

"Follow me and have no fear."

29

I watch him come. Tall black fin. Miles he has come to this. Drawn by the whale and the battle of his brethren calling him from the deep. I wrestle the machete out of the gunwale, pay no attention to the black smoke choking all around me, coughing out of the flue by the ladder. I'd have to let the engine cool to add oil. Howie Turnbull's maxim always right. Oil. You can get in as long as you have enough oil for every ten miles. No patience for that now.

The deep has urgency upon it. Calling to me.

Blind Bill chews on and the camber of the deck has my right boot swallowed by water. Gaff in one hand, blade in the other. The whiskey bottle rolls against my foot. I kick it away. I wave him in with the blade. Welcoming in the new one with the machete.

"Come on," I beckon. "You an' all."

I run the machete along the gaff like I'm sharpening knives for Thanksgiving. Like fathers might do, like good men might do.

"I'm still here, you bastards!"

He runs at me like a sub rising, the water folding away from his black hide just the same, faster every moment. I raise the gaff, wait for his head to break, wait for his show of teeth like they all do. I'll pluck him as good as I can for the first time. Show my measure.

Closer now. He's at the stern, not stopping, and I hold back, steel raised and following him as he goes. Goes past. Ignorant of me.

The fin is midnight black, too tall for a shark, and I think I know what is about to come.

I think I know.

I have heard the stories.

And then it happens. Happens too fast for me to recall correctly.

Besides us they are the most widespread mammal on earth. Every ocean, every quarter they call theirs, same as the shark does. Only different.

They eat sharks.

He rears up so I can see his white markings behind his eye and under his jaw and then there is only the explosion of water as he punches his ton weight into Blind Bill who is no longer at my boat, tossed aside by a freight train, and is surprised as hell.

Orcinus Orca. Named after Orcus. A Roman god of hell, of the underworld. Of the deep. Orcus.

Orcus. The Punisher of Broken Oaths.

If the deep is made up of columns, like the Greeks would have it, then he makes up its highest rank. The "Wolves of the Sea" seamen call 'em. *Ballena Asesina* the Spanish call 'em. The Assassin Whale.

They probably call themselves that.

Man, the grizzly bear, and the orcas. The absolutes. We're the apex predators of the whole earth. And don't we know it. Don't we show it when our moments come. The bears roar. The orca steam-rolls. We pull triggers and push red buttons to burn flesh from bones.

Blind Bill is spinning, rolling. He missed what happened. He was occupied. He shows me his two cocks and his remoras as his white belly comes up and then the orca is on him again, the white belly his cue. Flip 'em; that's what they do. Stuff the shark's fifteen foot up their asses with the weight of a locomotive running over 'em.

Old Blind Bill gasps at the air, my wood still in his mouth like some hick chewing tobacco while someone picks his pocket. A young man has got him.

He's alone. Away from his pod. A bull seeking a mate or lost a mate. It happens. They ain't invincible. And like us they ain't all the same. They got different races, different attitudes. Some just eat salmon and squid, some eat other mammals, and their own.

And some just eat sharks. Their teeth worn down because of the hide. Told you that before.

It's the liver they crave. The same liver we use for hemorrhoid cream. Look it up. Look at the label. Shark your only relief.

He's in warm waters. Maybe he's following the Gulf Stream and the breeding fish up from Mexico, same as Bill. But like I said: the apex predator. They own every ocean. They just don't come close enough to consider us food.

And it ain't a whale.

It's a dolphin.

Look it up.

He dives on Bill. Holds him in his jaws like that boy in my raft. Bursts him. Bursts and busts him like a water balloon just the same. Bill's head out one end, tail out the other.

Bill don't make a sound. His black eyes look at me, question me, and for the first time I think I see a thought. But like I said: I don't recollect it all that well.

A black tail crashes, soaks me. My gaff and machete still raised. And then nothing. Gone. Taking Bill home.

Ripples on the water, above the deep. The only sign he was ever there. If I wasn't wet again I might not have known he ever was. The churning of my engine the only sound. The water still. Red. Again. A red foam floating on it. It bubbles as something is happening below, something I've not earned the right to see. I'm abandoned, forgotten, looking about me alone, looking over my dead whale. The steel foolish in my hands. My evolution not welcome, not privy. The deep announcing its loneliness, its solitude. No sound beneath the film of its surface. Fury below. Beyond my reach. I was never here.

I only thought I was.

Only thought I belonged.

An ant among dinosaurs.

You could hang pictures on the silence.

"Help me, Father! Help, for I am dying!"

Father and son were really about to drown when they heard a voice like a guitar out of tune call from the sea:

"What is the trouble?"

"It is I and my poor father."

"I know the voice. You are Pinocchio."

"Exactly. And you?"

"I am the Tunny, your companion in the Shark's stomach."

"And how did you escape?"

"I imitated your example. You are the one who showed me the way and after you went, I followed."

30

I come into Amity with the sun and the tide. I'm on the flybridge and can see 'em all. The others, Ben Gardner and the rest, getting ready to head out. They stop their loading to look at me limping in. I'm standing under my diesel smoke clouding the harbor and all the swooping gull-rats screeching and following my catch, announcing me in like a trumpet fanfare.

All their charters are standing on the dock waiting to get on and I see their arms pointing and their gossiping like schoolgirls at the meat hanging from my gin pole. They're slapping each other's backs like they done something.

Ben Gardner walks slowly toward and I throw him a rope to tie me on and damn if he doesn't do it. He's eyeballing my sharks. He checks for someone else in the wheelhouse then looks up at me and nods, sucks on his mustache. He sees the broken stern and my low keel and rubs his chin. He turns his back without saying nothing.

I step off the boat into a crowd. I get a hundred questions fired at me all at once, a dozen slaps and handshakes. Bigger reception than when I got in from the war anyways. Nobody gives me a bottle of milk at least.

Every voice has the word "shark" in it. Every question. I tip my cap and walk through it all. Leave a trail of blood from my leg all along the dock and they follow it like dogs. They've forgot their charters.

I've lost this weekend. Gotta get the boat fixed up, but I tell 'em I'll charge five dollars anytime of the week or weekend next and show 'em how it's done. Come see me. Ask for Quint. Get your photo taken tomorrow. I'm tired now. I'll hang 'em from the dock. Two dollars a tooth for your kids. I'm tired now.

I close the harbor master's door behind me and wipe my forehead with my cap. Frank Silva's at his desk, smoking his pipe, his coffee steaming in his fist, every half-draw of either he glances through the window at my boat and its swinging corpses.

"I got one more dragging along," I say. "Just as big. I'll winch him up tonight."

"Three? Must be about thirty-six feet of fish," he says.

"Forty."

I'm standing at that picture of the Black boy surrounded by the porkers. Look at it long. Reading it, like you can to some paintings. "A ton of 'em."

"Don't do too much good to make folks think we got sharks about. Maybe you should drop 'em in the drink. Now. Before they worry."

"That ain't gonna happen," I say. "They were at the blackfish. I cleared 'em out. Moved the whale someplace safer so she don't wash up. So she don't bother the beaches."

He jerks his pipe to the window.

"Those other boys are taking their charters out to that whale. They were hoping to get them some of that shark. They won't like that you've moved it."

"Then they shouldn't let their mothers tuck 'em in so early."

I put my cap back. "You write up that license for me Monday. And you can tell everyone that Quint knows where the whale is."

He chews on his pipe.

"I don't like people I don't know telling me what to do, Quint."

I pull open the door.

"Get used to it. I got work to do."

I leave. Done with him.

I'm beat but can't sleep. Not yet. Kids follow me up main street, forgetting to go to their Sunday school.

"*Mister? Did you get those sharks all by yourself?*"

"*Mister? What sharks are they? Did you shoot 'em?*"

"*Can I stroke 'em? Can I get a tooth?*"

I put my hands in my jeans and don't stop walking. I mumble back to 'em over my shoulder.

"Just me. Porkers. Great Whites. No. No bullets. I caught 'em. You can have a tooth tomorrow. Tell your father I'll teach him how it's done."

Albert Morris runs Amity Hardware. I tell him to get down to the dock and look at my boat and ring the local newspaper, the Amity *Gazette*, and get 'em to meet me at my boat first thing. He never questions why I don't do this myself. People tend to do things when I tell 'em so straight up. Probably helps that I say I'll buy everything I need from him. That includes a new M1. No chance to get another Enfield. I ask for a shipwright. He tells me that the closest thing they got is a couple of carpenters, Danny and Armando Felix, Italian work-shy but they'll do, he says. I ask him where. Breakfast later. I've got something to do before I eat.

Danny Felix is already in his overalls so he can't be that much of a sitter. They got boats up in the air so that's good enough for me. I tell him my problems and he nods and writes numbers and dollar signs in his book.

"Can you get her round to our dock?" he asks.

"I'll do that. You get her out of the water today mind."

"On *Sunday*?"

"You can do it after Mass. If your mother lets you." I make this a statement and he nods. "You make letters?" I ask.

"*Letters*?"

"Boat names. I need metal letters."

"Sure, sure. What size?"

"To match what I got already. Boat's called '*Akron*'. I only need a C. Take off the K and the N. Move the others around. Take you ten minutes or I'll do it myself. Put up the C."

He looks at me puzzled, that Italian way that they do well.

"To spell what?"

"Put 'Orca', on her." I give him my hardest Irish jaw. "Quick, mind. Before she loses her luck."

And I'm done here too.

And I'm in the paper on Monday.

And not for the reason I thought I might be.

"I wonder where the old Pinocchio of wood has hidden himself?"

"There he is," answered Geppetto. And he pointed to a large Marionette leaning against a chair, head turned to one side, arms hanging limp, and legs twisted under him.

After a long, long look, Pinocchio said to himself with great content:

"How ridiculous I was as a Marionette. And how happy I am, now that I have become a real boy."

I'm writing this at Christmas in '68. I'm forty-four years old. Amity's my home and business. And nobody tries to tell me my business.

I bought a plot of land off South Beach's inlet from a smarmy jack-ass named Vaughn. He's the only realtor on the island but he acts like he's doing you a favor. He'll go far. He can hardly walk straight for his balls swinging. He'd named the plot "Promised Land". That's what realtors name shitholes when they don't sell.

The plot's just big enough to build a wooden two-story shack. No second floor just stairs and a sawed timber walkway, "mezzanine" they calls it. Built her myself, but you knew that. And didn't others follow me there? Trying to get a piece of my luck.

The Felix brothers, them carpenters, had a lot of army surplus green paint, light green, and I got the *Orca*'s deck and bridge painted up right smart. Kept the black and red of her hull. Black and red are the colors I see most of. Reminds everyone of what I do.

I took the biggest shark, "He-Who-Took-His-Brother's-Head", and mounted his jaws on the front of the flybridge just like I said I would. He's yellowed now, aged like me, probably as old as me. That's the only thing I ever did for show. And no one asks me about it no more. They've mostly forgotten or moved on, passed on.

I still clean up them shark jaws. Sell 'em to Albert Morris at the hardware instead of that shanty store on Merritt. And he goes one better and puts, "Caught By Quint" on 'em and I get half. It's good sales in the summer.

I got a phone, and a number in a directory. Nobody rings. No need. They all know me. Know how I earn a living. Still, I wonder, late at night and when the whiskey's past the label, if I could pick up that machine and ask for someone to find me a woman named Amanda or Carole. Just for talking. But I don't know if them machines work for things like that.

See, two things happened that made me come to this.

We got those rockets working real good and changed some of 'em into missiles when we didn't want 'em shooting at the moon. Thirteen days in October '62 we got close to our own Hiroshima. I stayed out on the ocean for a week. Took plenty of water, plenty of corned beef. Nobody wanted to go fishing anyways. We got commies all over us they say. But they would say that. Stops us looking into our own yard. Although, like those Japs and Germans, I don't know what they look like. I know I got a good Japanese woman who does my laundry once a month.

Once we got the rockets going someone thought Vietnam was another Asian place to take interest in. We had a generation of men grown up that we hadn't used yet. Them babies were old enough now. There was the Tet offensive, just this year, when we started drafting again and young men got to leave our shores again. I don't know if that had any part of what happened last month but it set me to thinking. That's the second thing.

You remember my captain? Captain McVay? Him who they court-martialed for getting his ship blown out from under him?

Well, Captain McVay was bounced down a hundred points and never set foot on a boat again 'cept the blue rowing boat he had on his farm in Connecticut for fishing and such. They kept him to a desk for the rest of his career. They didn't need to put a gun to his head. But I guess he did. He was seventy. He'd had three wives too.

I read it in the paper. He went out on the porch in his khakis, pressed as always. Just before lunch. He lay down, his head on the porch step. In his left hand he held his key-chain. On that key-chain was a wooden toy figure of a sailor that he'd had since he was a boy. Seventy years old and he still had it. He'd carried it around the oceans. He had it in the water. In the deep. In his right he had his service .38. That's how he was found. The same month those boys left.

Like I said I don't know if it had anything to do with the war now taking hold, I don't know if it was for the wars and the boys to come or just too many sleepless nights over the boys gone, never to become. I just read about it and thought that I kinda understood.

There are jaws bleach-steaming and rattling behind me in kettle-tubs as I finish this. I keep the money I get from 'em in a peach-tin. Forget it's there. I don't ever dip into it. It ain't about the money.

Tomorrow I'm going to the hospital.

Oh, I ain't sick.

Got an appointment to get a tattoo removed.

Stop folks asking me about it.

Glossary

Some terms used in the book:

Gaff—A fishing tool comprised of a very large hook, often barbed, on a detachable pole. The hook has a line attached which runs along the pole and is tied to a cleat. When driven into a large fish the hook detaches and the pole is removed. Thus the fish is tied via the hook and line to the boat cleat. Used to pull fish to the boat for securing in order to bring up the fish by tail rope and leader.

Fighting chair—A specialized seat used by anglers to assist them in reeling in large or powerful fish. The chair is typically mounted on a pedestal or swivel base, and is designed to provide a secure seating position while fighting a fish.

Flying gaff—A larger gaff used in commercial fishing to secure large, powerful fish. It is designed to be thrown at a fish while it is still in the water, allowing the hook to penetrate its skin and hold it in place. The same as a regular gaff a line runs along the pole (max 8 ft) with

265

one end to the hook or barb and the other end attached to the boat via cleat. Flying gaffs are often used with traditional gaffs and other tools to secure and land large game fish.

Flybridge—Deck area above cockpit of a boat accessed via ladder or stairs.

Gin pole (archaic)—In older commercial fishing, and land use, a manual hoist or winch used to lift large loads.

Kapok (archaic)—A life jacket filled with natural kapok fiber.

Leader—A short length of fishing line that is attached to the end of the main fishing line. The leader is typically made from a heavier material than the main line and is designed to provide additional strength and protection when targeting larger or more aggressive fish. It is safer and easier to pull up the leader rather than the line directly attached to the hook in the fish.

PT boat (or Patrol Torpedo boat)—A type of fast, light naval vessel used primarily for patrolling and attacking enemy ships during the Second World War.

PV-1—The PV-1 (Patrol, Lockheed Ventura Model 1) was a Second World War American patrol bomber aircraft used by the United States Navy and other allied forces.

Remoras—Sucker-fish or shark sucker. A fish that attaches itself to the underside of larger marine animals.

Strakes—A series of longitudinal ridges or flat plates that are attached to the outer surface of a boat or ship's hull.

Tail rope—A rope or line that is used to secure the tail or hind-quarters of a marine animal, such as a whale or a large fish, to a boat during the process of towing or hauling it aboard. Essentially a noose which will tighten as the animal is hoisted up.

Transom—A flat, vertical surface located at the stern (rear) of a boat or ship, where the hull meets the deck. On antiquated boats you may see the name of the vessel here.

Author's Note

"You all know me, know how I earn a living"

I had to make two assumptions when writing this book.

One: the reader is familiar with *Jaws* and Quint.

Two: the reader is aware of the sinking and tragedy of the *USS Indianapolis*, if only through the film.

But I didn't want this story to be a novelisation of the tragedy. That wouldn't work. It's a character story.

If we did not have Quint's mesmerising retelling of the sinking of the *Indianapolis*, we would not have the understanding essential to the appreciation of his character, or the understanding of his behaviour after the realisation of what he is actually dealing with.

"You're certifiable, Quint!"

What was most important was that I must not do wrong by the sailors and marines of the ship.

The stories of those days in the water relayed in the book are

269

drawn from actual survivor stories, but in no way should it be inferred that the protagonist's thoughts, actions and feelings are related to any of the survivors. My protagonist's attitude, his emotions, his character, all stem from my interpretation of the character from the motion picture only, and not from any group or individual associated with the tragedy.

Is this related to the original novel?

Yes, of course, and also no, of course.

There is little point in mentioning the differences between the novel and the movie, but this story is based from and related almost entirely to the character of Quint in the film and the incredible performance and writing contribution of Robert Shaw. That's the springboard.

I used place names and other characters from the original novel to connect to it and show my appreciation and respect to Peter Benchley for creating such a phenomenon. Spellings of names and places, if the character or place appears in the film, are from the movie rather than from the book.

Why *Jaws*, why Quint?

This movie has been a part of my life since I was five years old. That is not an exaggeration. And I'm not alone. After the internet became a thing, I discovered there was a whole wealth of knowledge and fandom that went far and beyond what I would have imagined. I wasn't alone, I wasn't mad.

Adult me found out that there were documentaries, books, analyses about the movie, a thousand copycats, a whole genre and sub-genres, filmmakers cited it as their inspiration, quotes had embedded themselves into pop culture, it created the summer blockbuster and changed cinema. The making and legacy of *Jaws* had become a phenomenon of its own. And one four-minute scene of dialogue had captivated generations. Even if a fan hadn't seen it first in the cinema, you'll find that they all have a story of when *Jaws* first, well . . . *bit* them.

There are two books (other than *Jaws*, obviously) that helped fuel the engine of this one, and I must acknowledge them enormously.

For the stories of the *Indianapolis*, I am gratefully amazed to have read Doug Stanton's *In Harm's Way*. It is *the* book on the events surrounding and concerning the tragedy. I mostly read history books and I can only say that this is the finest I've ever read. For the historical timing of events, and detail, this book was invaluable, as were the accounts from which portions of the survivor scenes of the book derive.

The other book was *In the Slick of the Cricket* by the late Russell Drumm. Many *Jaws* fans have this book as there's a contentious legend that the original novel's Quint was based on legendary fisherman Frank Mundus (who gets a shout-out in my novel).

Russell Drumm had written a near-biography of the man and had accompanied him on probably his last charter. I learned so much from this incredible book, which is part beautiful novel and part account, that I had to acknowledge and use some of the yarns and character tales, both Frank's stories and Russell's. The part where Quint cuts the shark open and shows it eating its own insides? That's pure Mundus (and also cut from the original *Jaws* script). When Quint becomes a fisherman and is offered to eat the heart of the first tuna he caught? That was Russell Drumm. All hunters and fisherman have these rituals, but I was acknowledging Drumm when I put that in.

As many people now know, Peter Benchley deeply regretted the aftermath of shark hate that followed the cultural impact of *Jaws* and spent the remainder of his life campaigning and raising awareness about the ignorance surrounding sharks, and actively promoting the conservation of marine ecosystems in partnership with his wife, Wendy.

But, as all things balance out, his book and the film also inspired people to understand and appreciate sharks. Children that grew up loving *Jaws* didn't go out murdering the creatures of the sea. That was the adults above them.

If anything, the generation that followed appeased Benchley's regret for him, and the shark is now once again a subject of fascination and respect, as it was when civilisations once recognised them as gods. Benchley played no small part in that, and Wendy Benchley continues this work to this day.

I was also conscious in this work not to make the sharks the object of horror (after all, I'm one of those children that grew up to admire them). The violence is all Quint's. The sharks are not his demons.

And Quint?

I'm not going to analyse the film or novel but I'm with a lot of those who have when I say that, if you break down what *Jaws* is about, it's another four-letter word.

Fear.

All the characters, major and minor, are afraid of something. This is what we feel, what makes us afraid when we watch.

But only one character has a unique paradox of fear. Quint is only afraid of fear itself. The fear of it coming back.

He alludes to the word once, describing when he was waiting for his turn to be rescued from the sinking, and his answer to that fear was to never put a lifejacket on again. He has beaten it and won't go back. Won't allow it to come back.

Most attempts to dramatise or create a story around the events of the *Indianapolis* have disappointed, in my opinion, because they show the subject and the action itself, relying on that being enough, believing that is the story. I didn't want to write that story.

What I intended was to take the most famous fictional character related to the tragedy, and take him out of that water. Before, after, and up to where we think we know him. And I feel, like many, many others, that I do know him.

Take him all the way out of the water.

For only then do you get the head, the tail. The. Whole. Damn. Thing.

Q and A: Robert Lautner

1. No famous yellow barrels?

The only reason the barrels are used in the film, to great effect, is that the mechanical shark wasn't working as well as hoped. The barrels replaced the non-existent shark. They're not an actual thing for game-fishing.

Also, as with some other visual aspects in the film (looking at you, leather drum seat) I felt sure it would be better if Quint and the Orca were not as fully formed as in the film, as it takes place a number of years before.

It would also not be practical or possible for Quint to employ the barrels (or harpoons) on his own.

2. In the note from Larry Vaughn that precedes the story you mention 'Salvatore' as a fisherman who sometimes helped Quint with his charters - but this character does not appear in the story. Is he another of the not 'fully formed' aspects that come after the conclusion of the story?

As many *Jaws* fans know, there are deleted scenes which feature a character named Herschel or Salvatore, depending on which version of the script you're reading. He can still be seen in the town hall meeting with Quint, and helping load the Orca. This character, like many others, was played by a Martha's Vineyard local. I put him in to mark his deleted contribution from the film.

3. Why is the note dated 1977?

The great Murray Hamilton, who played Vaughn, also appeared in *Jaws 2*. I set the letter prior to the events of that film for timing.

I did a similar thing with Quint's age. In 1968, at the time of the novel, my Quint is 44 years old. If we move the timeline forward to the events of *Jaws,* my Quint would be the same age as Robert Shaw when he died at only 51. I felt that fitting and respectful. Everyone thinks Quint is older, but he was only 48 in Jaws, just five years older than Roy Scheider's Brody; but he plays off the 'old man of the sea' so brilliantly that everyone interprets him as older.

4. Quint insults the shark with a line about making douches out of their lungs. Surely he knows sharks don't *have* lungs?

Throughout the shark fight Quint pulls himself up for giving human emotions and thoughts to the sharks. But he can't help it. At this point the insult reflects his continued anthropomorphisation of them, springing from his rage.

5. Why is Quint's boat named Akron?

The original lobster boat that would become the film's Orca was named 'Warlock', and as much as I thought I should call it that

I just really didn't like the name and didn't feel it fit Quint's character. Akron and Orca have the same hard sound and there's a scene in the book where Quint talks about four- and five-letter words. Akron is a five-letter word, Orca is four letters. Fate has four letters. "Quint" means five. In the film, Quint is the fifth and final victim of the shark. I like the accidental symbolism of it.

Acknowledgements

This book originally began around 2011, very much as a personal project. For it to finally see the light of day I'm forever grateful to a number of people.

I would foremost like to thank Wendy Benchley for granting permission to pay respectful homage to Peter Benchley's wonderful characters and work.

To all the team at The Borough Press and HarperCollins over the years for believing we could do this. Particular thank you to Suzie Dooré for her enthusiasm and contribution on what turned out to be a fair stretch of road to publication.

Much gratitude to my agent, Jim Gill, and all at United Agents for their support and dedication.

I'd like to acknowledge the financial support of the Royal Literary Fund which enabled me to dedicate time to work on the novel.

Lastly, I'd like to thank Robert Shaw for his inspirational performance and writing contribution to the *JAWS* phenomenon, and for transfixing me to sit and watch countless times over the decades and still feel five years old and in the dark again each and every time.